Aiko's Dive

Aiko's Dive

Chase Gamwell

Published by Vulpine Press in the United Kingdom in 2024

ISBN: 978-1-83919-583-9

www.vulpine-press.com

For Anastacia and Bagheera

1

The only view of the outside world I've ever had is the rough-hewn oval skylight set directly above the center of the Alphanax Orphanage's common area. Crimson sunlight beams through the opening, painting a complementary shape on the unyielding stone floor. It's a far more comfortable resting place than the cold corners of the wide room, where condensation drips onto soggy mounds of rags. Beds, the Headmistress calls them.

Sitting on the floor, I settle against Fallah's leathery flank. My best friend is a Quiloh: bigger than all the other children and twice as strong, with four stubby legs poking from a round torso and a blue stripe tracing her spine. Her triangular head is tipped with huge nostrils beneath milky, sightless eyes. And floppy, yet surprisingly articulate, ears indicate her mood.

Her head swivels toward me, ears twitching as she grins.

"Aren't you glad you have a friend as big as me?" she rumbles in her native tongue, tilting her head at the children we'd kicked out of our spot in the sun. They try to take it every day, but Fallah is just too large.

"Hey! I watched your back!" I stumble over the reply. She's managed to teach me some Quiloh over the years, but my parts aren't meant for the same sounds. Fallah understands, however,

1

and that's enough to keep the others from eavesdropping when we don't want them to.

"Sure," she teases, before dropping her meaty chin to the worn stone floor. *"As long as we're the ones in the sun."*

I nod in agreement.

"How long?" Fallah asks after a moment; the same question she asks every day.

"This is day 3745 in the sun," I answer.

Before that—before Fallah arrived—I crouched in the cold, damp shadows, teased and bullied by all the other children. For as long as I can remember. And maybe even before that. Back then, Ki'leh was the one in the sun. He stared at us now with blood-red eyes, a bristling nest of white feathers framing a hooked beak that gleamed like liquid gold.

Fallah smiles, but shakes her head. *"You* know *that's not the number I asked for. How long until—"*

"Freedom," I finish for her, readjusting the number in my head. *"Only 725 days left."*

Rough, sun-warmed skin shifts under my shoulder blades. *"So close."*

The daily exchange is a ritual. A reminder. A promise.

I squint up at the sun. The sky framing it is pink and traced with wispy gray clouds. One day, we'll stand under the open sky together. Free. Able to go wherever we please.

"Tell me about Quil again," I say.

"You know I barely remember my home," Fallah replies.

"Please?!" I plead. *"I like hearing about what you do remember."*

"Well"—Fallah shifts under me—*"Quil is warm, and there's always a gentle breeze blowing across the fields. The soil is soft, and loose, and cool. Nice to lay on…"*

"It sounds like paradise," I breathe. Compared to the stone prison of Alphanax, at least: the only home I've ever known. But even if Quil is the only other place I ever get to see, I'll be happy. Because Fallah and I will be together. And free, instead of just two more unwanted orphans waiting for a Kaisin to give them a 'home'.

"There are other places beside Quil," Fallah says, turning her wide face to me, ears raised. *"I'm sure there's a planet full of other smooth-skins."*

The made-up name tugs my mouth into a frown, but neither of us know how else to describe what I am or have any idea where I come from.

"How do we even know there are any more like me out there?" I ask.

"There have to be," she says, *"somewhere."*

Her heartwarming insistence brings a smile to my face. Fallah has always been adamant about finding others like me once we leave. She says it's important I know more about my kind. I want that more than anything, but I'm not confident like she is—not enough to get my hopes up, anyway. But even if we never find another 'smooth skin' beyond these walls, I'll be happy as long as we're together.

"Maybe," I concede.

Fallah returns the smile and opens her mouth to say something else when the jingle of keys pierces the air. A heartbeat later, the heavy iron door at the far edge of the room creaks open, and the Headmistress stalks into view. A wicked grin twists her thin lips, pulling them apart to reveal jagged, yellowing teeth.

That look is *never* a good sign.

Jittery blue eyes sweep the room in a silent warning as two other Kaisin saunter in on her heels, just as tall, pale, and appraising.

"This is what I have," the Headmistress says, in a lazy drawl.

"No others?"

The Kaisin who asked is covered from head to toe in a dusty jumpsuit and wrapped in a tattered, shapeless coat the same shade of brown as the stone walls.

The Headmistress crosses her wiry arms over a slender torso. "What did you have in mind?"

"You got anything large?" the other Kaisin asks. He wears ill-fitting slacks and a baggy shirt that makes his torso seem miniscule.

Fallah stiffens under me.

"You'll be fine," I whisper.

"How do you know?"

"I just know," I soothe, patting her side.

Fallah nods, but the nervous flops of her ears suggest she isn't convinced. *"What about you?"*

"I'm an 'anomaly', remember?"

That was the Headmistress' name for me. She mumbled it in passing, like a curse, or a sickness to be excised. But for some reason, the Headmistress always makes it a point to divert attention away from me. And most Kaisin that *do* give me more than a lingering glance are disgusted by whatever I am. Maybe it's my smooth skin. Or my thick mane of raven hair. Or my dark eyes.

4

But *these* Kaisin don't seem to notice, or care, as their eyes sweep over me. Then again, I'm not big like Fallah. I swallow the lump rising in my throat.

"The Rhandannan," Tattered Coat says, pointing at Ki'leh.

Oversized Shirt shakes his head. "They look big, but they're all feathers. Also, hollow bones."

Tattered Coat gives a thoughtful frown and scans the room again. His gaze lands on Fallah, and her flank hardens like stone against my back.

"What about the Quiloh?"

Suddenly, the lump is so big that it's hard to breathe.

"Maybe." Oversized Shirt turns to the Headmistress. "Can we get a closer look?"

"Of course."

She walks toward us, keys jingling like death bells.

"Out of the way," she snaps at me. Then her glare shifts to Fallah. "Stand up."

Fallah's milky-white eyes widen as I scramble toward the edge of the crimson circle, and when I turn, she's trembling.

"You're fine," I call in her native tongue, my heart drumming in time with the deepest, soothing notes of the words.

"Quiet," the Headmistress hisses.

All the warmth drains from my body as the Kaisin inspect Fallah. My skin crawls as they run spider-like fingers across the leathery hump of her flank, along her bright blue stripe running down her spine, and toy with the simple wooden pendant always hanging around her neck. She's quiet, but every inch of her screams distress: her big ears press flat against her bald head; her prominent brow draws down above narrowed eyes; her lips press into a thin line; her wide shoulders hunch in a defensive posture; and all four of her legs are bent slightly. She's ready to bolt, but there's nowhere to run.

Oversized Shirt, hands still on Fallah's back, glances sidelong at the Headmistress. "Can this one carry a load?"

"All of the children can."

"Can any of the others carry as much?" Tattered Coat presses.

"I don't know," the Headmistress growls, "but these are the only children I have. Find one. Or don't. But don't waste my time."

The pair converses in the Kaisin native tongue, a scratchy grumble that's so familiar I can almost grasp its meaning; always could. But comprehension hovers just out of reach. Finally, Tattered Coat turns back to the Headmistress.

"We'll take the Quiloh."

My heart skips a beat. This isn't right. This isn't supposed to happen. Fallah and I are going to leave Alphanax together. Be free together. But if they take her away, I'll be left alone. And she'll be all alone with these Kaisin, wherever they take her. No. That can't happen! But, I'm frozen in place, as if my feet have fused with the smooth stone of Alphanax. All I can do is watch as the Headmistress replies.

"The fee is fifteen hundred credits."

"So much?" Tattered Coat complains.

"Surely, only a thousand will do," Oversized Shirt offers.

"Fifteen hundred, or you leave without the Quiloh," the Headmistress snaps, planting balled fists on her hips.

"Fine," Tattered Coat grumbles, pulling a pouch off of his hip and dumping the contents into her cupped hand. "That should be enough."

Maybe it isn't. Maybe they'll be short and the Headmistress will send them away without Fallah. The glimmer of hope dwindles with each counted credit. But then, the Headmistress finishes and raises an eyebrow.

"Fourteen hundred." She glares at the two Kaisin. "And I suppose you didn't bring a credit more?"

It isn't enough! Fallah will stay!

They both grin.

"What do you say?" Oversized shirt asks.

"Do we have a deal?" Tattered shirt adds.

She lets out a heavy sigh. "Go ahead. Take her. Before I change my mind."

The Kaisin bow their heads in thanks. Their mouths move, but the words are muffled, as if uttered far away. Then, they turn to Fallah.

But... No! They didn't have enough. The Headmistress was supposed to turn them away!

"Wait!" I cry, leaping in front of her. "Take me too! I can carry as much as she can! More!"

"Out of the way!" Tattered Coat growls.

"Scrawny pest!" Oversized Shirt shoves me with rough, spindly hands.

Fallah's milky eyes widen in terror as unfamiliar hands nudge her away from the sun's warmth. Then, her wide lips open in a panicked cry. *"Aiko! What do we do?"*

"Run!" I shout in reply.

Fallah bucks away from Tattered Coat and Oversized Shirt. The Headmistress' cry for her to stop is drowned by the pair's angry barks and the sudden babbling roar of children. They cheer as Fallah sprints for the open door and freedom. It's always left open, because no child has ever tried to escape. Fallah will be the first.

And I'll be the second.

My two legs aren't as strong as Fallah's four, but I'm quick enough to keep up with her headlong rush. I yank the iron door shut behind me, pausing long enough for the solid click of the latch to echo in the empty hall. Then, I'm on Fallah's heels.

"Do you know where you're going?" I pant at her wide flank.

She shakes her head, then says, *"I'm not letting them take me!"* Tears flash in her sightless eyes.

"No," I agree. *"We're supposed to leave together, so that's what we're going to do."*

There's a junction at the end of the hall. Left is a short offshoot that ends at a narrow door. A dead end. But right stretches further in the distance.

"That way," I cry, pointing.

We hurry along a hallway with dripping stone walls and crumbling floors. Up ahead is a set of wooden double doors. Maybe that's the way out? It has to be! Harsh voices echo behind us, joined by a chorus of pounding feet. But freedom is only a few dozen paces away. We're going to make it!

Stumbling to a stop in front of the door, I shoot a glance over my shoulder. The Headmistress is in sight, flanked by Tattered Coat and Oversized Shirt.

Fallah's ears flick at the chorus of footsteps. *"Hurry!"*

8

I fumble with the latch. Why is it so hard to grip and turn? Why is the door so heavy? Why is the air so thick? Why are my legs so shaky? My hands tremble as the latch turns. And turns. And turns. Then, the door is open and we're outside.

Worn paving stones trace a path to a ship in the distance. It belongs to the Kaisin. More mill around the base of an extended ramp, their stark white skin at odds with the ruddy landscape and the crimson sunlight.

"Not that way," I say, gripping Fallah's shoulder and steering her off the path.

The gentle slope of loose dirt and rock stretches on forever. In the far distance, what looks like a mountain range reaches for the sky. Between, there's nothing but barren wasteland.

I skip a step staring at the open expanse. How will we survive out there? Can we? A glance over my shoulder reveals the alternative: Fallah will be taken away, and I'll return to the dank cold of Alphanax.

No. We don't have a choice.

I clap a hand on Fallah's wide flank and urge her on between gasped breaths. *"Don't...stop..."*

She trundles ahead and I use the hand on her back to keep myself upright. I can hear Tattered Coat, Oversized Shirt, and the Headmistress in our wake, but they're falling behind. On even ground, in a straight line, they might have been faster, but Fallah's four legs make up for, in stability, what she lacks in raw speed.

"We're going to make it," I pant. *"Just—"*

My words are cut off by loud pops. Geysers of dust and dirt explode around us. The echoing chorus is joined by the

Headmistress' shrill shouts that I can't make out over the pulse pounding in my ears. I hunch and squint, but don't stop.

Ahead, the slope steepens, then swoops behind a mound of stones. Fallah slips, stumbles, and plants her feet to keep from falling. For an instant, she's as stiff as a statue. Then, there's a pop. A zip. A muffled thump as something hits her leathery hide. She wavers. Falls.

She doesn't move. She doesn't get up. And as I shuffle the handful of steps toward her, the ruddy dirt darkens. Is that…blood? The parched ground guzzles her life eagerly, and the breeze pushes fine sand against her limp form as if trying to swallow her whole. I collapse to the moist patch of ground and place a hand on her side.

"Fallah?"

Her sightless eyes blink and swivel toward the sound of my voice. *"Aiko?"*

"I'm here," I say. *"You're going to be alright."*

"Go," she wheezes. *"Be free."*

"I can't. I won't."

"Run." Her eyes flutter. *"Before it's too late."*

"Not without you!" I cry, wrapping my arms around her and struggling to heave her back onto her feet.

But…Fallah doesn't respond. Or move. Or breathe.

"No!"

This isn't supposed to happen! None of this was supposed to happen!

Reaching out, I brush limp ears back from her face and look into her milky-white eyes. They're beyond sightless, staring, glassy and empty, into the rosy sky. All of a sudden, my chest tightens and a lump the size of the sun lodges in my throat. I suck a shuddering breath around it and try to swallow. I can't. My hands shake. My eyes are dry. They burn. Blur with tears.

Fallah is…gone? How can she be gone? We made a promise…

Somewhere in the distance, I hear the scrabble of boots. Then, a familiar voice.

"You fools! What have you done?"

"She ran," someone snaps. "We have no use for runners."

"It wasn't your place." That's the Headmistress.

"We paid for the Quiloh," another voice chimes in. "How about the other one? Want us to deal with *it* as well?"

The Headmistress spit something in the Kaisin tongue. Boots scuff stone. Metal chatters on the ground.

"Take your credits and go."

There's a moment of silence, then a grumble from one of the Kaisin. Boots scrape anew. Metal clinks as it's gathered. Finally, footsteps retreat into the distance.

Fingers close around my bicep in an iron grip that should hurt. And the way I'm yanked upright should prompt a cry of pain. But I'm numb. My bare feet no longer feel the shards of stone underfoot. My suddenly dry eyes don't water when the breeze tosses sand into them. And the crimson sun's light no longer warms me. I'm cold. Empty.

I glance up at the Headmistress' face. It's creased with anger. Jittery blue eyes flick down to me, then quickly return to Alphanax. Her grip tightens. Her pace quickens.

From a distance, the orphanage is no more than a squat rectangle of brown stone against a flat horizon. This is the first time I've seen it from the outside. It's so unassuming. Yet, the mundane collection of tricks seems more sinister now. Without Fallah, Alphanax isn't a place I can call home. It might as well be a tomb, because the freedom I dreamed of for so long is pointless now. Before, even if I was the only 'smooth skin' at the orphanage—maybe anywhere—at least I had Fallah.

Now, I'm really, truly all alone.

2

The Headmistress turns away from the cart and pushes the iron
door closed, testing the handle to make sure the latch catches.
She's done it every day since—

The memory of Fallah's empty eyes churn my stomach. And
a fresh lump rises in my throat, choking me. I shrink deeper into
the damp shadows as if I can disappear into the darkness completely. I'd prefer that to the—Days? Weeks? Months? I've lost
count—of empty, meaningless solitude.

Her hard gaze wanders in my direction, but doesn't quite
make it to my spot in the corner. Does she feel guilty for her part
in what happened? Does she blame herself in any way for letting
those two Kaisin... I clench my teeth and shake the memory out
of my brain. It's still too fresh. Too raw.

Knees pulled into a frock still stained with dirt and blood, I
glare at the Headmistress. She paces from one child to the next,
ladling a scoop of slop into a bowl before holding it out like a
king's ransom. When she nears me, most of a scoop makes it into
the bowl. And most of the rest jostles over the sides when she
hastily slides it toward me.

I stare daggers at her back until the iron door crashes closed in
her wake. Then, swallowing my pride, I scoop as much of the
spoiled gruel as I can manage back into the bowl. It already tastes

bad enough without extra sand. And the puddled liquid gives it a bitter bite I'll never get used to.

But nothing rivals the thick bile at the back of my throat. It's always there, like the ghost of Fallah. Even though I do my best to forget, nothing can erase the sight of her glassy eyes and the dark liquid seeping from her motionless body. She's gone, and I'm truly alone in this place.

Pausing mid-scoop, I drop my head to my knees and bite back tears. There has to be a way out; a reprieve from being left behind. Freedom. Or something like it. Life has become even more like every bite of the slop the Headmistress serves us: bitter and un-fulfilling. But I eat it all the same.

Not too long after I finish the bowl, the jingle of keys pierces the air again. The Headmistress is back already? So soon after the midday meal? But why?

I dab my eyes on the soiled frock before looking up. The Headmistress is in the doorway, and someone is with her. Not a Kaisin. The man is as tall as the Headmistress, yet solidly built. His skin is darker than the stone of Alphanax, and his head is dusted with hair as white as Ki'leh's feathers. He's different. As different as *I* am. Another smooth skin?

"Here's what I have," the Headmistress says. "What are you looking for, exactly?"

Her eyes drift across the open space, hopeful.

"Something unique," the man says, in a resonating baritone.

"Well, take a look," the Headmistress replies, her gaze straying toward me a second time.

The strange man dismisses her with an absent nod and sweeps the room with cold gray eyes. They find me and stop. His brow furrows. And his lips twist into a frown.

"Her," he says.

I'm taken aback. So are the other children. But the Headmistress doesn't react.

"Are you sure that's the child you want?" she asks evenly.

The man nods again and reaches under his coat. The hand reappears holding a glowing slip of glass. He studies its surface, then glances at me. Those eyes hold a secret only he knows.

"What's your fee?" he asks.

The Headmistress chews on her bottom lip as she stares at me. There's regret in that gaze. Remorse. And...guilt? But also fear. She wants me gone. Today. *Now!*

The Headmistress breaks eye contact first and glances at the man. "Standard adoption fee is fifteen hundred credits. But since she's a runner, you can have her for half."

"That's fine," the man says.

He reaches under his coat a second time and removes a small pouch. Pouring the contents into one wide palm, he gathers a number of small circular chips and dumps them into the Headmistress' hands.

"That should be enough. Count it if you like."

The Headmistress shakes her head. "I'm sure it's all there. The girl's yours."

She turns her back on the man and stalks toward me. Her lips quiver, and the fist gripping the ring of rattling keys at her side is so tight that white knucklebones gleam through already pale skin.

"This man's your caretaker now," she mumbles under her breath. "Good luck and good riddance."

My contempt for the Kaisin doesn't dull the shock of her words. I blink and slip my gaze to the man standing next to the iron door. He stares back and beckons with thick fingers. A simple motion that communicates haste. I heave to my feet. Slow steps carry me out of the shadows and across the stone floor, but my heart races.

I can feel the weight of dozens of eyes on me, and the confusion of the other children Mine stray to the crimson circle in the center of the room. Ki'len glares at me, feathery mane bristling, beak hanging open. He'd been master of the spot since Fallah died. I'd always hoped to take it back from him one day, but he can have it. I won't step foot in it ever again.

When I reach the strange man, he offers me a shallow smile, though that flicker of surprise plays across his grizzled face again.

A moment later, the Headmistress walks up to us. Ignoring me, she addresses the man. "This way, please."

She leads the strange man out of the vaulted stone chamber. I follow in a daze.

We walk down a familiar hall and turn right. At the far end are the wooden double doors I've passed through only once before. That time, the result had been a tragedy. Now, however?

I stare at the strange man walking a step ahead of me. I've never seen anyone like him before: not among the children at Alphanax, and not among the few non-Kaisin who'd come to buy children over the years. He is as much of a mystery as I am. But he's also an opportunity. He's an escape. And maybe, just maybe, I'll have the chance to strike out on my own once we're away.

We pass through the double doors, and I squint under the full light of the crimson sun, brilliant after so long in the shadows. I walk away from Alphanax without looking back, even when I hear the Headmistress clear her throat and shuffle her feet on the worn paving stones. It feels good to ignore her for once, despite walking headlong into the unknown.

I look up at the strange man again. He might be as dangerous as any of the Kaisin who come to Alphanax for children, but I sense only curiosity. Why? What does he know that I don't?

He leads the way to a ship in the distance: an oblong tube balanced on slender legs that barely seems suited to the job of supporting such a large object. Its shiny gray hull is at odds with the ruddy dirt, pink sky, and hellish sunlight. Only the wispy gray clouds come close to sharing something in common with the ship.

A ramp stretches from the ground to a dark opening in its side. The man walks to the top, but I hesitate. It feels wrong pausing so close to freedom, but I can't shake the doubt gnawing at the back of my mind. What if going with the strange man is no better than remaining at Alphanax? What if he's no different than the Kaisin?

My doubt is erased by the sudden memory of Fallah's smiling face. While this isn't the freedom we originally wanted, it's a chance to escape. To live. To thrive. And since Fallah grasped at opportunity with both hands, so will I.

Meeting the strange man's expectant gaze, I climb the ramp and follow him into the ship. The smooth metal floor inside is cold enough to sting my bare feet, but the white lights lining the upper corners of the narrow hallway are far softer on my eyes than the harsh, red sun.

The man turns right and walks to a doorway. At the threshold, he glances over his shoulder.

"Come on."

The cramped room beyond is dominated by a single chair set in front of a wide viewscreen. Through it, I catch a glimpse of the drab stone of Alphanax huddled in the dirt. And a mountain range in the far distance.

The man ignores the sweeping vista, drops into the chair, and taps controls on keypads affixed to its armrests. Glowing pictures spring to life in the air around him in a dance of color and light.

"Take a seat," he calls, as a vibrating hum runs through the ship's hull. "And strap in."

He indicates a pair of chairs beside me.

I slide into the nearest one, but don't know for sure what he means by 'strap in'. There are loose belts hanging by my shoulders and hips. Maybe those have something to do with it?

He looks over his shoulder and makes a pulling motion with his hands, then taps closed fists together. "Small ends go in the big ends. Quickly."

I'm still not sure what he means, so I grab the straps and tie the ends together. Just in time.

With a piercing wail, the landscape rotates and Alphanax disappears from view. Then, the ground recedes altogether. Pink sky dominates the viewscreen, and a crushing weight—like Fallah's ghost settling on my chest—presses me into the cushions cradling me. I feel sluggish. Lightheaded. And the roar of blood rushing in my ears rivals the scream of the ship's engines.

The pink sky fades to blue. Then purple. Then black. Finally, an impossible number of stars pepper the infinite darkness. In the span of minutes, I've gone farther from Alphanax than my legs could have ever carried me.

Sudden tears blur my vision. I have well and truly escaped. But I've also left Fallah behind. For good. On top of that, I have no idea where I'm headed or what this strange man has planned for me. Worst of all, I'm alone.

A deep breath holds back the flood, and another drives the tightness from my chest. I can be sad later. Now, there are questions that need answers.

"Who are you?"

"Name's Fletcher," the man replies, shooting a thin smile over his shoulder. "And this is my ship, the *Undertow*."

He gives the chair's armrest an affectionate pat.

"Where are you taking me?"

"Now, hold on." Fletcher twists to get a better look at me. "I told you my name. What's yours?"

"Aiko," I say hesitantly.

"Nice to meet you." Fletcher dips his head, then glances at one of the hovering pictures in front of his chair. "There's a station at the edge of Kaisin space. About six hours from here. That's where we're headed."

"Why? What's there?"

"Friends. And safety," he says, with a slightly warmer smile this time.

That sounds too good to be true. Maybe it is.

"Why me?"

The smile falls from Fletcher's face.

"What is it?" I ask.

"Because of what you are." He glances to an empty corner of the cramped space. "Someone like me..."

I frown. "What do you mean 'someone like you'?"

He rubs the stubble on his chin, then answers my question with another. "You've never seen anyone else like you, have you?"

"No," I say. "But I grew up at Alphanax. I'm sure there's plenty I haven't seen."

He chuckles and gives a conceding nod. "Yes, but it's a bit more complicated than that."

In the back of my mind, memories of the Headmistress drawing attention away from me float to the surface. Is he suggesting there's something to those memories? That he knows what I am? I lean forward in anticipation of what he's about to say.

"You and I belong to a race of beings called Humans," he continues.

"Humans? So that means there are others like me? Can you take me to them?"

Fletcher frowns. "That's the thing: there are no more Humans. You and I are it."

"What?" The hope building inside me shatters like glass. "How do you know?"

"It's—" Fletcher shakes his head. "I'm not really sure how to begin."

He falls silent for a moment.

"My mentor was obsessed with Humans. He's the one who found me. He's the one who told me about them. I'd always hoped to learn more, before—" He takes a deep breath. "He's gone now."

I stare past him, into the speckled starlight, and shake my head. This is a lot to take in. Fletcher doesn't seem like he's lying—*he* believes the story he's telling—but I'm not so sure. I've never heard of Humans. Or seen another like me. But I also spent my entire childhood cooped up in a tiny room with only a sliver of sky connecting me to the outside world. Can it be true? Maybe, but I have other questions.

"How did you find me?"

A wistful smile touches Fletcher's lips. "A friend of mine heard about you."

"How?"

"She only said someone like me was at Alphanax," Fletcher replies, with a frown. "I had to see for myself. And once I did, there's no way I was going to leave you there."

It's a nice sentiment. And it got me away from Alphanax. But there's a question stuck in my mind. "What happens when we reach the station?"

He shrugs. "I don't know."

"Will I be free?" I ask.

He blinks. "It's dangerous to be by yourself."

"So you're going to keep me?"

"No, it's—"

"What, then?" Sudden, irrational rage burns in my chest. Sure, Fletcher took me away from Alphanax, but what's the point of escape without freedom? I didn't leave the orphanage to be a slave; his or anyone else's. Fallah died grasping at freedom. It would be a disservice to her memory if I didn't do the same.

"Listen," he says. "Let's make it to the station first. We'll figure everything else out there."

21

"Fine," I snap.

"For now, feel free to get some rest." He points down the hall. "There's sleeping quarters behind each door. Pick whatever room you like."

It's a dismissal. Or an opportunity to ignore me. Either way, Fletcher turns back to the collection of glowing screens hovering around his chair.

I wrestle with the knotted straps, then storm out of the cramped chamber. Frigid metal sears the soles of my feet. And cool air sends icy fingers trailing down my spine. But it's fresh. Dry.

I approach the nearest door, but it doesn't open when I push. Taking a step back, I study the featureless slab. A single button is set on the wall beside it. I press it, and the door slides open. Inside is a tiny room. Plain. Unadorned. Every surface is made of the same smooth metal, except for a cushioned mattress against the far wall and a narrow door beside it.

Just another prison.

With a deep sigh, I shuffle to a bed that's softer than anything at Alphanax. Is everything beyond the confines of the orphanage like this? If so, maybe it won't be so bad to—No. I want freedom. I *deserve* freedom after everything that's happened. So what if Fletcher saved me from that hell hole? So what if I'm a human like him? That doesn't mean I'll defer to his whims; not when I'm so close to the freedom Falah and I dreamt of! I have to be ready when an opportunity presents itself again. And for that, I need rest. I lay back on the almost-too-soft surface, close my eyes, and drift into darkness.

3

A knock on the door snaps me awake. I bolt upright and stare at the metal slab. It doesn't open.

"Aiko?" The door muffles Fletcher's voice. "We've landed."

I climb off the bed and cross to the door, opening it with the press of a button. Fletcher stands against the wall opposite my door, a messy bundle clutched in one hand. He pushes it at me.

"Here."

"What is it?"

"Clothes," he says. "Probably won't fit, but it's better than that."

I look down at the bloodstained smock and see it clearly for the first time since—

"Th—thanks."

He nods. "Get changed."

I close the door and untangle the garments. Sandals flop to the floor, along with the trimmed arms and legs of a too-large jumpsuit. It's just as baggy as the smock when I slip into it, but far softer. And the arms and legs are all different lengths. Did Fletcher cut them himself?

Folding the stained smock, I place it on the foot of the bed, step into the oversized sandals, and walk back to the door.

Fletcher is still waiting on the other side of the hall.

"Ready?"

I give him a silent nod and follow as he turns down the hall.

The ramp is already extended, and tepid air filters in from outside, carrying a pungent odor that stings my nose. A smooth metal floor stretches in every direction, occupied by ships of all shapes and sizes. Fletcher's is the largest, but also the ugliest. Other ships have soft lines and swooping curves, but his is just a dull tube...

He pauses at the bottom of the ramp and beckons impatiently.

"Come on. Stay close."

I walk at his shoulder into the maze of ships. Crates litter the floor around each, and countless beings go about the task of loading or unloading. Most I don't recognize. The rest are Kaisin. They stand apart, clustered into their own tight-knit groups, casting disapproving glances at any that veer too close. A scowl tugs at my lips, and it takes all of my force of will to keep my eyes glued to Fletcher's back and not meet jittery, blue-eyed glances with smoldering ire.

At the opposite end of the space, a massive set of double doors creak open as we approach. On the other side, towering structures stretch toward a roof made of glass. The clear plates are fitted together between octagon-patterned metal scaffolding. Beyond, countless stars twinkle in a kaleidoscope of color. I sigh in wonder, then drop my eyes to the dense crowd filling the street.

Here, there are even stranger beings.

Against the wall of a nearby building, a blob of flesh with saucer-sized eyes balances on a trembling nest of tentacles. A few feet past it is another being with a razor sharp beak and a tufted feathery mane. Beyond are countless others in shapes and sizes I never dreamed possible, each speaking a different language.

Craning my neck to see over the crowd, I scan for *anything* familiar. Neon signs hanging over storefronts at the sides of the street are scrawled in dozens of strange languages. In the distance, a line of glyphs I recognize stand out from the rest. Fallah taught me the Quiloh alphabet, though I barely know enough of the letters to piece together the sign's meaning. Something about food. And drink.

That's enough.

I glance at Fletcher. He's busy shoving his way through the crowd, not paying attention to me. It's now or never.

Slipping into the relentless press is easy. The flow of beings carry me away from Fletcher like one of Ki'leh's feathers on a breeze. I make my way to the edge of the street as the sign draws closer. And I scramble out of the flow just in time. Taking slow, deep breaths to calm my racing heart, I scan the crowd for any sign of Fletcher, but he isn't there. He didn't notice.

Good.

The sign hangs over a rickety door that seems less kept than any of the others on the street. No beings loiter around the entrance. No light shines through the narrow gap between metal and frame. No one even acknowledges the door exists. That doesn't inspire confidence, but Fallah had been kinder to me than anyone else at Alphanax. She was more than a friend. She was family. As near to blood as I'll ever be able to manage. If there's a Quiloh inside, they'll be just as friendly. I feel that much in my gut.

Neglected hinges groan when I push the door open. Inside, a low roof lined with yellow lights hunkers over a dingy space. Circular tables are arranged in front of a wide counter stretching across the back wall. Behind it, bottles of various liquids are stacked on shelves that seem inadequate to handle the job. Soft melodies drift through the air, more of an ambient sway of sound than a structured rhythm. And as I'd hoped, a Quiloh is behind the counter. They sit on powerful haunches and balance their front two legs on the faded surface.

Their ears swivel in my direction as I walk to the counter.

"Hello there!" They—he—greets me in a baritone rumbling lilt I didn't expect to hear again so soon.

"Hi," I rumble in reply. My suddenly dry tongue stumbles over the word.

His ears flick in surprise. *"You speak Quiloh?"*

"Yes," I say with a wistful smile.

It hurts thinking about Fallah, but being able to speak in the language we'd shared for so long sends an odd serenity washing over me.

"What can I do for you?" He asks.

"I need your help. If you're willing,"

Thick, stubby fingers wiggle in time with his flicking ears, as sightless eyes narrow. *"What kind of help? You're not in trouble, are you?"*

"Nothing like that," I rumble quickly. *"I'm just…lost."*

Lost? Is that the best I can come up with?

The Quiloh's ears swivel forward so I can see their full, round shape. It means he doesn't believe me. *"Are you sure you aren't in trouble?"*

"No. I'm just—" Lying to the Quiloh anymore won't help. He already doesn't believe my little white lie. So, all I can do is tell

him the truth. I take a deep breath. *"I'm new here. I don't know where I am. I don't know where I'm going. I need help."*

It stings to be so forthright, so vulnerable—but it's easier to plead for help from a Quiloh than any of the other, stranger aliens on the station. I just hope he'll pity my situation and lend a hand. I'll take anything as long as it helps me grasp the freedom Fallah and I sought.

The Quiloh gives a heavy chuff, and his ears relax. *"Wait here."*

My heart pounds as he heaves his front legs off the counter and lumbers to a door in the back wall. He returns a moment later, limping on three legs, with a large bowl of a soupy substance that smells more edible than it looks balanced on the fourth. He places it in front of me.

"Eat."

My stomach grumbles thanks as a mouth-watering aroma washes over me. I grab the bowl with both hands and raise it to my lips. The liquid has a smooth texture and complex flavor. Bitterness bites the tongue, before a wave of spiciness sets my mouth on fire. The finish is sweet and savory. And unlike anything I've ever tasted.

I lower the bowl to gasp for air.

The Quiloh chuckles. *"Good?"*

"The best," I reply. *"What is it?"*

"Gundor-tail soup," he says.

I give a slow nod. I've never heard of a Gundor, but its tail is delicious!

"Do you mind if I ask you a question?" I say, after another deep draught of soup.

"Sure." The Quiloh lifts his front feet back onto the countertop.

"Do you know what a human is?"

Round ears flap a negative. *"I don't know this word. Where did you hear it?"*

I frown. Did Fletcher make the whole thing up? *"No place important."*

With an absentminded shrug, the Quiloh lumbers to check on a patron at the far end of the counter.

I glance down at the already nearly empty bowl and ponder my future in the droplets of grease glistening in the dim light. Fletcher insisted it was dangerous on the station, but was it really? So far, I haven't seen anything as worrying or threatening as the many things I witnessed at Alphanax. There are Kaisin on the station, but they seem to keep to themselves; a far cry from watching them drag children into the unknown. And none of the other beings have paid me more than a passing glance. The Quiloh has been accommodating so far. Maybe he could help me find a place to stay? Somewhere I can think about what I want to do next. Maybe he'd even let me stay with *him* for a little bit.

I take a deep breath to rumble the question at the Quiloh, but the door swings open with a stuttering creak.

A tall Kaisin swathed in dark, loose-fitting robes slips past the threshold like a looming shadow. I hunch forward as jittery eyes scan the establishment. They sweep past me and settle on a pale figure sitting in a dim corner: another Kaisin, wrapped in a hooded robe as dark as the shadows around him. The two make eye contact, then look at me.

28

Before I can slip off the stool and beeline for the door, they are on either side of me, staring down with glassy, unfocused eyes.

"Can I help you?" I ask.

The tall Kaisin leans closer and looks *through* me.

I frown. "Hello?"

Neither answer. Neither move.

This is strange. Unsettling.

The Quiloh shuffles down the counter and shifts his gaze from me to the two looming Kaisin. It says a single, heavily accented word. "Problem?"

Both Kaisin remain perfectly still, but the tall one offers a stiff reply. "No."

The Quiloh looks at me and rumbles. *"Problem?"*

The heat of the Kaisin squeezed on either side of me is as smothering as the hottest midsummer day on Alphanax.

I clench my teeth. *"Trouble? Maybe? I don't know."*

The Quiloh blinks and shifts his gaze from one Kaisin to the other. "Excuse. Disperse."

Spider-like fingers close around one of my biceps, then the other. But otherwise, the Kaisin remain perfectly still. Silent.

"Let me go!" I cry out as their iron grip forces me off of the stool. I try to twist away, but their grip tightens.

"Excuse!" The Quiloh shouts after them. "Release!"

The Kaisin ignore him and drive me into the street.

I squirm as they march, in lockstep, parallel to the bustling crowd toward a nearby alleyway. I twist in their grip, kick at their shins, and shout. "Help! Somebody! Anybody!"

My cries fall on deaf ears. Some aliens simply don't hear. Others cast sidelong glances at me, then quicken their pace, unwilling to intervene in whatever business the Kaisin have with me.

We're steps away from the alley. This is it. This is how it ends. At the hands of Kaisin. Just like Fallah.

"Excuse me."

My heart jumps at the familiar voice. And I struggle with renewed fervor when Fletcher slips out of the crowd.

The Kaisin pause and sweep Fletcher with their glassy-eyed stares. For a moment, they freeze, then a flicker of recognition mars their stony expressions.

"Another," the tall one drones.

Suddenly, the other Kaisin lunges. The motion is stiff, and Fletcher is ready. He catches the Kaisin's slender wrists and spins it against the nearest wall. It smashes into the textured polymer with a hollow thud and collapses to all fours, gasping for breath.

The tall Kaisin doesn't move, and his grip doesn't loosen, but this is my chance! Planting both feet firmly on the ground, I bend my knees, then straighten, whipping my head back into the Kaisin's flat nose. It lets go and stumbles. I spin and follow with a shoulder to his abdomen, knocking him to the ground.

Fletcher grabs my wrist. "Let's go!"

I scramble into the thick crowd after him. His grip is so strong my hand throbs, and my shoulder aches from the incessant pulling as he weaves through the press. Even when I run out of breath, he doesn't stop; not until the streets are narrower, emptier, and lined with squat buildings that blot out the glittering stars overhead.

When he finally releases my hand, I sag against the wall of the nearest building.

"I told you it was dangerous," he says with a chiding tone.

"Why do you care?" I ask defensively.

"We're both human. We should stick together."

"Why?"

He grimaces at my blurted question, but offers no reason.

I look over my shoulder, down the street. "What were those Kaisin going to do with me?"

"No clue," he replies. "Never seen that happen before. Did they say anything to you?"

I shake my head. "They were quiet the whole time. Except when they said 'another'. Do you think they meant—?"

"Human," Fletcher finishes for me. "Probably. But why, I wonder?"

"You said your mentor told you about them. Did he mention anything about why Kaisin might be interested in Humans?"

"Nothing." Fletcher rubs the stubble on his chin. "But he was Kaisin, which might explain how those two knew what you were."

He doesn't sound so sure.

Phantom fingers still grip my biceps. And the memory of the duo's empty stares sends a shiver down my spine. "Where were they taking me?"

He chews on his lip, then shakes his head. "I don't know."

Stepping away from the wall, he glances up and down the street, then motions for me to follow. "We shouldn't stick around to find out. Let's go."

I want to refuse, but the thought that those Kaisin might still be looking for us—for Humans—twists my insides. With a reluctant nod, I fall in line behind him, but this time stick close to his shoulder. As we push through the crowd, I ask, "How did you find me?"

"Noticed you were gone and started asking around," he says. "Lucky for me, you stick out enough for a few beings to remember you. Then, I heard you yelling."

"Thanks," I mumble. "Where are we going now?"

"To visit an old friend," he says, glancing over his shoulder with a forced smile. "And with any luck, get a few answers to our little problem."

4

Glowing letters I can't read flicker above a worn door.

"This is it," Fletcher says, glancing up and down the street for what feels like the millionth time. We turned off the crowded thoroughfare a while ago, so it'll be easy to spot an approaching Kaisin. But they'll be able to see us as well.

He steps toward the door, pulls it open, and motions me inside.

Bright white lights glint off a pristine metal floor, stretching to walls covered in shelves bursting at the seams with mismatched parts. Across from the door is a wide workbench. The small being sitting behind it doesn't look up when we enter. I've never seen one of its kind before, but something in my gut tells me it is a 'he'.

"I'll be with you in a moment," the small being calls out in a high-pitched voice.

"Just like you to keep me waiting," Fletcher calls back.

Wide eyes look up at him, then flick to me. The small being's lips stretch into a grin. "Gohk sold you more than just another story this time?"

"At Alphanax, just like she said," Fletcher replies.

The small being skewers me with an appraising stare. "Come here, girl."

I don't budge.

"I won't bite," he prompts.

With halting steps, I shuffle across the open floor, remembering all the times the Headmistress trotted me out in front of prospective buyers. But at Aphanax, I was never alone. Now, however...I stifle a frown as I stop in front of the small being. He studies me with large eyes, sharp teeth bared in a grin, bushy eyebrows wiggling. Finally, he reaches out a hand.

I stare at it. What does he expect me to do?

Spindly fingers dart out to grab mine, and soft fur tickles my palm as he gives my whole arm a gentle shake.

"Pleased to meet you," the small being croons. "My name is Rhuk."

"I'm Aiko," I reply, with a wary smile.

"Are you done?" Fletcher asks behind me.

Rhuk drops my hand and shuffles to one side.

"I'm being nice," he says. "Easing her into this wide, new world you've dragged her into."

He looks up at me and winks, then walks past.

"Now, out with whatever you're bursting at the seams to say."

"A couple of Kaisin just tried to grab us off of the street."

Rhuk frowns. "Both of you?"

"Well, they were in the middle of carting her away," he replies. "And when I intervened, they made a grab at me.

"Why?"

"I'm not sure," Fletcher says with a frown. "They only said a single word—'another'—so I'm guessing it has to do with..."

He trails off and motions to me, then himself.

"That's new." Rhuk's eyebrows twitch. "This ever happen to you?"

"Never."

"And they didn't say anything else?"

"No. You think Gohk would have anything to say about this?" Rhuk gives a thoughtful nod. "You could go ask her."

"How about you call her, instead?" Fletcher shoots back. "I'd rather stay off the streets for now. Just in case."

"Good idea," Rhuk agrees. "I'll give her a shout. In the meantime, you two head upstairs. Get comfortable."

Fletcher beckons as he passes and heads for a spiral staircase tucked between a shelf and the wall. I follow. The grated metal digs into the balls of my feet through the thin sandals, and the corrugated walkway at the top is no better. I glance down, past the ill-fitting garment Fletcher gave me, to the tops of my dirty feet. Even though I escaped Alphanax, its memory still clings to me. Haunts me. And there's nothing I can do about it.

The walkway ends at an open door. Inside is a small room lined with supple carpet; probably the softest, springiest surface I've ever walked on. Fletcher drops into a cushioned chair to the right of the door. There's another beside it, with a small table in between. Across from the door, a bed is pushed into the corner. To the right of that is a counter, cabinets, and a collection of instruments I can't identify. But nothing is small. Wouldn't Rhuk prefer everything to be his size? Maybe not. I just know it would make me feel weird.

Stepping away from the door, I settle on the seat beside Fletcher. It's as soft as the carpeted floor and the bed on the

Undertow. I close my eyes and relax into the enveloping cushions. I could get used to everything being so comfortable.

"How long were you at Alphanax?"

I open my eyes and look at Fletcher. He's leaning forward, elbows on his knees, gray eyes fixed on me. He seems genuinely interested in my answer.

I shrug. "I can't remember a time I wasn't at Alphanax."

"How old are you?"

"Twenty-seven," I reply.

He blinks, then asks: "How long is a year on Alphanax?"

"Two hundred days." The number is etched into my head. And my heart.

Fletcher mumbles under his breath for a moment, then: "So, 15 by the standard calendar."

I furrow my brow. "Standard?"

He nods. "Everything out here is based on a common 'standard': money, time, measurements, language."

"And who decided on those?"

Fletcher frowns. "I'm not sure, actually. It's just always been that way."

I nod slowly. "And how old are you?"

"By the standard calendar? Fifty. But I'd be ninety-one on Alphanax," he says with a grin.

Ninety-one!? He's so old! But he's seen so much, been free all that time.

"What's it like?" I blurt out.

He cocks his head to the side. "Being fifty?"

I shake my head. "Being *free.*"

"Oh," he pauses, thinking. "Better than living in an orphanage, but not really any easier."

I blink. "Wait...Did you—?"

"Yep," he replies. "Fifteen years in an orphanage, just like you."

That catches me off guard. I didn't expect us to have so much in common. Then again, with what he told me about Humans seemingly being true, it makes sense. Doesn't it? I lean forward, toes curled on the stiff sandals, fingers digging into the plush arm of the chair, heart racing. "And then?"

"My mentor showed up."

The Headmistress' watchful eye was bad enough, but being adopted by a Kaisin? Having to live with one? The thought makes my skin crawl.

"By Kaisin standards, he was kind. But..." He trails off. There's something he won't say.

I'm about to ask what when Rhuk appears.

"You two getting along?" he asks.

"Well enough," Fletcher says quickly. "Gohk on her way?"

"Yeah, but she isn't happy," Rhuk replies.

"You *told* her what happened, right?"

"Of course," Rhuk says with a shrug, "but you know how she is."

Fletcher sighs.

I shift my gaze between the two of them. "Who is Gohk?"

"She's an information broker," Fletcher replies.

"The best in the sector," Rhuk chimes in, crossing to the bed and hopping on top of it without a second thought. He sits facing us.

37

Fletcher nods in agreement. "She's the one who told me about you."

"And you think she might know what's going on?" I ask.

"If anyone does, it'll be her," Rhuk suggests. "If not..." He shrugs.

Is Gohk really so knowledgeable that they'd put so much faith in the chance she knows something? And *how* will she know? I lean back in the chair and shake my head. I've been away from Alphanax for less than a day and my life is already more complicated than I could have ever imagined. Not only am I human—whatever that is—but the Kaisin want me for some unknown reason.

"What if she doesn't?"

They both frown at my question.

"Then I'll find someone who does."

The snapped reply is as harsh as the deafening crack of a gunshot. My eyes snap to the door and the tall, wiry figure standing there: a Kaisin.

I stiffen against the urge to recoil.

She's so tall, her bald head nearly brushes the doorframe. Jittery blue eyes stare out from a nest of crow's feet, and wrinkles line the rest of her pale face. Her flat nose is crooked, and her impossibly thin lips are stretched into a permanent grimace, granting a better view of pointed, yellowed teeth.

The Headmistress always frightened me. But Gohk? Aside from being the oldest Kaisin I've ever seen, she's truly, honestly terrifying. Just looking at her sends an icy shiver down my spine. And my legs tremble from muscles clenched and ready to flee at a moment's notice.

"But lucky for you, I happen to have *some* useful information."
Gohk's lips stretch into a grin as spider-like fingers slip beneath
the folds of a worn canvas coat. They reappear holding a glowing
slip of glass similar to the one Fletcher had briefly studied at Alphanax.

"As usual," Fletcher says with a sigh. "And for a price, I bet."

"You're lucky I'm willing to give you anything at all," she
snaps, "considering the trouble you got into today."

I stifle a grimace. Fletcher was the one getting scolded, but her
sour mood tinges the air like a cloud of choking dust. Then her
hard gaze drifts to me.

"This the one I told you about?"

"Human after all," Fletcher says.

A slight frown touches Gohk's lips. "Lucky her."

She left a lot unsaid in the tone of those two words.

Fletcher clears his throat.

Gohk skewers him with an annoyed glance, then looks down
at the pad. "Lorn—" the muscles in Fletcher's jaw bulge at hearing that name "—had thoughts about the relationship between
Humans and Kaisin."

"Lorn?" I ask.

"The one who found him." Gohk says, motioning to Fletcher
with her free hand.

Fletcher hadn't used that name. He'd simply said 'my mentor'. What happened to Lorn that Fletcher won't say his name?

"Anyway, Lorn had thoughts—"

"What does this have to do with the Kaisin that tried to grab
us?" Fletcher interjects.

"Hush," she grumbles. "I'm getting to that."

Fletcher holds up his hands in mock surrender.

"Lorn knew about Humans long before he found you," she continues. "They're"—she takes a deep breath and cocks her head to the side as if choosing her next words very carefully—"more or less a legend."

"What do you mean?" I blurt out.

"A story. A fable. A fairy tale." Gohk shrugs. "Take your pick."

"What kind of stories?" I ask.

"Not the good kind." Gohk's lips purse. "Which may explain why those Kaisin had such a negative reaction to you."

"So Humans are what? Monsters?" I ask.

"Nothing like that," Gohk says, shaking her head. "More like a bad omen. Or an example of hubris."

"What does that even mean?"

Gohk shrugs again.

"So, what? It's nothing to worry about?" I press. "Just some Kaisin taking those stories too literally?"

Gohk blinks. Then quickly nods. "Sure, kid. You hit the nail on the head." The answer sounds disingenuous, at best.

A confused look twists Fletcher's face "But what about Lorn? How does he fit into all this?"

"Lorn—like most other Kaisin—thought they were just stories." Her lips stretch into a tight-lipped smile. "Until he found you. Then, he suddenly wanted to know everything about Humans."

She starts counting on her fingers.

"Where did they come from? How did they get here? Where did they go? And why did the Kaisin—and only the Kaisin—have so many stories about them?"

"And?" Fletcher leans forward.

"He…" Gohk hesitates.

"Well?" He urges.

Her brow furrows for a moment, then she shakes her head. "I gave you the information you wanted. The rest is in the past."

She turns to leave.

"Wait a damn minute," Fletcher growls at her back.

She pauses and turns, a sweet, dangerous smile curling her lips. "Excuse me?"

"I mean"—the hard expression on his face softens—"what else is there to tell? I'd like to hear it."

Gohk stares at him for a long time. Appraising. Motionless. Finally, she sighs. "Have it your way."

She crosses her arms and leans against the door frame.

"Like I said, Lorn started looking for answers. That's why he was always sneaking off on his own; disappearing for days, sometimes weeks, at a time."

"You knew?" Fletcher demands.

"Of course I knew," Gohk shoots back. "He was getting all his information from me."

Fletcher frowns. "And where was he going?"

Gohk scoffs. "Every place that might have a connection to Humans, no matter how small. Led him all over the sector. And beyond."

The corners of Fletcher's lips dip even further, into a scowl. "So, did he ever find the answer?"

Gohk gives him a grim smile. "Yes and no."

"What does that mean?" Rhuk rocks forward so far I'm sure he'll tumble from his spot on the bed.

She pauses again, head cocked to the side, obviously thinking. Then, she sucks in a deep breath, holds up the pad, and thumbs its surface.

"I've done it," a deep voice begins.

Fletcher stiffens, and Rhuk's wide eyes grow wider.

"I've found the ship that brought Humans to this sector of space. It's massive. The ship isn't in bad shape, so I wouldn't be surprised if a few systems still function. If not, I can always find the memory cores, pull them, and figure out how to extract the data later. Maybe this ship'll have the answers I've been looking for. Only time will tell. I'll send updates when I can. Be back soon!"

Gohk lowers the glass pad, the whisper of a frown touching her lips. "That was the last message I got from Lorn."

"You've known all this time." Fletcher's lips press into a thin line. "Thirty years and you never said a word. To me. Or Rhuk."

The pain in Fletcher's voice suggests an old wound has just been torn open.

"I had my reasons." Gohk's permanent grimace stretches even wider.

"Like what?" Fletcher snaps in an accusing tone.

"Like keeping *you* safe,' she shoots back. "Lorn didn't want you following in his footsteps because he knew where the path might lead."

She crosses her arms.

"He was right. So was I. And you're still alive."

Fletcher looks away and his lips move, but he doesn't speak.

Rhuk fills the tense silence with a question: "Where did he go?"

"To wherever these coordinates lead," Gohk replies, waving the pad.

"You ever go after him to find out what happened?" His eyebrows wiggle.

She frowns. "No."

Fletcher's fiery gaze snaps back to Gohk.

"Why not?" he growls.

"If he thought it was too dangerous to go, why would I?" Her free hand balls into a fist and drops to her hip as she looms to her full height. "He's gone. Finding his bones wouldn't have made that any easier to swallow."

Fletcher scowls. "You're so sure he's dead?"

"Lorn never came back," Gohk deadpans. "That's proof enough for me."

"Maybe I want to find his bones!" Fletcher fixes her with a defiant stare. There's pain behind it; pain I understand. Even though the thought of being so close to a Kaisin sends a chill down my spine, it doesn't diminish the magnitude of his loss. And it hasn't diminished over the intervening years. I stifle a grimace. Will the gnawing emptiness in the pit of my stomach ever disappear? Or will the ghost of Fallah haunt me for the rest of my life?

"It's too dangerous," Gohk repeats. "If he didn't come back, you won't either."

"I need to know what happened." Fletcher half-rises out of the chair. "And he deserves to be found and laid to rest. Properly."

I give a shallow nod. Presented the opportunity, I'd have done the same for Fallah.

But that isn't the only reason to go after Lorn. Fletcher and I are both human. I don't know what that means. Fletcher doesn't seem to know either. So, won't it be worth following in Lorn's footsteps just to see what he might have learned? Isn't it worth the risk to discover the truth about what we are? What we really are? Smooth skins. Humans.

"Maybe we should go," I blurt out.

The three of them look at me.

Gohk frowns. "Have you been listening, girl? It would have been dangerous enough for Fletcher to go alone. But the two of you…?"

She shakes her head.

"On top of everything else, he doesn't have time to babysit you."

Fletcher is poised to give a scathing reply. His eyebrows are drawn together, his mouth is twisted into a scowl, and his hands are clasped, knuckles white. But a hollow, echoing knock interrupts him.

Rhuk vaults from his spot on the bed, scurries to the door, then slips out of view. A moment later, his high-pitched voice echoes back through the open door. "Sorry to keep you waiting! How can I help you today?"

Eerie silence answers him.

"Were you looking for something in particular?" Rhuk asks slowly. Cautiously.

Fletcher leaps up first, but I beat him to the door. A quick peek reveals Rhuk standing beside his work bench, facing two Kaisin. Even though their backs are to us, I can tell they aren't the two from earlier. These are close to the same height, and their remarkably similar robes are just as dark. Just as loose.

"Hello? Can I help you?" Rhuk asks again, walking up to the duo, but staying well out of reach. I don't blame him. Kaisin are bad enough. But *these* Kaisin? Just looking at them makes me want to run as far and as fast as I can.

The one on the right pulls out a glowing pad and offers it to Rhuk.

His eyebrows twitch as he studies it. "What is this?"

The two Kaisin share a blank look. Neither speak. But after a moment, they point at the pad in perfect unison.

"I haven't seen anyone that looks like this," Rhuk says and hands it back.

With a coordinated nod, the Kaisin accept the pad. As they begin to turn, slender fingers grip my shoulder and yank me away from the door. Then, Gohk slips in front of me, hiding me from view.

Momentary silence is broken by Rhuk's high-pitched trill. "Another customer."

"We were in the middle of a transaction," Gohk grumbles. "You're interrupting, so I'd appreciate it if the two of you move along."

Paired with the words, her dismissive wave seems more like a command. But it works, because after a few more tense moments of silence, Rhuk appears at the door.

"They're looking for you two," he says.

Gohk fixes me with a hard stare. "Are those the two that tried to grab you earlier?"

I shake my head. "No"

"So there's a group of them after you," she says with a frown. "I wonder how many more are traipsing around the station."

I blink. "There might be more?"

"How many do you think?" Rhuk asks.

Gohk shakes her head. "Impossible to tell. A dozen? A hundred?"

My chest tightens, like a giant, invisible hand is squeezing my heart. "What do we do?"

"Perhaps it's best if they leave the station for a few days," Rhuk suggests.

Gohk nods in agreement. "Not a terrible idea, but—"

"Where would we go?' I cut in, furrowing my brow and looking at each of them in turn.

"After Lorn," Fletcher says.

Gohk scoffs. "Again, no."

The muscles in his jaw bulge. "Where, then?"

"Anywhere else. But"—she waggles the pad at him—"I'm not giving you the coordinates. Besides, you have another problem: how are you going to get to your ship? It's definitely *not* safe on the streets if they're carrying pictures of you two around."

She raises a finger to her lips.

"How did they get those, anyway?"

"I don't know about that, but I have an idea about getting them back to the *Undertow*," Rhuk chimes in with a saw-toothed grin, "though I doubt either of you are going to like it."

5

"You've got to be kidding," Fletcher grumbles.

The cargo container towers over us, but that isn't what he's complaining about. I glance at the two suits standing nearby.

"I'm not doing it," he continues.

"It won't be that bad," Rhuk urges. "And it's only from here to the *Undertow*."

"Without power, the suit's a coffin," he replies. "Take too long to get us to the ship and it really will be."

"I'll be with him," Gohk chimes in. "The Kaisin won't stop *me*."

It's clear Fletcher wants to protest, but he holds his tongue. After all, how can he argue when she got the other two Kaisin to leave so easily? I'm certainly not going to protest. If Gohk and Rhuk feel leaving the station is for the best, I'll trust them, though I don't really have any other choice. The alternative is being dragged away by the Kaisin, whatever their intentions.

"How is this going to work?" I ask, shuffling toward one of the suits.

The steel frame stands two heads taller than me; solid, yet elegant. Thick arms sprout from an oval torso, planted on powerful legs that bend twice: once at the knee and again, backwards, where the boots should be. The suit balances on a collection of stubby appendages that look like a Quiloh's fingers. Maybe they're supposed to? The hands look Kaisin. And the helmet has an odd backswept shape, like a teardrop.

Rhuk sidles up beside me. "You'll get in, squeeze into the cargo container. Then I'll pull the batteries from each suit to make sure there are no accidents on the way to the ship."

I frown. "I get the cargo container, but why the suits?"

"They're Fletcher's," Rhuk replies. "He dropped them off for service before heading to Alphanax."

"Sure," I say, scratching my head, "but couldn't we make two trips?"

"Exactly," Fletcher agrees.

Gohk drums her fingers on the cargo container. "It would be a risk.

"Why?" I press.

"It's a big container," Rhuk offers. "The only way to get it to the dock is through the streets, so we're going to get noticed. Once we could get away with, but twice?" He shakes his head. "We'll definitely draw undue attention. Maybe get stopped. And if they want to open the container…"

"Do we *need* the suits?" I shift my gaze between Rhuk and Fletcher.

It takes a few heartbeats for Rhuk to give a noncommittal shrug. "I suppose—"

"Yes," Fletcher interrupts. "I don't have any suits on the *Undertow* right now, and space is dangerous enough as it is. I'd rather be safe than sorry." He pauses, then mumbles. "It's still a terrible idea, though."

"You just said you wanted the suits, so quit whining and get a move on," Gohk snaps. "I don't have all day."

Fletcher storms toward one of the suits in a huff.

Rhuk scurries to the other and disappears behind its bulk. Then, his furry head pokes back into view. "Aiko! Come here!"

I hurry to join the small being. The bulging back of the suit is tilted away from the torso. The entire inside—what I can see, anyway—is covered in sectioned pads. Like cushions, only much smaller and chopped up into awkward shapes.

"Climb up," Rhuk says from his perch on the tilted section.

It's easy enough to mount the suit. My sandaled feet find solid footing on the thick legs. And there are bright yellow handholds strategically placed to be out of the way, yet reachable. With one final heave, I drop to a seated position beside him.

"Slide in," he commands.

Swinging my feet into the torso, I scoot forward. For a heartbeat, I fall, then the plush lining catches me. The suit feels like the bed on the *Undertow*, too soft and way oversized.

"Good," Rhuk says at my shoulder. "I'm going to close the suit now. Don't get pinched."

The back seals with a hiss, and my world descends into silence so complete, the rush of blood in my ears rumbles like rolling thunder. Then, I hear a click followed by Rhuk's voice, clear but digitized through the suit's audio system.

"Can you hear me?" He vaults up the suit's arm and taps on the curved glass visor in front of me, eyebrows twitching in question.

"Yes."

"Excellent," he replies. "Now this next part is tricky, so I'm going to need you to do exactly what I say, alright?"

I nod.

"Okay. Put your arms into the holes on either side of you, and slip your hands into the gloves."

I do.

"Now, hold very still."

Rhuk slips out of sight, and a creeping hiss rises out of the silence. A moment later, the cushions around my arms and legs begin to grow. Tighten. Squeeze. Then, the cushions around my torso do the same, until I'm not sure whether my pounding heart and gasped breath is because of fear or the constricting surroundings.

"Calm down," Rhuk calls out, as the firm pressure equalizes across my entire body.

The soothing tone of his voice cuts through the panic. I manage a slow breath. Then another.

"This is normal," he continues. "Each pad has a sensor built in that measures the movement of your muscles, transferring them to the suit. It takes firm contact to get a decent reading. How does it feel?"

"A little uncomfortable," I admit.

"You'll get used to it." he says. "Now, I want you to take a step forward. Be gentle."

I lift my foot, and the suit responds like a second skin. Even though it wobbles when my foot lowers, I feel weightless. Invincible.

"Good," Rhuk says. "Think you can follow Fletcher?"

Craning my neck to look past Rhuk, still perched in front of the visor, I watch the other suit slip effortlessly into the cramped container.

I flex my fingers and feel a vibration through the cushions as the massive gauntlets do the same. "Sure."

"Alright." Rhuk drops out of view, then reappears next to Gohk. "Go ahead. And be careful."

Ginger steps make the suit respond in kind. The wobbling walk isn't pretty, but I make it to the container, and then inside with only the slightest nudge against Fletcher's suit.

"Great," I hear Rhuk call. "I'm going to strap you guys in, then disconnect the batteries. Hang in there."

In the dim light, Rhuk looks like just another shadow, flitting across the surface of the two suits, connecting straps to anchor points on their surfaces. It's no wonder everything in his room is 'normal' sized; he doesn't have to care. I wouldn't either, if I was capable of such acrobatics.

It takes only a few minutes for Rhuk to finish with the straps, then he goes to work on the suits. Mounting Fletcher's, he opens a panel in the center of its bulging back. A twist here and a pull there frees a bundle of wires, and the suit sags against taught straps. He disappears, and I feel as much as hear him poking around the back of my suit. Then, it goes limp, and the pressure of countless constricting cushions releases as if the suit just let out a deep sigh.

Once again, the silence is filled with the beating of my heart and the rush of blood in my ears. And the rhythmic cadence quickens when the world descends into darkness. Were it not for light rocking as the cargo container moved, I'd panic. Even now,

I can feel it gnawing at the back of my mind, clamoring for attention.

I draw in a deep breath, then another, and think about Fallah. Remembering her is equal parts painful and comforting, but it grounds me in the darkness; reminds me why every step is worth it. Freedom was snatched from her grasp, but I won't let it be taken from mine. For both of us.

The memories of everything we shared and planned to share buoy me through the darkness, until a flicker of light returns. Then, the suit comes to life. Fresh air drives away the sticky funk that had filled the cramped space, and the cushions balloon, squeezing the fresh air out of me.

The tap of Rhuk's tiny feet takes my mind off the uncomfortable press; then his wide eyes appear in front of the visor. "Back out. Slowly."

I do.

"Stop," he commands.

I do.

"Alright, you're done," he says with a smile. "Now, you need to open the suit."

"How?"

"Raise your left hand. Slowly."

The metal arm moves like one of my own.

Rhuk scoots aside. "You see that red button? The one under the clear plate?"

There's a control panel on the suit's left wrist, covered in buttons winking like so many stars. Nearest the wrist is a clear plastic cover framing a bright red circle that reminds me of the sun on Alphanax. "That one?"

Rhuk nods. "That's the master release. If you press it, the cushion will deflate and the back will pop open."

I reach out with artificial fingers for the cover. When they touch, a light whisper brushes the end of my glove. I yank the fingers back.

"Force feedback," Rhuk says with a chuckle. "It's easier to handle things if you can feel them."

I nod and try again. It's a strange sensation to feel something with hands that aren't mine, but Rhuk is right. Without any trouble, I flip the plastic cover open and press the button. This time, the suit stiffens when the cushions deflate, and cold air washes over me as the suit's back tilts away.

"You alright?" Rhuk asks when he lands behind me.

"Yeah." I shoot a smile over my shoulder.

"You did good for your first time," he says.

"Thanks!" I grab the yellow handholds overhead—they bookend an ominous red lever—shimmy out of the suit, and hop to the floor. "It was fun!"

"Not all of it," Fletcher chimes in. He leans against the leg of his suit, sweaty and flushed.

So was I. The oversized jumpsuit is wrinkled and damp with sweat. Wherever we're going, maybe I could get some new clothes. At least something that fits better and isn't so musty.

"Well," Gohk saunters toward him. "Safe travels, wherever you decide to go."

She sticks out her right hand. The other is bent, hooked in the collar of her coat. It drapes over her shoulder, and sticking out of the pocket is a glowing slip of glass. The same one she waved in Fletcher's face when he asked where Lorn had gone.

She said going after him was too dangerous, but so was growing up at Alphanax. Fallah and I spent every day worrying about what might happen if either of us were bought by Kaisin. And when it finally happened, Fallah paid the ultimate price. So, I know what danger is. Besides, how bad can the sunken ship Lorn found really be?

Gohk's back is to me, blocking Fletcher's view. And Rhuk is giving Fletcher's suit a once over. It's now or never!

My sandaled feet are whisper-quiet on the smooth metal floor. And Gohk doesn't feel a thing when I pluck the pad from her coat pocket. I spin away and try to bury the slip of glass in the thick folds of the jumpsuit. But there isn't that much extra fabric; it won't stay bunched around the pad.

"You too, Aiko."

My next step falters, and I nearly drop the pad. I can feel Gohk's jittery stare piercing the center of my back. It will look odd if I don't turn. But the pad! She'll see! Maybe this isn't such a good idea after all?

"Everything alright?" Fletcher asks.

I half turn. As expected, Gohk is staring at me. Fletcher stands beside her, eyebrows raised in question. Even Rhuk stopped working to look in my direction. This isn't great.

"Yeah, it's just—" What can I say to redirect their attention *away* from me?

"Don't worry," Rhuk says from his perch. "You two'll be safe once you're off the station."

"Of course," Gohk adds, her blue eyes softening. It's strange to see a Kaisin look so…amicable. "I'll keep an eye on our friends and let you know when everything settles down."

"O—okay," I stammer. They all misread what was happening. But why? Because I'm an orphan? Young? Innocent? Whatever the case, as long as I keep the pad hidden, I'll be home free.

"In the meantime, be careful," Gohk says, turning to Fletcher. "I don't know how many Kaisin are looking for you or whether they have any friends. So, don't go anywhere too crowded. Or maybe don't go anywhere at all. It's up to you."

Fletcher frowns. "I'll figure something out."

Gohk nods, smiles, and stalks toward the door.

"I think she knows more than she's telling us," Fletcher says, when Gohk is finally gone.

"She always does," Rhuk replies from atop Fletcher's suit. He's threading a harness under its arms. "But that's why *she's* the information broker."

Fletcher shrugs and disappears through the wide double doors across the room.

Rhuk shakes his head and lets out a deep, exasperated sigh.

"Do Fletcher and Gohk not like each other?" I ask.

"It's not like that," Rhuk replies, sitting on the suit's shoulder. He looks like a toy perched atop the metal behemoth.

"They're hard on each other—always have been—but ever since Lorn disappeared—" Rhuk's lips purse. "There's this…tension between them. It's hard to explain."

He sits quietly for a few moments, then scoffs. "Hard to believe it's been thirty years."

"And all this time you never knew where Lorn went?"

"I knew he went somewhere," Rhuk replies. "He told me he was leaving Fletcher with me; that he'd be back soon. But…"

He shakes his head.

Gohk keeping such a secret for so long explains Fletcher's re-action. And maybe even the tension Rhuk mentioned.

Behind my back, I slip the glass pad from one hand to the other and dab my sweaty palm on the jumpsuit's baggy thigh. Knowing how long Gohk has kept this particular secret dulls the guilt gnawing at my insides and lends a measure of vindication to my decision to swipe the pad. Maybe we'll both find something worthwhile following in Lorn's footsteps.

"Anyway..." Rhuk heaves to his feet. "It'll take me a few minutes to finish this up, so you can be on your way."

He turns back to the harness loosely secured around the suit's torso.

I walk across a large, closed hatch in the center of the floor, to the double doors Fletcher slipped through earlier. Harsh light glints off of the brushed steel floor and walls. Even the crate-packed shelving to either side reflects the spotlights overhead. The room looks brand new, as if it had just been put together.

The one beyond, on the other hand, is dim and dull, closer to the worn interior of Alphanax, but different enough to be comfortable instead of concerning. Or frightening. Cross-hatched metal floors stretch to matte metal walls. A low ceiling supports lights that are more yellow than white. Against the right wall of the space is another set of double doors. Beside it, a counter stretches to a window, beneath which is a table surrounded by four chairs. Left is another closed door. And on the far side of the space, the passageway that leads to my room.

I shuffle to the hall, past my cramped quarters and the closed entry door, to the bridge. Fletcher sat in the center chair, sur-rounded by glowing projections. He glances over his shoulder when I enter. A frown twists his lips. Worry furrows his brow. Giving the barest nod, he turns back to whatever he was doing. Sagging into one of the chairs beside the door, I stuff the glass pad between the cushion and the jumpsuit's extra fabric. I'll give it to Fletcher as soon as Rhuk is gone and we're off the station—once it's too late to turn back.

For a while, only Fletcher's nervous tapping of the controls fills the room. Then, the patter of tiny feet joins the chorus, and Rhuk appears in the doorway.

"Done," he says with a smile.

"Thanks," Fletcher replies, twisting in his chair to face the little being.

"You know where you're going yet?" Rhuk asks.

Fletcher's lips stretch into an obviously forced smile. "Not yet, but there are plenty of options. We'll figure something out."

"Well"—Rhuk flicks his gaze to me, then back—"be careful.

The muscles around Fletcher's eyes tighten. "Sure."

Without another word, Rhuk slips from view. A moment later, the main door opens and the ramp extends. Then, it closes. Fletcher and I are alone. *Finally.*

More tapping sends a shudder through the floor. A whining scream, like a tortured animal, fills the air as the ship lifts off of the dock, spins, and thrusts toward a massive set of double doors. They creak apart as the *Undertow* approaches. And after a moment, a second set heaves open to reveal the twinkling of countless stars in a kaleidoscope of colors.

Fletcher sits back and lets out a heavy sigh. The slump of his shoulders hints at weariness. I feel its shadow looming over me as well.

"So—"

He cuts me off with the wave of a hand. "I still haven't decided where we're going."

There's a twinge of annoyance in his voice.

"I have an idea," I say, holding up the pad I swiped from Gohk's pocket.

Fletcher looks over his shoulder, eyes widening when he sees the device. "When did you—"

"She was distracted, and I couldn't pass up the opportunity."

His lips purse.

"You want to follow in Lorn's footsteps." I wiggle the pad. "So do I."

"Why?"

"Because it's worth the risk to learn the truth about what I am," I reply. "And I owe it to Fallah."

"Fallah?"

I swallow the sudden lump in my throat. "She was my best friend."

His eyebrows lift slightly. "Was?"

"We tried to escape. Failed. Kaisin killed her." The memory of her glassy eyes staring up at the sky twists my stomach into knots. "We were supposed to leave together. Be free together. If I can learn about what I am—what I really am—maybe I can leave the past behind." Earn forgiveness. Forge a new future. "Maybe you can too?"

Fletcher frowns and eyes the glowing pad.

"It'll be dangerous," he finally says.

I take a deep breath. "I'm used to dangerous."

He holds out a hand, and the whisper of a smile touches his lips. "Then I think we have a destination."

6

"That has to be it!"

I follow Fletcher's pointed finger to an azure sphere, no larger than a marble, hidden amidst the glittering starscape in more ways than one. The *Undertou's* charts label this system as unremarkable: a lonely star hanging in the void. And yet...

"A planet?"

Fletcher frowns. "Hmmm."

"Why wasn't it marked on your charts?"

"Who knows?" Fletcher shrugs. "Maybe it was overlooked? Or forgotten?"

He doesn't sound convinced.

Nor am I.

It can't be a coincidence that this planet is just within the bounds of Kaisin space, uncharted, *and* holds the secret to Humans' origins. He ignores my skeptical frown and turns back to the ballooning sphere.

The planet fills half the viewscreen, now. Solid blue resolves into a gradient. Large swaths of navy—nearing black—are interspersed with areas the soft blue color of a moon moth under the glow of ethereal starlight. And clouds as soft and fluffy as Ki'leh's feathers swirl across the surface in myriad patterns.

I frown. "I don't see any land."

"There might not be any," Fletcher offers. "But, we'll see."

Leaning forward, he taps a few buttons. A shudder goes through the *Undertow's* hull, and I feel a tug on my insides. The planet continues to grow, but shifts to one side of the viewscreen. Then, the ship spins until we're looking down at a gentle curve stretching in either direction.

"Low orbit," Fletcher says, standing and stretching.

I stand as well. It's a relief after a few hours in that chair, however comfortable. "What now?"

"We let the *Undertow* do her thing," he says, then continues when he sees my furrowed brow. "A surface scan to find the sunken ship and an atmospheric scan to determine the smoothest way down."

"How long will that take?"

"An hour? Two? Depends on the planet's size." He pauses and stares at me for a moment. "In the meantime, let me see if I can find you something better to wear."

I glance down at the jump suit. It hangs awkwardly from my slim frame, and the poorly cut arms and legs make each of my limbs seem a different length. I've gotten used to it, though. And it's far better than the rough, threadbare smock stained with dirt and Fallah's long-dried blood. Sudden heat burns my cheeks at the reminder of Fallah's death. I won't wear that garment ever again, but the thought of discarding the only solid thing I have to remember her by freezes the breath in my lungs.

Without another word, he strides from the bridge. I don't follow. Can't. Instead, I stare out at the blue and white sphere. This is a whole new world, the first I've seen since Alphanax. And Fallah isn't with me.

Sudden, wet streaks warm my cheeks.

We were supposed to do this together.

I look down. The soft fabric in my lap is darkened by tears, then my vision blurs.

The truth Fallah and I had always wondered about hid somewhere beneath the waters of this planet. But I'd be finding it alone.

Fletcher's heavy footsteps prompt me to wipe my eyes, but I still can't look at him when he walks through the door.

"Here," he says, pushing a folded bundle of cloth into view. "These should fit a bit better."

They smell stale, as if left untouched for a long time.

"Thanks," I mumble, still unable to look him in the eye.

"You okay?" he asks.

"Fine," I lie.

He crouches in front of me. "Listen, I understand how you feel."

I look up at him, poised to insist he doesn't, but the expression on his face twists my tongue into a stuttering knot. There's deep-seated sorrow in his eyes. And his mouth is twisted in pain from a thirty-year-old wound that's suddenly been ripped open.

"The pain passes," he says.

It doesn't look that way from where I'm sitting; doesn't *feel* that way. Maybe he's right. But maybe I don't want it to pass. After all, once it's gone, my memories of Fallah will follow. She'll disappear. Fade to a shadow. She doesn't deserve that. I *want* to hold on. Need to. Somehow. "I—"

Fletcher shakes his head and pushes the clothes at me again.

I accept them with silent gratitude. There's so much I want to say, but can't. And not just because of the lump in my throat.

He leaves me alone, then. To sulk. Or grieve. Or whatever he thinks I'm doing. I'm simply content with a moment of silence, the chance to be alone with my thoughts. For better or worse. Memories of Fallah are painful, but they ground me in reality and lend a searing clarity to the slash of blue across the screen. Then, the world blurs again. This time, I don't fight.

At Alphanax, crying was a weakness. But here there's no one to watch the tears streaming down my face. No one to judge. No one to prey on the momentary lapse. So, I cry. And when the tears dry up, I shuffle to my room. This time, it feels less like a prison. It's cozy. Comforting.

The bed looks inviting, but I'm in no mood for sleep. There are too many thoughts pinging around in my head; too many memories casting shadows in the dark recesses of my mind. Tossing the bundle of clothes on the bed, I pull open the narrow door next to it. Inside is a tiny cubbyhole with a toilet, sink, and shower.

Scalding water burns away dirt, and grime, and nagging doubt. Well, most of it. I come out clean, but my mind is still in turmoil. I can't stop thinking about Fallah: about how every step leads further away from her and her memory; about how doing what we always said we'd do together is just creating an indelible separation between us; and about how the gulf is growing by leaps and bounds by the day. No, hour.

Freedom. Clothes. Identity.

I've attained all of these things without her. And yet—my gaze drifts to the soiled frock folded beside the bundle of fresh clothes—her memory is what kept me moving forward. It always will.

The new clothes Fletcher gave me are baggy, but fit better than the stained, shapeless frock from Alphanax or the chopped-up jumpsuit. My feet rattle in the oversized boots, though they're more comfortable than the floppy sandals. Best of all, I'm not cold at all. For the first time since... I close my eyes and can almost feel the warmth of Alphanax's crimson sun on my face and the gentle rise and fall as I rest against Fallah's leathery hide.

Wait. No. That movement is real!

I stumble out of my room on unsteady feet as the deck jostles under me, and a loud, rushing roar fills the silence. Fletcher is in his chair. The projections around him blink and flash as if the *Undertow* is concerned about what's happening.

"What's going on?" I shout.

"We're entering the atmosphere," Fletcher calls back. "Should be over in a moment."

I slide into the seat behind him and grip the armrests to keep from being shaken onto the floor. But that doesn't stop my insides from doing flips of their own.

"You could have warned me!"

"Sorry," he shouts over his shoulder. "I'm still used to being alone."

"Well, you aren't anymore," I shout back.

He gives a halting nod and turns back to the viewscreen.

For a moment, solid blue is obscured by trails of liquid fire, then the viewscreen clears and the thundering roar fades to a whistling rush.

"We're through," Fletcher calls.

I relax into the chair, glad the violent shaking is over, but still a bit queasy. "Where are we going, exactly?"

"Surface scans pinpointed a massive ship," he replies.

"The one Lorn found?"

"I suppose so…"

Past him, baby blue sky and darker waves glitter under a white sun, stretching to the horizon and beyond. There isn't an inch of land in sight. "How are we going to get to it?"

"That's what the suits are for," he says.

"We can't take the ship?"

He shakes his head. "The *Undertow* is only able to dive to a few hundred feet."

"Why?"

"Salvage as deep as this is rare to begin with. Besides, it's far more comfortable to park beneath the surface. Less rocking."

My eyebrows screw up. I didn't understand almost any of that, but one thing did stick out. "Salvage?"

"Pulling apart wreckage and selling the most expensive bits. It's what my mentor did. And how he got so interested in stuff like Humans, I guess."

I blink. "And you do it, now?"

He nods.

"Do you like it?"

I expect another nod, but Fletcher doesn't move.

"It's okay," he says. "Pays for food and fuel."

The water is an azure blur now, only feet below the *Undertow's* belly. With a throaty growl, the ship slows to a hover above the foam-tipped waves.

"Hold on!" Fletcher calls.

A moment later, the roar of engines is drowned out by deafening silence, and gravity yanks the *Undertow* to the water's surface. I grip the armrests and clench my teeth against the sudden churning in my stomach as the ship bucks on the rolling waves. Then, we sink.

Panic quickens my heart as water swallows the viewscreen. But the bucking stops, and the harsh crash of waves on the *Undertow's* hull is replaced with silence, pierced by only the faintest hum. Taking a deep breath, I stare out into the crystal-clear water. It's still. Quiet. Empty.

"Wow…"

"It is something," Fletcher agrees.

"Have you done this before?" I ask.

"Ocean salvage?" He looks over his shoulder, a thoughtful frown twisting his lips. "A few times. Though, it's never been my favorite."

That doesn't inspire confidence. "You know what you're doing, right?"

"Of course," he scoffs. But his lips dip into a troubled frown.

"Are you sure?" I press.

Fletcher takes a slow breath.

"It's a deep dive," he finally says. "It will be every bit as dangerous as Gohk claimed."

I wait for a 'but'. There isn't one.

"Lorn made it to the ship," I say hopefully.

He nods. "Yeah…"

I furrow my brow at the placid water pierced by shimmering beams of sunlight. "How deep is it?"

"A few miles at least," he replies, "but the suits'll be able to handle it just fine."

"Then why is it so dangerous?"

Fletcher purses his lips and turns to the viewscreen.

"The unknown," he says. "You can do everything right, and it's the stuff you don't expect that gets you. Every time."

"Is that what happened to Lorn?"

The question catches Fletcher off guard. He struggles for an answer. Finally, he just shrugs.

"I'm not sure. I suppose we'll find out. Speaking of which"— he stands—"we should get moving."

I give a calm nod, but my heart is trying to pound its way out of my ribcage. Time seems to slow to a crawl as I follow him down the hall, through the common area, and into the room where the suits are secured. Without a glance in my direction, he crosses to the armored behemoths and begins undoing Rhuk's work. I watch his singular focus from the door, forgotten. And I remain so until the suits are free and the door in the center of the floor creaks open, to reveal pale blue water so still it could have just as easily been a pane of glass peering into the depths.

Fletcher looks at me. "You sure you're ready for this?"

"Y—yeah!" I'm not, but don't want to turn back.

He gives me a thin smile. "It'll be fine. Just stay close and do exactly as I say. Alright?"

I manage to squeeze a deep breath around the lump in my throat. "Sure."

"Great," Fletcher says, turning to his suit. "Now mount up, so we can get going."

He leaps up onto the folded-open back, then slides inside.

The thick rubber soles of my boots slip on the suit's slick metal, so I take them off. They were oversized anyway, and I'm used to bare feet. The icy floor burns, and so does the armored leg as I clamber up, but the familiar feeling is oddly comforting. Calming. And I'll need to be calm for what comes next.

"Can you hear me?" Fletcher's voice crackles inside the suit.

"Yeah," I say, swinging my legs into the cushioned interior.

"Great." Through the visor, I see his suit swivel toward mine. "Let's get you set up."

His left arm raises so I can see the glowing panel attached to its wrist.

"Usually, everything on your suit is controlled from this panel," he continues, "but there are a few controls inside the suit you need to know about. Look up."

I do. "There's a covered button and a red handle."

He nods. "Pressing the button opens and closes the suit. The handle is an emergency release. Pump it twice and it'll pop the back of the suit open."

"Got it," I say, reaching up and flipping back the clear cover. A chime sounds when I press the button, and the back of the suit swings closed. There's barely enough room to wiggle my arms down the sleeves and into the gloves. Once in place, the pads around me begin to constrict. They squeeze until the pulse thunders in my ears.

I must have looked panicked, because Fletcher's voice crackles in my ear. "Calm down. This is normal."

"How? Why?"

"Rhuk got you dialed in back at his shop. After the first time, putting your hands into the gloves inflates the cushions."

"How do I get out?" They hug me like a second skin.

"You pull your hands out of the gloves," he says. "You'll have to really yank 'em out, but that'll deflate the cushions holding you in place."

"Good to know." It was, but my heart still batters against my ribcage and the suit's vice-like grip. "Anything else?"

"Not right now." He swivels toward the opening in the center of the floor and steps to the edge. "Let's get going."

I sidle to within an inch of the metal floor's edge so I can peer into the crystal-clear water. It fades from pale blue to black somewhere in the depths. "It'll be dark at the bottom?"

"We have spotlights," Fletcher says, holding up his left arm and indicating a button on the keypad.

He indicates another. "And sonar."

Then, a third. "And dark vision."

"Sonar? Dark vision?"

Fletcher chuckles. "The suit has plenty of gadgets, but let's focus on one at a time. First, spotlights."

He points at the button again.

I lift my hand to press it.

"Not yet," Fletcher says quickly. "You'd blind both of us. Just remember the button. You'll want the light when it starts to get dark."

He pauses, then edges closer to the mirror-still water. "We go on three."

"One."

My insides cinch tighter than the cushions hugging my body.

"Two."

Legs trembling, I inch toward the pale blue portal into the depths.

"Three!"

Fletcher drops into the water.

The splash peppers my visor with tiny droplets. But I don't flinch. Can't. I'm frozen in place. My legs tremble, but won't move. The next breath catches in my throat. And tranquil silence is suddenly drowned out by the rush of blood in my ears. What am I doing? How did I ever think this was a good idea? Why did I want to follow in Lorn's footsteps knowing he hadn't made it back?

"Aiko!"

Fletcher's voice cuts through the panic as I teeter on the edge.

"Come on!" he urges "Jump!"

I waver, stumble, and fall forward. For a moment, weightlessness fuels the veil of panic overshadowing my mind, then the suit hits the water's surface. Bubbles obscure the visor's clear curve, then slide away to reveal crystal clear water pierced by shimmering shafts of sunlight. Fletcher is already a small dot, barely distinguishable from the darkened depths. But I'm gaining on him.

"For a second, I wasn't sure you were going to follow me," he says when I draw even with him. The soft glow of his helmet light illuminates the deep frown twisting his lips.

"Me either," I admit, meeting his steely gaze.

"You can't hesitate down here." His eyes sweep the navy emptiness around us. "When something happens, you only have seconds to make a decision and stick with it."

I manage a halting nod. "O—okay."

"Anyway, it's about five miles to the bottom," he continues, checking the readout on his left wrist. "Might as well settle in."

"How long will it take us to get there??"

"A few hours," Fletcher replies.

"Hours?!" I squirm. "I'll be squished by then!"

"Pull your hands out of the gloves," Fletcher says, waving a free hand in front of his visor. "It'll make the drop a bit easier."

I tug my hands out of the gloves, and when they pop free, the pads around me deflate. The suit is still cramped, but I'm thankful for the wiggle room. "So, what do we do for the next few hours?"

"Rest. Sleep if you can." His eyes are already closed. "We'll need the energy when we reach the bottom."

"For what?"

He takes a deep breath. "That's what we're going to find out."

7

The ocean floor is an endless desert of fine silt. And the water is so crystal clear that I could be standing on dry land under a cloudy midnight sky. But there's no sign of the ship we're here to find.

"I thought you said it was right under us?" I ask, spinning to take in the empty darkness.

"It is," Fletcher says confidently.

"Did we miss it?"

Fletcher looks down at the display on his wrist. "No. We're right on top of it."

"Where is it?" I glance at the loose silt around my suit's fingered toes.

"Buried, most likely." He taps a few buttons on his wrist, then says: "There you are."

"I don't see anything," I complain.

Stepping toward me, he reaches for my left wrist. When I offer it, he taps one of the buttons there, sending a wave of soft blue sweeping across my suit's visor. It traces the endless expanse of soft silt, highlighting a contoured surface a few feet below it.

"That blue wave is the sonar I mentioned earlier," Fletcher says. "You see the solid blue under the ocean floor? That's the ship."

"How do we get inside?"

"That's the million-credit question." He taps his foot, sending a puff of fine silt into the crystal-clear water.

"How did Lorn get inside?" I ask. "Did he make his own door?"

"I don't think so," Fletcher replies. "I doubt he would have chanced filling the ship with water by cutting a hole in it."

"So, he found a door, then?"

Fletcher looks like he wants to scratch the stubble on his chin. "That seems most likely."

"Well, how did he find it?"

Fletcher chews on his bottom lip for a moment, then shakes his head.

"How would you usually find an entrance to a ship?"

"Usually, ships aren't buried," he shoots back, a twinge of annoyance in his voice.

I sigh. "Too bad you can't just scan for a door…"

He blinks at the backlit keypad on his wrist. "Maybe I can."

Metal fingers jab at keys until a slight smile twists his lips. "Let's try that."

He starts a slow spin, then pauses when his back is to me.

"There's a slight change in hull thickness over there." He points. "About a hundred paces."

"A door?"

"No clue," Fletcher says, starting in the direction he pointed. "But it's our best bet at the moment."

I pace to one side to avoid the clouds of silt kicked up in his wake and scan the ocean floor ahead. It remains as smooth as the soft blue surface projected beneath us. But Fletcher stops short as if one section of silt is somehow different from every other identical inch.

"It's here." He drops to his knees. "Help me."

We begin scooping away handfuls of the slippery stuff. The ocean floor disappears, obscured by billowing clouds of sediment. And the dampened beams of Fletcher's spotlights in the muddled water are the only hint he still kneels across from me. Regardless, we continue to dig, until—

My fingers scrape across metal with a hollow moan. I recoil. Sit back on my heels. Wait for the sediment to settle in eerie silence. It might have taken minutes. Or hours. It was hard to tell. However long, my legs are stiff by the time Fletcher fades back into view. When our eyes meet, he gives me a tight-lipped smile, then glances down at the hole we burrowed into the loose ocean floor. It's a two-foot-deep funnel ending at the ship's hull. The silvery metal glints in our suit's spotlights, at odds with the blue surface still projected against my visor.

"Is it a door?"

"It's the ship, at least," Fletcher grunts as he scoops more of the silt away from the hull. He disappears in a shifting cloud of sediment, and a moment later his breathless voice crackles over the comm. "Help me clear a bit more."

I sink my fingers back into the soft ocean floor, scraping and clawing until my arms ache. But when the water clears again, the funnel is a six-foot circle of shining metal glinting up at us.

Success! Sort of. "I don't see a door."

"The hull is definitely thinner here," Fletcher replies, stepping from silt to metal. "I'm guessing"—he bends down to get a better look at the pristine surface—"yep…there's a seam."

I scramble down the shifting slope and kneel beside Fletcher. There's an oval scoured into the otherwise blemishless metal surface. "A door!"

"But how do we get inside?" Fletcher mumbles.

I trace the seam to another: a perfect square a few inches away and half buried by silt.

"How about this?" I ask, wiping the square clean.

At the touch of my metal fingers, the surface springs to life. Text I can't read brackets a large red square with an "X" in the center.

Fletcher sidles up beside me. "Looks like the control panel." Then, he offers me most of a grin. "You've got a keen eye. Keep it up and you'll be better at this than I am someday."

He shoulders past me before I can respond.

Just as well. All he missed was a grimace.

Fletcher and I may both be human, but I still haven't decided to stay with him. Sure, he's nice enough—so is Rhuk—but I need to live my own life. Find my own freedom. For myself. And for Fallah. Her memory deserves that much, at least. How, exactly, I'll do that remains unclear, but one thing at a time. First, we find the truth we came here for. Then, everything else.

I take a deep breath and peer over Fletcher's shoulder. "Is it a good sign there's still power?"

"Good?" He shrugs. "At the very least it'll make getting in easier. And moving around once we're inside."

"So, that red button will open the hatch?"

"There's only one way to find out." Without hesitating, he presses a metal finger into the center of the red 'X'.

For a heartbeat, the ocean floor is still. Silent. Then, a low groan pierces the deep. The oval pops up from the hull, and a flurry of bubbles stir silt into the water around us. My suit's spotlights play across a shadow that sets my heart raging against the inside of my ribcage. Is there something inside the ship? Have we set it free? I hold my breath and remain perfectly still until the silt settles once again. The shadow had only been the door swinging open. And where it once sat is a six-foot-wide hole.

"There we go," Fletcher says. His voice is just as tense as the muscles between my shoulder blades.

"After you," I say, waving him ahead of me.

This time, there's a moment of hesitation before he drops out of sight. Then, his voice crackles in my ear. "It's fine. Come on down."

I do, unsure of what to expect. Not this.

The room is twelve-foot square. Plain. Almost familiar. To my left is a row of lockers. Across from them, a row of hooks line the wall. The remains of a suit made of some kind of shiny weave drifts in a nearby corner. The water must have knocked it loose. But besides the single bench bolted in the center of the floor, the room is empty.

"This looks almost like the dive room on the *Undertow*," I mumble, disappointed.

"It's an airlock," Fletcher says.

"A…what?"

"It basically functions like the dive room on the *Undertow*," he replies. "A transition point between inside and outside."

He points at a large hatch in the wall ahead of us. "There's our way inside."

"Won't the water—?"

"We'll close the outer door behind us," Fletcher cuts in. "I doubt the ship was designed to drain the water out of the room, but at least it'll limit how much we take inside with us."

He walks to the hatch and swipes his hand across a section of blank wall. Another panel, with another red button, springs to life.

"This is a little bit too easy, don't you think?" I ask before he can press it.

"Easy is relative," he replies, motioning around us. "Look what we had to do to get here."

"Yeah, but shouldn't the ship be locked? Or something? Wouldn't the humans have wanted to protect it even if they were leaving it behind?"

"Maybe so," Fletcher admits with a thoughtful nod, "but Lorn did get here before us. Maybe he took care of whatever safety measures were in place."

"And if not?"

Fletcher's lips dip into a frown. "Maybe that's why he didn't make it back."

The unsettling realization fills the silence. Twists my insides. Squeezes the breath from my lungs. Maybe this isn't such a good idea after all?

"Last chance to turn back," Fletcher mumbles, as if reading my thoughts.

It would be safer to go back to the *Undertow*, but… "No. We came here for a reason."

"Alright then." His finger is poised above the red button. "Hold on."

Nothing happens when he presses it. Or nothing seems to. But then there's a hollow clang above us as the outer door slots back into place. Moments later, the inner hatch pops open with a creaking hiss and a flurry of bubbles.

Water thunders out of the room.

I stumble to my knees under a sudden, tremendous weight. Then, dark waves take hold of my suit and drag it toward the opening. I flail for a handhold and manage to grab the bench beside me. I hold on until only the six inches of water trapped beneath the hatch's bottom lip remain.

Fletcher wades toward me and offers a hand. "I told you to hold on."

"Yeah…" I take it and hop to my feet. "Thanks."

Fletcher nods, then turns to the new opening. His suit's spotlights illuminate a small alcove of three walls and a ladder plunging into the unknown. "Only one way forward. Easy enough."

He steps through the hatch and peers down.

"What do you see?"

"A hallway," he answers. "Wide. Runs in either direction."

I splash my way to the hatch. "Anything else?"

"Can't see from up here," he replies. "Wait. I'm going down."

There isn't time to protest before he drops out of sight. He hits the bottom of the hall with a solid clang.

"You okay?" I call out.

"Fine." His reply sizzles over the intercom.

"Safe to come down?"

"Looks like it."

I slip through the hatch, sit at the edge of the opening, then slide off. The drop is short, but sends a jarring shudder through my spine nonetheless. Groaning, I spin to take in our new surroundings. They are as plain as Fletcher described them. A single, straight hall stretches in either direction. Textured floors are bracketed by slightly curved walls. And the ceiling overhead is dotted with rows of circular lights, all dark. There are no breaks in the unending corridor as far as our spotlights can reach. The soft blue projection on my visor paints the hallway stretching even further into the distance. Though, *that* image fades eventually, as well.

"Which way?" I ask.

"Tell you what." Fletcher swivels in each, identical direction. "Let's split up."

"W—what?" I stammer at the prospect of venturing into the dark alone.

"You'll be fine," he says. "It's just us down here. And as far as I know, shadows don't bite. Besides"—he gives me a thin smile—"we'll cover more ground this way. Means we won't have to stay down here as long."

I manage a shaky nod, though I'm not convinced. "Okay."

"I'll go this way. You go that way," he says tapping the side of his helmet with a metal finger. "We'll keep in touch via radio. Let me know if you find anything."

He turns away before I can answer.

Watching his spotlights fade into the distance is like falling out of the *Undertow* all over again. Only this time, I'm heading into the unknown alone. Panic surges. My chest tightens. I take a deep breath and try to remember why I'm here. Why am I here? What can possibly be worth stumbling around in the dark? That isn't helping. It definitely doesn't calm the anxiety in my mind, as it crashes through my thoughts like untamed waves. But then Fallah's kind face enters my mind's eye, and the roiling sea of emotion calms to a gentle flow.

That's right. This is for her as much as it is for me. Her memory, anyway. I have to keep going. For me. For her. For the freedom we both wanted.

I take another deep breath and force myself forward. Eventually, the halting pace turns into something resembling a normal walk. Though, I'm still less than enthused to be trundling along in the dark. Into the unknown. Alone. But there isn't much to see. The plain, straight corridor remains so. For a hundred paces. Two hundred. I'm starting to wish something *would* happen by the time I reach the first intersection.

My spotlights only pierce a dozen feet of darkness, but soft blue traces what my suit's lights can't. Three identical paths forward. I frown. "Fletcher? You there?"

"What's up?" His voice is marred by static fuzz.

"I, uh…" Hearing his voice is more comforting than I expect. It fills the silence, and the sudden urge to drag more words out of him overwhelms me. "You find anything yet?"

"Just more hallway." He sighs. "I take it you have?"

"An intersection."

"Pretty straightforward," he mutters. Is there a twinge of annoyance in his voice?

"Sure." I frown. "But which way should I go? What should I be looking for?"

Fletcher sighs again. "I don't really know. Lorn is in here somewhere. Well… was…"

"Fletcher?"

"Yeah…sorry." He sounds distracted.

Fallah's death is still fresh. Just the thought of her stings like rubbing a raw wound. But for Fletcher, it must have been like tearing open a long-healed scar. In the days following her death, I learned distraction was the best way to keep the pain at arm's length. But how can I distract Fletcher from the pain? The memories?

"You—uh—ever think of doing anything else?"

"Huh?"

"Other than salvage."

Fletcher doesn't answer, and for a moment it seems he ignored my question.

"Never really thought about it," he finally mumbles.

"Why not?"

"It was the only thing I knew. And after Lorn disappeared…"

So, he'd been trapped in a different kind of prison.

"Have you ever wanted to do anything else?"

"I—No."

I stare into the dark emptiness and rack my brain for another question. None come.

Lorn is down here. Somewhere. And I doubt Fletcher will be able to focus—really focus—until we find out what happened to him; why he disappeared thirty years ago. But how do we do that? Stumble around in the emptiness hoping to run across Lorn's remains? Or is there another way?

How had Lorn gotten here? A suit like ours, most likely. So, isn't it still here somewhere?

"Hey, Fletcher," I blurt into the intercom. "Can you use one of your gadgets to scan for Lorn's suit?"

"Huh?" The question seems to catch his interest. Barely.

"If it's still here, wouldn't it give off some kind of signal that would lead us right to it? To him?"

The new line of questions snaps Fletcher back to reality. "Yeah. Yes. Good thinking."

He's silent for a few heartbeats, then: "I've got a signal."

There's a measure of excitement in his voice.

"Lorn?"

His grunted response is the vocal equivalent of shrug.

"Where?"

"Your direction," he says. "Hang tight. I'll be there in a second."

Even though we only parted a few minutes before, it feels like an eternity before the glint of Fletcher's spotlights appear in the distance. And it takes just as long for him to reach me.

"Hi," I say, once he's close enough to see his face past the blinding spotlights and soft blue corridor projected against my visor. I'm tempted to ask him how to turn it off, but it's comforting to know what's past the limit of my lights.

"Hey." His gaze sweeps past me, to the intersection.

"Which way?" I ask.

"Left," he says, pointing.

This corridor is just as long. Just as straight. Just as featureless. Seen in twelve-foot snippets, but traced for a few dozen after that by the projection on my visor. After a while, the darkness becomes less of a worry and more of an annoyance. I want something different, something new.

"Here."

Another turn. Another corridor. More darkness. More walking. If nothing else, the plodding emptiness makes ample room for wandering thoughts. How far from the signal are we? How much longer will it take to get there? What will we find when we reach it? Lorn? Someone—something—else? Or just more emptiness?

A third turn reinforces the latter eventuality. The ship, though large, is as dead and dark as the ocean it's buried under. And the longer we walk, the more it seems we might not find anything at all in the barren hulk. Had Lorn? Or had he gotten so turned around that he simply lost his way inside the maze of endless, doorless corridors?

"Where are we going?" The complaint slips past my lips in an impatient growl. I have to suppress the urge to slap a metal hand over my mouth.

"We're getting closer," Fletcher says without looking at me, "but I think we're going to have to find a way down."

That piques my interest. "Down?"

"Deeper into the ship." He motions toward the floor just past the limit of our suits' spotlights. "The signal is coming from that general direction."

"Any idea how it's still working after all this time?"

He shakes his head. "No, and I doubt I will until we reach it."

A mystery. Is that good or bad?

"And how far away is it?"

"Still pretty far," Fletcher deadpans.

We continue in silence. Along more, featureless corridors. Past countless, identical junctions laid out in a grid. But are we making any progress at all? Or are we just wandering aimlessly? Also, what are these corridors for? Where are they supposed to go? Why aren't there any doors?

"Where are we?" I mumble, if only to release some of the frustration building within my chest.

"If I had to guess? Maintenance corridors," Fletcher replies. "Right under the ship's hull."

I frown. "Will they ever end?"

"It feels like they won't, huh?" He gives a strained chuckle. "We just have to find an elevator. Stairs. A hatch. Something that'll grant us access to the rest of the ship. Smooth sailing after that."

The way he trails off doesn't inspire confidence. But we don't stop. We can't.

After that, I start paying more attention to the corridors wrapped around us. Before, I only gave the featureless walls and floor a cursory glance, but now I study every inch of metal plate fading out of the darkness. I make note of every seam. Every blemish. Every glint of light. Paying attention reveals that the ship isn't nearly as pristine as it appears at first glance: that was just an illusion. In reality, the ship is old. Worn. Put through its paces by years in space; frozen in time after a plunge into the black, watery abyss of an alien world. And also that the way forward has been in front of us the whole time. We've just been too preoccupied to notice.

In the center of the next intersection, the hatch sticks out like a sore thumb. The circular seam is just like the one on the hull, but battered. Used.

"Wait," I call out to Fletcher, pausing at the edge of the scoured line. Have we really been missing them this whole time?

He stops and spins. "What is it?"

I grin and point at the rough circle. "Our way down!"

8

Beneath the hatch, another hallway stretches into endless darkness. But we've made undeniable progress.

"Which way?" I ask. There are only two possible options.

"The signal is stronger in this direction," Fletcher replies, pointing, then trudges off into the dark.

I follow.

This darkness is no different, but the hallway is. It's wider, and there's a matte texture to the metal plates underfoot. The walls are lined with panels that seem almost decorative. And the ceiling overhead has the slightest curve, inlaid with wavy trails that catch light from our spotlights and carry it far down the hall. The resulting glow illuminates the way forward dozens of feet past the limit of the soft blue tracing into the distance.

Fletcher walks with renewed energy. I feel it too, bolstered by the spacious corridor and nurtured by the amplified light. Although...it reminds me of the circle of sunlight Fallah and I shared back on Alphanax. I frown, swallowing the bile rising in the back of my throat, and stare at the back of Fletcher's suit. But as hard as I try, I can't brush the memories aside. They haunt me, like Lorn's memory haunts Fletcher. Still. After all these years. I don't want Fallah's memory to fade—she deserves to be remembered—but not as a ghost. As a friend. A companion. A—

I barely stumble aside when Fletcher stops walking. "What is it?" I ask, scanning the dimly lit corridor ahead.

"A door. Writing." He points ahead to a rectangular slab set in the center of the next molded panel. Next to it, a blocky script spells out strange words. And yet, they're vaguely familiar. As if...

"What do you think it says?" I muse, drifting toward the door. "What's inside?"

"Come on. Signal's up ahead." He swivels to fix me with a piercing gray stare. "We can come back later."

I glance at him and stifle a frown, but he's right. We're here to find Lorn. And the truth. Those things take precedence over wandering through the ship's likely empty rooms.

"Alright," I agree, with a nod.

Fletcher turns down the hall and picks up the pace. He doesn't sprint. Or run. Or jog. But the brisk walk carries us past more doors and intersections so fast there isn't time to grant them any more than a cursory glance. I thought Fletcher would be just as compelled to peek in every nook and cranny of the rooms we passed as I was, but who knew how much time we'd waste wandering through the wreckage. Or how off-track our curiosity might take us.

Is that what happened to Lorn?

Eventually, Fletcher slows.

"What's wrong?" I ask.

He motions ahead. "We're close."

I stare into the dimly lit distance. "I don't see anything."

"Just up here," he insists.

The corridor remains straight. Empty. Then, a door appears.

"There! That's gotta be it." Despite the excitement in his voice, he slows to a cautious advance.

The door is no more remarkable than any of the others we've passed thus far: a single rectangular slab set in the center of a decorative wall panel, labeled by text I can't read. And that's it. There's no glowing panel like the one that granted us access to the ship.

"How are we supposed to get inside?"

"We should be able to pry it open," Fletcher says, then points at some scuff marks along the doorframe. "Looks like that's what Lorn did. Let me try."

Metal fingers scrabble for purchase at the edge of the door. Slip. Scrape. The screech of tortured metal echoes down the endless hall, a terrible sound amplified by darkness and imagination. I glance away from Fletcher's concerted effort and immediately wish I hadn't. Shadows flicker around us. Harmless. And yet...

I draw in a deep breath and shuffle at Fletcher's shoulder.

"Do you think Lorn is inside?" I ask, to take my mind off the nightmarish wandering of my imagination.

"Dunno," he grunts. "Can you give me a hand? Grab the edge and pull."

It's a tight squeeze, but I manage to reach past the bulk of his suit and slip my fingers into the tiny gap between the door and the molded panel. The door barely budges.

"Harder," he urges.

I strain against the inflated pads pressing into me. The suit whirs and jitters. For a moment, the tension holds, then the door gives with an angry hiss.

The space beyond is cramped: only a few paces across with panels and screens lining the far wall. I poke my head inside, and the breath catches in my throat when my gaze sweeps across the figure standing in the corner.

"T—there's—" I stumble backwards, bumping into Fletcher.

He slips past me, and a moment later, laughter crackles through the intercom.

"It's only Lorn's suit!"

"Is he inside?" I hover at the threshold. The room is too small for three suits to comfortably fit.

"No," Fletcher mumbles. "Although…"

His spotlight sweeps across the abandoned suit—the same general shape as ours, but not nearly as sleek—pausing on a wrist-mounted panel attached to its right forearm. A thick wire runs from beneath the darkened screen to the nearest control console on the wall.

"What's that wire?" I ask.

"It's a power cable," Fletcher replies, leaning closer. "That's why there's still a signal after so long. The suit's leeching energy from whatever reserves the ship has left."

He reaches out to the darkened panel as if touching it might reveal some long-hidden secret. When his fingers brush across the screen, it springs to life.

"Woah." I squeeze further into the room and crane my neck. "It still works?"

Fletcher nods. "This is definitely where the signal's coming from. But why did Lorn leave his suit here in the first place?"

I can tell he's frowning.

"He sent a message to Gohk. Maybe he left another with the suit?"

"Yeah…" There's a tinge of hopefulness in the word as he swivels the arm up and begins tapping on the panel. After a few heartbeats, Lorn's familiar voice fills the silence.

"I've done it. I've found the ship that brought Humans to this sector of space. It's massive. And at the bottom of an ocean."

"This is what Gohk played for us," Fletcher says as Lorn drones on in the background.

"Is there any more?" I ask, edging closer.

"Lemme see," he says, fiddling with the panel.

The recording cuts off abruptly, and another begins to play.

"The ship looked large on orbital scans, but I had no idea. I can say beyond any doubt that Humans were industrious. No other ship I've ever seen even comes close to this size. What was it for? What were they doing way out here? How did it end up at the bottom of an ocean? The answers to those questions—and others—are somewhere on board. I just have to find them."

Lorn's voice fades to silence.

I hold my breath and wait for him to start speaking again.

The silence drags on, filled by the rhythmic rush of blood in my ears. Surely, there's something else. Lorn would have left more than two messages behind. Right? I'm beginning to doubt when one of the screens on the wall sputters to life. A Kaisin is framed in its center, jittery blue eyes set in a pale face that seems almost good-natured. For a Kaisin, at least.

"It worked!" Lorn exclaims.

"Took me long enough, but I got the suit spliced into the ship's emergency power. Miraculous that there's still any juice left. But

there's something wrong with the capacitors in my suit. They're drain-ing faster than I anticipated."

A frown flickers across his pale face.

"This is some sort of ancillary control room. With a bit more luck, I'm hoping I can get some of these computers working. Maybe find a map of the ship and figure out where the central command center is located. I'll update this again when I come across something worth-while."

The screen goes dark, then Lorn reappears, looking weary. Haggard. There are bags under his eyes, and his pale skin is smeared with grease.

"So, I found a map…" His strained voice trails to silence. How long had it taken him to get the ship's computers working? Hours? Days?

"The Human language is easy enough to read," he continues. "But their damned maps are symbol-based, which makes them almost useless."

"Almost," he repeats, stepping back from the screen.

The sight of him doesn't stir up the same nervous roiling in my gut as other Kaisin. Maybe it's the oversized jumpsuit over-whelming his slender frame? Or the warm, half-smile twisting his thin lips? Or the steady, deliberate movements that set him apart from the usual Kaisin jitteriness?

"A map is a map, so I can find my way around the ship once I determine a reference point. I planned on being here a while, but I think my stay might wind up being even longer than I initially an-ticipated. The capacitors in my suit aren't charging. And what's left of the ship's emergency power might not be enough to keep it *operational for much longer—I can't really be sure. At the very least, I'll have to leave the suit here. For now."*

He scratches his bare chin.

"More later."

This time, the screen remains dark.

"Is that it?" I ask, shifting my gaze to Fletcher.

He frowns, swiveling to the pad on Lorn's suit, and taps glowing buttons. Nothing happens.

"I guess so," he says with a sigh.

"But Lorn was here," I offer.

He nods in agreement. "Was…"

"So, where did he go?' I ask.

Fletcher is quiet for a moment. Pensive.

"He didn't," he finally says.

"What do you mean?"

"The capacitors in his suit weren't charging." Fletcher frowns. The arms of his suit raise, then lower, as if he'd tried to cross them, and then realized he can't.

"Without them, he wouldn't have been able to move the suit back to an airlock. Or float it to the surface." He gives a sorrowful shake of the head. "Lorn got trapped down here. Died down here."

"But he's still here," I offer hopefully. "Maybe we can still find him?"

"He could be anywhere." Frustration tinges Fletcher's reply. And it would take us ages to find him without some sort of clue. If we ever find him at all."

It's like a glorified game of hide and seek. Only, Lorn isn't hiding. He's lost. And the play area is an endless maze of rooms and corridors neither of us can begin to fathom. So, we've taken one step forward and a dozen back.

"Any ideas?" I almost grimace asking the question.

"None," Fletcher grumbles and blows a breath out of his nostrils. "It might be better to just leave."

"No!" The word escapes my lips before I have a chance to clamp them shut.

Fletcher's brow furrows. He fixes me with an icy stare, but doesn't speak.

"There's got to be a way to find Lorn," I say quickly. "Maybe if we looked at the map—"

"Lorn had enough trouble reading it. What makes you think we can?"

He stares at me for a few heartbeats, then shakes his head. "No. We're done here. Come on. Let's go."

He shoulders past me and stomps down the hall. I stare after him, dumbfounded. We came so far, and he's giving up? Just like that? Sure, finding Lorn will be hard, but he's been here! Is still here. *Somewhere.* And so are the answers I've come so far to find! No. I can't leave. Not yet. Turning my back on the truth when I'm so close will be a disservice to Fallah. She grasped at freedom knowing it could cost her everything, because it was worth it. So, I will too.

Turning my back on Fletcher's shrinking spotlights, I head in the opposite direction.

I'll find the truth we came here for. And I'll find Lorn. No matter the difficulty. Or danger.

Pausing at the next intersection, I frown at three identical paths forward. One is as good as another, but before I can choose, Fletcher's voice crackles over the intercom.

"Aiko? Where are you?"

I hold my breath and swivel just enough to glance down the hall. Only darkness peers back.

"Aiko?" He repeats, an edge of annoyance in his voice.

I ignore him and consider the path forward. Which way would Lorn have gone? How would he have chosen? He had a map, but he'd said it was useless. Well, almost. But without a frame of reference, what would he have done? I frown and drop my gaze to the center of the matte intersection.

Is that...a circle?

I blink.

The shape had been etched into the metal by hand, and a messy number '1' is scratched inside it. I walk to the circle's edge and drop into a crouch, leaning as far forward as the bulk of my suit will allow. This definitely isn't part of the ship's design. Did Lorn do this?

I scan the rest of the floor for more unnatural marks.

A messy X is scrawled a dozen paces to the left of the circle. And another straight ahead. But to the right, a neat triangle points into the unknown as if to say 'this way', even though my suit's spotlights and the soft blue outline tracing into the distance suggest only more, featureless corridor.

"Aiko!"

This time, my name is accompanied by the clink of metal on metal. And a moment later, a heavy hand lands on the shoulder of my suit.

"What the hell—?"

"Look at this."

I don't know if Fletcher expected an explanation, an apology, or something else, but the interruption catches him off guard.

"W—what?" he sputters.

I point at the numbered circle, then the scratched shapes nearby.

Fletcher's lips twitch.

"Looks like Lorn figured something out," I say.

The twitch dips into a frown.

I motion at the triangle. "We should see where it leads."

"Aiko, listen…" Fletcher lets out a deep sigh. "Gohk was right. It was a mistake coming here. We should leave. Head back. Figure out how to sort out this whole Kaisin mess."

Heat burns my cheeks as anger bubbles to the surface. Why is he giving up so easily?

"We came here for a reason," I snap. "And I'm not leaving until I find the truth."

"What truth?" Fletcher counters. "So far all we've found are empty corridors and the ghost that haunts them."

The pain behind those words reminds me of Fallah. Of watching her fall as we sprinted toward freedom. Of holding her as the blood drained from her lifeless body. Of the emptiness in the days—Weeks? Months?—that followed. I understand how he feels; the crushing weight borne by those left behind. Us.

A heavy sigh slips past my lips as I stand.

"Lorn came here to find out how Humans and Kaisin are connected. He believed the answers were here and gave up everything to look for them. If they really are that important, we have to find them. And him." Fletcher tries to respond, but I speak over him. "I won't give up. Neither should you."

Fletcher chews his bottom lip and stares into space. He might as well have been chewing on my words. Why would they matter to him? Why would he listen to me? He's already made up his mind, hasn't he?

"We'll follow the markings," he starts slowly, "but if they don't lead anywhere, we head back to the *Undertow*. Agreed?"

It's more than I expected. "Sure."

"And you listen to what I say," he continues. "No more running off on your own."

I stifle a frown. Running off on my own is the only reason we found the way forward, but if that's what it takes to follow the trail to its end, I'll oblige. For now. I nod. "Alright."

He offers a thin, approving smile before walking in the direction the triangle points.

I follow in reluctant, dutiful silence.

The trail leads to another junction, with the same hastily scrawled collection of shapes. Only the number '2' is scratched inside the circle. Each junction is labeled with another number, until we reach a massive door spanning the entire width of the hall, stretching from floor to ceiling. In front of it is another circle, with the number '9' scrawled inside. The quick strokes suggest haste. Excitement. Had Lorn expected to find what he was looking for on the other side? The possibility sets my heart racing.

But the door is shut tight. Although...there's a darkened panel on the wall beside it.

"Maybe we won't have to pry our way inside this time," I mumble, more to myself than Fletcher.

"Maybe," he agrees, sidling up to the panel and tapping it with a metal finger. It springs to life just like the others. But when he presses the red button that appears, he's answered by a belligerent warble.

"Access denied," a strangely accented voice booms into the silence. "Quarantine lockout in effect."

Fletcher's hand yanks back from the glowing screen as if he's been stung.

I blink at the door, dumbfounded. "What was that voice?"

"An automated message?" His eyes dart from the pad to the door.

"No…I mean…it spoke our language. How? Why?"

"Because this is a Human ship?" he guesses.

"But why would Humans speak the—" I search for the term Fletcher used once before "—standard language?"

"I can't even begin to hazard a guess," Fletcher answers quickly, as if he hadn't wanted to hear the rest of the question. As if the possibilities frighten him.

"Fine." I frown, trying to ignore the sudden uptick of my heartbeat. "What does it mean?"

"That the way forward is blocked."

The word 'lock' implied as much. "And what's 'quarantine'?"

"It's…" Fletcher pauses, and his lips press into a thin line.

"It can be a few things," he finally says, "but usually it's an imposed isolation."

That sounds familiar. "Like Alphanax."

He scoffs. "Not quite. The word usually implies quite a bit more danger."

"Danger? What kind?"

Fletcher shakes his head. "I can't say for sure."

So what if there's danger beyond the door? We've come this far, and I'm not ready to turn back. Not yet.

"How do we open it?" I ask, determined.

His lips dip into a pensive frown. "I can cut through it. As to what's on the other side—"

"I'm sure it'll be fine," I offer quickly, though I say it more to put myself at ease.

For the first time since leaving the *Undertow*, a creeping uneasiness settles into the pit of my stomach like a stone. It isn't like a fear of the dark. Or jumping at shadows. It's raw, primal, as if every cell in my body has an inkling of what might be waiting for us on the other side. But the feeling can't be anything more than an overactive imagination. Everything has been fine so far. What would a locked door change?

9

"Done!" Fletcher shouts over the fizzling hiss of what he called a plasma torch.

The metal is still glowing faintly when I look up, tracing a border around a square big enough for a suit to slip through.

"What now?" I ask, pushing my hands into snug gloves and climbing to my feet. Despite its cramped interior, I found a seated position marginally comfortable once the cushions were deflated.

Fletcher motions to the outlined square. "Help me kick this in."

I sidle up beside him.

"On the count of three," he says. "One…Two…Three!"

We kick with opposite feet: my left and his right. The metal barely budges, so we kick again. And again. On the fourth kick, the slab gives and falls with a creaking groan, slamming into the darkness beyond with a resounding clang of metal on metal.

Fletcher squeezes through the opening first. I follow, expecting the same pristine hallways as before.

A dark substance smears the floors, spatters the walls, and, at some point in the distant past, had dripped from the ceiling. It reminds me of the stained frock folded in my room back on the *Undertow*.

"Is that…blood?"

"No," Fletcher says with a frown.

"What—?"

"I don't know what it is, but we should keep moving." There's a clear note of apprehension in his voice. "Don't touch anything."

A complementary twinge of uncertainty sends a shot of adrenaline through me as I hurry to keep pace with Fletcher's brisk walk. What had Lorn found in these stained corridors? The truth? Or something else? Something worse? I brush the questions aside before my imagination can produce any answers.

The next intersection is no farther than before, but the condition of our surroundings makes each step feel like slow motion. By the time we reach the circle with the number '10' scrawled inside, sweat drenches my clothes, drips from my brow, and stings my eyes. Each breath leaves a fog of condensation on the suit's visor that makes me glad I didn't ask Fletcher to turn off the blue pulse of the sonar tracing the corridor into the distance. It's the only thing keeping me headed in the right direction.

Fletcher pauses beside the messy script, obscured by the black smear it had been scratched through.

"How did Lorn get past the door?" I ask, breathless.

Fletcher peers down at the encircled number. "The door must have been open when he got here."

"So why is it closed now?"

I see the muscles on either side of his neck flex. A shrug?

Ginger steps bring me closer to the center of the junction.

"What is all this stuff?" I wonder aloud, casting a wary glance at the stained floor. And walls. And ceiling. Something about the smears, splatters, and dried droplets above set off alarms in my head.

"It could be anything," Fletcher says, spinning in a circle. "But it doesn't seem like something we need to worry about. Not now, anyway."

"Are you sure?"

"No," he admits, "but whatever caused all this"—he motions to the streaked walls—"has got to be long gone."

"Then what happened to Lorn?"

"That's what we're here to find out," he replies with a strained smile. "Remember?"

There's no more uncertainty in his voice. I can't tell whether it had really passed or if he's putting on a show for my benefit, but the words are soothing either way and make trudging further into the unknown that much easier; even if the knot in my stomach persists. It disappears like smoke on the wind when we reach an empty circle in front of a wide doorway. This has to be our destination, because there are no more X's or triangles to guide us.

One half of the door is missing. The other hangs crooked in its frame, withdrawn just enough that we can squeeze through. On the other side is a large, oval room. The back half is covered with screens over darkened control panels. A bulky chair sits in the center of the space, slightly behind two more curved panels. The far wall is lined with what used to be a massive curved screen, but whatever happened to the ship shattered it, leaving darkness and cracks—like a spider's web—behind.

"This must be the control room," Fletcher guesses. "This had to be what Lorn was looking for. Which means…" He scans the dark consoles and broken screens for any sign his mentor has been here.

While he remains near the ruined door, I pace along the back wall, metal fingers trailing along curved consoles, the cushioned gloves squeezing my hand mirroring the smoothness of the surface. But there's no sign of Lorn anywhere. How can that be? His numbers led us here. He had to have been here. So, where's the message he left behind? Where would he have left it?

My gaze drifts past, then back to, the bulky chair in the center of the room. There! It has to be!

I walk to the ancient monolith of command and peek past the edge of its high back. Eyeless, lidless sockets peer back at me over a toothy grin. I recoil and cry out, stumbling backwards over my own metal feet.

"What is it?" Fletcher appears at my side.

"I—It's a—"

My throat squeezes around the explanation. Why is it suddenly so hard to form words? Instead of stammering on, I point.

He shoulders past me, around the edge of the high-backed chair, but only a slight frown creases his lips.

"A skeleton," he deadpans.

I blink. Is finding a skeleton so normal? His response makes it seem as much. I ask the next question that pops into my head.

"Is it Lorn?"

"Can't be," he says. "Bones are too small. And the skull is too round to belong to a Kaisin."

"Human, then?"

Fletcher's eyebrows lift. "Maybe."

My heart skips a beat, and I edge forward just enough for the bleached bones to slide into view. At second glance, they aren't as frightening. The grinning skull rests atop a scrambled pile of what used to be a fully formed being. And a deep sadness settles over me when I consider what must have happened to cause this being to die here. Alone.

But what *did* happen? Despite the broken doorway, there's no sign of the black smears inside this space. Why not? Why is it any different? Lorn must have found out *something* during his time here. Surely, he didn't waste away wandering through the empty corridors in search of an answer that isn't here. We just have to find it. If it is here to find at all.

While most of the skeleton is an unruly pile on the seat of the chair, its left forearm, and fingerbones, are balanced on the wide arm. They're reaching for a group of buttons arrayed beneath a small screen, swiveled to face where the being had once sat. The panel beneath it has been tampered with, bent upwards, albeit gently, so as not to disturb the being's eternal rest. Did Lorn—?

I lean closer and reach out.

"What are you doing?"

Fletcher's sudden voice in my ear makes me jump. My finger slips, jamming into one of the buttons.

The screen flickers to life, and Lorn's grinning face peers out at me.

"You know," he begins cheerily, *"the longer I spend on this ship, the clearer the connection between Kaisin and Humans becomes. I can see the overlap. The technology. It's almost a mirror image of what the Kaisin use. As if whatever the Humans brought with them into this sector of space was frozen in time and carried into the present. But how the Kaisin got a hold of Human technology is still a mystery."*

He glances away from the screen to scan his surroundings.

"As to the state of the ship itself: something happened here. Some-thing monumental that changed the fate of the Humans onboard, but I haven't found any records that explain what it might have been."

"This one might have known." He chuckles and indicates the bleached skull just poking past the bottom of the screen. *"But they carried their secrets to the grave."*

Lorn's tone drips with disappointment.

"It's a shame, really. One account from this one would have been enough to connect all the dots. I'm so close. There's only a few gaps left to fill, and the answers feel like they're at my fingertips. But I'm starting to doubt they're here. Anymore, anyway. I'm hundreds of years late. Maybe more."

Lorn lets out a deep sigh.

"I think it might be time to go. If it's not too late..."

The screen goes dark.

"Is that it?" The twinge of disappointment that sweeps over me seems like an understatement. We've come all this way to learn Lorn hit a dead end!

"I guess so," Fletcher mutters, obviously just as unsatisfied.

"What now?"

"There's nothing left for us here," he scoffs. "Might as well get off of this godforsaken wreck and leave the past where it belongs: dead and buried."

With that, he turns his back on me and storms toward the door.

"Fletcher! Wait!"

I scramble to follow and trip over my own feet, flail for a hand-hold, and grab the first thing my hand touches. A crunch vibrates through the gloves cradling my hands. When I look down, my fist is closed around the button panel Lorn tampered with. It's crushed. Destroyed. Blue sparks arc from damaged circuits to metal fingers. And when I pull back, there's an electric sizzle, a flash, then the screen flickers and a strange voice splits the silence.

"I'm the only one left."

Fletcher freezes mid step.

"All the others are gone."

He turns, mouth hanging open

"But I'm not sure it was enough."

The screen flickers again, then snaps to life. A woman fills it, blood dripping from her mouth and nose, and seeping from a deep gash across her forehead. But most remarkable of all: she looks like me! Dark hair frames a round face, and dark eyes seem to pierce through the screen.

"It was all my fault, of course," the woman continues.

Her speech is tinged by a strange accent that twists familiar words in ways I could have never imagined.

"When the scientists told me about the object, I should have handled the situation with more caution. But I was just as excited about their discovery. It's not every day you find life floating through the void of space. And who was I to quash the first sign of hope in generations?"

"I should have been." The woman's lips press into a thin line. *"Instead, I caved to their wishes; let them bring it on board. That was a mistake, but hindsight is always 20/20."*

She looks away from the screen.

"It was my responsibility to protect everyone on this ship. I failed. Those that weren't killed by what we brought on board are now trapped in cargo vessels, short range shuttles, and landing vehicles that

weren't meant for sustained deep-space travel. They'll have to endure cramped quarters, restricted rations, recycled water, stale air. And inevitable equipment failures. Many more—maybe all of them—will die. And it's my fault."

Her piercing gaze sweeps back.

"Their only hope is finding a habitable planet soon. Otherwise..."

She shakes her head.

"As for me...I'm going down with the ship, like any captain should. It isn't enough to simply point it at the nearest star and hope the autopilot fulfills its purpose. I have to be sure what we brought on board is dealt with. Permanently. There can't be any chance it isn't destroyed. And I can't risk the colonists coming back out of fear or hardship."

Her eyes hardens.

"There's a planet at the edge of the system suited for the job, and I've already set a course. Hopefully, I last that long."

For the first time, the woman's piercing glare wavers. Her lips twist into a grimace, and a crimson-stained hand rises into view.

"This will be my last act. I hope it serves my people well," she says, through clenched teeth. Then, she sits up and squares her shoulders. *"This is Captain Ehko Shen of the Colony Ship Kaisin, signing off."*

The screen goes dark

I blink. "Did she say—?"

"Kaisin," Fletcher finishes for me.

"What does it mean?" I ask.

"I have no idea," he answers. "But there may be a way we can get some clarity."

He reaches out and gently plucks a tiny bone from the pile, then looks at me. "I'll explain when we get back to the *Undertow*. Now, let's get out of here."

Fletcher hurries to the door, then out into the hall. His brisk pace is hard to keep up with; it's clear he wants to get off of this ship as soon as possible. Then again, so do I.

"What about Lorn?" I ask between gasped breaths.

"What about him?" Fletcher grumbles dismissively.

"He's still down here somewhere," I say. "Shouldn't we look for him?"

"I don't think so," he mumbles.

"But maybe he found something else?"

Fletcher stops walking and lets out a heavy sigh. "You heard Lorn's message: there's nothing else here."

"We found the captain's recording."

"By accident," he interjects.

"There's gotta be more stuff like that down here," I press.

"And how are we gonna find it?" He scoffs.

I don't have a good answer for that question.

"Listen," he starts, a pained look wrinkling his brow "I want to find Lorn—and the truth—just as much as you do, but I think we've reached the end of the line."

"But Lorn—"

"Is dead," Fletcher snaps, then takes a deep breath.

"You can't be sure," I say.

His lips dip into a scowl. "His suit's still here. That's proof enough."

I open my mouth to protest, to push back against his stubborn insistence that Lorn didn't figure *something* out, but Fletcher doesn't give me the chance. He spins away and stomps down the hall, heavy steps echoing in the darkness. He doesn't want to be convinced. So, I let him stew in his own anger and follow at a distance, well within view, but far enough behind that I feel separated from his dour mood.

But that leaves me alone with my thoughts. And my imagination.

The captain of this vessel—a colony ship—mentioned bringing something on board. Was that what made the black streaks on the walls and floor? Is that what once dripped from the ceiling? What is the stuff? How did it kill her crew? Why did it force them to evacuate? And, maybe most importantly, is it still dangerous?

Regardless of the real answer, flickering shadows quicken my pace.

Then, there's the name of the ship we're on: *Kaisin*. At the very least, it proves that Humans and Kaisin are connected. Somehow. So many questions swirl around in my head. I have no idea where to start looking for answers. Are there any answers to be had? Here or anywhere else?

I frown at Fletcher's back. Will he even be interested in finding them? He gave up so easily on Lorn. Maybe—

A distant sound interrupts my thoughts. Though barely a whisper, it sticks out in the silent emptiness. I strain to pick it out from the stomp of metal footsteps, Fletcher's steady breathing over the intercom, and my own pulse pounding in my ears. For a while, the ship is quiet. Then…There it is again!

"Fletcher," I call over the intercom. "Did you hear that?"

"Hear what?"

"Some kind of shuffling in the distance," I reply.

He stops in his tracks and turns to face me. His eyes narrow. "Are you sure?"

"I swear I heard something!" I insist.

Fletcher's lips dip into a frown, and he cocks his head to listen for a repeat of whatever I heard. Only eerie silence accompanies the dark emptiness surrounding us.

"I don't hear anything," he finally says. "It's probably just your imagination. Happens a lot on dark, abandoned ships like this."

"But—!"

He shakes his head. "I'm sure it's nothing."

I want to protest, but give a reluctant nod. He isn't going to listen. His mind is made up.

We continue along the dark-streaked corridors, through the hole Fletcher cut into the massive door with the number '9' scrawled at its base, all the way back to the beginning of Lorn's trail. And whatever sounds *we* make are the only ones I hear the entire way. Maybe the distant shuffling was a figment of my imagination. The thought is somehow comforting as we reach the room with Lorn's suit.

The abandoned husk is far more sobering now. If Lorn hadn't been able to use it to escape the sunken colony ship, what happened to him? Did he lose himself in the endless corridors? And if so, where did he spend his final moments? My pulse throbs at the thought of getting trapped down here in the dark and wasting away, escape just out of reach. How did Lorn feel? I glance at his abandoned suit, but it offers no answers.

Fletcher doesn't seem to have the same thoughts. Or doubts. Slowly, deliberately, he steps up to Lorn's suit and bends over the panel on its arm.

"What are you doing?" I ask.

"Taking his computer," Fletcher mumbles. "I'll have Rhuk look at it when we get back."

"Do you think he recorded anything else?"

"It's the least we can hope for," Fletcher replies with a remorseful sigh. "We won't be getting anything else from him."

Nodding, I glance down the hall as I wait for Fletcher to finish. A flicker of movement catches my eye. I blink. Hold my breath. Stare into the darkness. Nothing. But then, something shifts at the edge of my vision: a shadow among shadows, accompanied by the same echoing shuffle as before.

"Fletcher?" I call out, not taking my eyes off of the shape in the distance.

"I'm almost done," he replies.

"Fletcher!" I pour every ounce of urgency I can muster into his name.

Heavy footsteps hammer metal, then he's beside me.

"What is it?" He sounds annoyed.

I point at the flickering shadow. It's closer than before.

"What the hell is that?" he mutters.

We have our answer a moment later when a pale figure stumbles out of the dark. Tattered clothes hang from an emaciated frame. But the face, however thin, is familiar.

Fletcher's mouth drops open. "Lorn?!"

10

The Kaisin stumbles toward us on unsteady feet. His eyes are dull, staring into space. And his skin is ashen.

"Lorn!" Fletcher's voice is confused. Frantic. Elated.

The Kaisin doesn't respond. He doesn't even seem to notice us as he wanders closer. But then he falls.

Fletcher's cry is drowned by a heavy hiss and the whine of hydraulics. Movement on my periphery draws my eye to his suit. It's opening! And he scrambles out before the back swings completely out of the way.

"Fletcher? What are you doing?"

He ignores me and hurries to the Kaisin's side.

"Lorn!" He cries out a third time, shaking hands reaching out to the collapsed Kaisin.

I can only stare in confusion as Fletcher cradles the strange, yet familiar, Kaisin. Is it really Lorn? Where has he been? How has he managed to survive for so long down here? An involuntary frown twists my lips.

"Aiko!" Fletcher fixes me with a wide-eyed stare. "Help me!"

"Fletcher, I don't think—"

"Damn it, girl," he snaps. "This is Lorn. And he needs us. So, get out here and help me!"

Every fiber of my being screams in protest when I pull my hands free of the suit's gloves. And I can barely steady them enough to uncover and press the red button overhead. A heavy hiss is accompanied by a waft of stale air, tinged with something unsavory I can't identify. It's cold and damp, adding to the sweat already drenching my clothes and slicking my skin. Climbing out of my suit, I pace to Fletcher on unsteady legs. The frigid metal floor sears the soles of my feet. This is real. This is happening.

"What do you want me to do?" I try to sound calm.

"Get the Medkit. Left thigh compartment," he snaps at me, then returns his attention to the groggy Kaisin. "Everything's gonna be alright."

The soothing words seem to pierce the fog dulling the Kaisin's senses. Sluggish eyes slowly focus and begin to sweep the empty hall. The suits. Me. Fletcher.

They freeze on him and widen.

"Fletcher?" The Kaisin wheezes. "Is that you?"

"It's me," Fletcher says with a wavering smile.

Lorn struggles to sit up, but fails. "W—what are you doing here?"

"I came after you," Fletcher replies. "What happened?"

"I…" Lorn's eyes lose focus.

Fletcher helps Lorn upright.

The Kaisin leans back on his slender arms, eyebrows drawn in concentrated thought. At the same time, his now-alert blue eyes study his surroundings. They stop on me.

"You found…another," he says with a genuine, warm smile.

Fletcher scoffs. "She's the one who convinced me to come."

"Oh?" A twinkle enters Lorn's eyes, and his smile widens to a grin.

Fletcher's hand tightens on Lorn's shoulder.

"What happened to you? What's the last thing you remember?" He asks again.

The question seems to sober Lorn. His grin is replaced by pouting lips, and his brow tightens.

"I remember coming aboard. Making my way through the ship. Leaving my suit behind." He pauses and squints. "Then, I..."

"What?" Fletcher urges.

Whatever color there is drains from Lorn's face. His blue eyes widen and flick to Fletcher.

"You shouldn't be here," he hisses.

In a sudden burst of energy, Lorn surges to his knees. Gnarled hands find Fletcher's shoulders. White knuckles bulge through nearly transparent skin. And Lorn's thin lips stretch into a grimace. "You shouldn't have come!"

"Why not?" Fletcher asks. "What happened here?"

Lorn shakes his head. "There isn't time to explain. Get in your suit and go. Now!"

The final word is punctuated by a savage, frantic shove.

Fletcher's mouth drops open. "Lorn—"

"Leave!" The Kaisin shouts. "Before it's too late!"

His hands begin to shake. Then his body.

"Lorn?!" Fletcher reaches out, but the Kaisin grabs his wrist.

"Go!" Lorn spits. His voice is strained. Distorted.

"We can't just leave you here!" Fletcher cries.

"You. Must." Lorn struggles to squeeze the words between clenched teeth. The convulsions racking his body are so powerful that he falls again.

Something about the jerky movements send fingers of ice trailing down my spine. What is happening to him? I force myself to take a step forward. "Fletcher…"

"Help me," he interrupts, bending to try and hold Lorn still. "Fletcher!"

He fixes me with a stare as cold as the sunken ship's metal hull. "Are you going to help me or not?!"

I open my mouth to tell him I won't and that I think we should leave. But Lorn surges to his feet and sends Fletcher flying with a wild backhand. He hits the wall and crumples to the ground.

The Kaisin's eyes snap to me, but they're no longer blue. Both the pupils and whites of his eyes have turned black. A dark substance begins dripping down his gaunt cheeks like nightmarish tears. And more flows up past his collar, out of the cuffs of his tattered sleeves, and from the bottom of his pants. In mere heartbeats, the entirety of his pale skin has been engulfed in dripping darkness.

I want to run to Fletcher, yank him off the ground, and shove him back into his suit, but fear keeps me rooted in place. Even though the Kaisin's face is a featureless expanse of undulating darkness, I can feel his gaze. It's like a whispered breath on the nape of my neck. Or the creeping scuttling of a thousand insects on my skin.

This isn't Lorn. Not the Lorn Fletcher remembers, anyway. But what happened to him? What is the stuff covering him? Is this what the humans brought on board? Is this why the ship is down here in the first place? Is this why Lorn never came back? My heart pounds in beat with the questions racing through my mind.

Everything stops when the Kaisin takes a heavy step forward.

"I told you to leave," he says in a ghastly wheeze.

"W—we'll leave," I stammer.

My feet are still glued to the floor. And my legs barely tremble when I try to force a step toward Fletcher. He's still crumpled at the base of the wall, groaning in pain but finally beginning to move.

"Too...late..." the Kaisin growls. The words are garbled. Strained. Painful. "It...wants...escape..."

In a flash, the Kaisin is inches from me, its featureless face even with mine, spider-like fingers poised to grip my shoulders. Instinct screams for me to flee, but fear holds me in place. I can't even close my eyes as tendrils of the black substance strain toward me.

A massive metal hand sweeps the Kaisin aside, and Fletcher's voice echoes down the corridor. "Aiko! Your suit!"

I stumble backwards as Fletcher pounces. A flurry of heavy strikes connect with the Kaisin, but the undulating fluid shifts in response to the attacks, thickening where the blows land. Blocking them? Then, a black fist smashes into the center of Fletcher's suit, driving him back against the wall.

The Kaisin pivots and lunges at me.

My suit is only feet away, but it's already too late. The Kaisin fills the gap, looming over me. There isn't time to slow down, but maybe...I duck and slide into a tumbling roll across the textured metal floor. Momentum carries me under the Kaisin's wild swipe. I'm going to make it!

A sudden explosion of pain along my left arm bursts like stars outside of the *Undertow's* common room window. I grit my teeth against the raging fire searing my skin and suck in trembling breaths. The Kaisin crouches over me, poised to strike again, fingertips shaped into savage claws by the black substance. I open my mouth to scream.

Metal fingers close around the Kaisin's wrists and yank it backwards.

"Your suit!" Fletcher repeats, as the creature begins to struggle. Black tendrils inch across the surface of his suit, probing for a way in.

I scramble for the idle behemoth standing nearby. Blinding pain cripples my arm. Hot liquid soaks my sleeve and slicks my fingers. They're numb. And they don't work when I haul myself inside the metal cocoon. Waves of cold sweep over me. Sweat beads my brow. I shake Searing pain builds to a crescendo when I push into the suit's gloves. And the blinding agony as the cushions cinch around my arm would have knocked me to the ground had the suit not kept me upright.

Fletcher is still holding the Kaisin at bay. Barely. His suit whines and shakes as if evenly matched.

"Aiko!" His strained voice pierces the haze of pain. "A little help!"

I trundle forward, barrelling into the Kaisin with the full weight of my suit. The force of the blow drives Lorn into the wall, and he slumps to the floor, stunned.

"Come on!" Fletcher snaps at me, grabbing my hand and yanking me down the corridor.

Shadows flicker and flash. Sculpted metal slips by in a blur. Time slows. The pain in my arm throbs in time to our pounding steps. Are we headed in the right direction? Is the Kaisin still following us? Lightheadedness scrambles the questions. Dizziness obscures the answers. But…There isn't time to…I need every ounce of focus to put one foot in front of the other. And each step is harder than the last.

"Here," Fletcher's voice crackles over the intercom, snapping me back to a reality of searing agony.

Through tears, I recognize the opening we dropped through earlier. Above are the empty corridors that lead to the airlock. And escape. Fletcher leaps up. Then, a hand pokes into view.

"Take my hand," he calls.

A stumbling leap is barely enough, but he grabs hold and begins to haul me up.

Something crashes into my dangling legs. And I hear a violent scrabbling on the thick metal. I crane my neck to peer down. A dark figure among the shadows is clawing its way up. Climbing faster than Fletcher can pull. The featureless face peers back, as piercing as any stare, even without eyes. I kick and swing at the Kaisin with my lame arm, but he sticks to me as if glued on.

Fletcher yanks me over the edge and grapples with the Kaisin again. The creature struggles, and sputters, and roars, an even match for Fletcher's bulky, armored suit. For once, I appreciate the overbearing pressure of cushions pressed against me. Despite the throbbing, searing fire in my arm, at least I'm safe.

"God *damn* you," Fletcher spits with a savage shove that drives the Kaisin back. Then, a kick sends it flailing into darkness.

"Almost there," Fletcher pants, pulling me to my feet and sprinting down the corridor.

Every twist and turn looks the same in the oppressive darkness, though now it seems more sinister. It hid so much from us, until it was too late. That thought is punctuated by the growling roar of the Kaisin on our heels. Will we be able to get away?

Hope appears in the form of a ladder. Above is the airlock. And beyond, fathoms of open water.

Fletcher leaps onto the ladder and I clamber up on his heels. Heavy footfalls echo down the corridor. Gaining. Fletcher disappears, then his hands dip through the opening and hoist me up seconds before the Kaisin, his snarling gasps fizzling over the intercom, reaches the base of the ladder.

I frantically fumble over the lower lip of the outer door.

"Close it," I shout, the words deafening in the confined space of my helmet.

Fletcher leaps for the glowing button on the wall, but a shadowy blur careens into him. He stumbles backwards over the bench in the center of the room, the Kaisin perched on the torso of his suit, fists poised to rain blows on his glass visor. Ignoring the pulsing throb in my arm and the slick warmth making my hand slip in its glove, I spring to Fletcher's aid.

Gripping the Kaisin's shoulders, I yank him off of Fletcher. The creature is lighter than I expect and flies farther than I intend. It hits the far wall with a heavy thud, but lands on its feet and lunges toward me. I catch its outstretched claws, teeter, then fall back.

My right arm holds the Kaisin's straining fist at arm's length. My left is heavy, as if the weight of the ocean is pressing down on it. Agony spears into my shoulder joint. Creeping warmth seeps down my sleeve and into my hair. The smell of iron fills the air, so strong I can taste it. Then, my grip wavers. I can't keep this up for much longer.

"Hold on to something!" Fletcher cries over the intercom.

What is he planning? I buck, throwing the Kaisin off balance, then twist free and clamp both hands around the leg of the bench. Black hands, fingertips sharpened into talons, raise to strike. Whatever it is, he better hurry!

A hollow thud shakes the hull beneath me. For a heartbeat, time stops, then water washes the world away. Frothy white waves batter my suit like a chorus of hammers. The cushions hold my body in place, but my head smacks against the back of the helmet. Swirling stars join the searing agony of my arm as the relentless flow loosens my grip one finger at a time. There's no way I'll be able to hold on. A final, heavy slap of fluid as hard as concrete knocks me free, and I tumble away from the bench. My suit slams into one wall, then another, and an explosion of pain carries me into darkness.

11

When I open my eyes, it's dark. The air is no longer damp. Or stale. Or freezing. And I feel like I'm floating. Pressure cradles my left arm like it's bound, and I can't move it. But no sign of the searing agony from before is present, only the barest throb of my pulse beneath the bandage.

Where am I?

I squint until the dark emptiness resolves into the familiar walls of my cramped quarters on the *Undertow*. A shallow sigh of relief escapes my lips, and I relax into the cushioned mattress. Fletcher must have dragged me out of the wreckage, dressed my wounds, and deposited me here. I'll have to remember to thank him when—

A twinge of pressure beneath the bandage interrupts the thought. I frown down at the stark white wrapping, so clean it's nearly glowing in the darkness, and pick at its edge. Something beneath wiggles.

What's that?

I peel the bandage away to reveal a jagged rip from elbow to wrist. It's deep. Angry. Red. The gash isn't bleeding, but clear fluid seeps from the wound. I raise my arm to get a better look at the gash, but nothing seems out of the ordinary. Maybe it's just my imagination?

Another twinge is accompanied by a shadowy flicker deep in the crevasse of the wound. I bring my arm closer to my face, straining to see in the near darkness. What *is* that?

A dark tendril works free of my split flesh, followed by another. And another. And another. Holding my arm out, I watch in horror as the same black liquid that devoured Lorn begins to flow from my wound. It puddles on the bed, drips down the side, and coats the floor with an oozing sheen of darkness.

The fluid begins to coalesce, compressing into a blob that shifts and shakes as if alive. Then, it grows taller and taller until it looms beside the bed. Still, more of the darkness flows from my wound, bolstering the figure as it continues to twist into something more familiar. Two arms and two legs emerge from the whole. The top of the blob morphs into a round head. With hair. And the blank place where a face should be shivers and trembles as features appear.

Mine.

A sinister grin twists the dark imitation's oozing lips to reveal black teeth.

I scream.

Its gaping maw opens in a complementary screech. Then, it lunges.

The ooze engulfs me, shrouding the world in darkness and squeezing the breath from my lungs. The throbbing pain in my arm resumes. I'm warm. Hot. Burning.

My eyes snap open, but I'm not in my room on the *Undertow*. And there's no sign of the oozing darkness anywhere.

The bed beneath me is soft and wider than I'm used to. Dim light reveals plain white walls. A wide door is set in the wall to my left, and a massive window dominates the wall across from it. Beyond, there are no stars. Or lights. Only darkness. A chair occupies the corner beside the window. Fletcher sits slumped in it, chin resting on his chest, slow breaths bobbing his head up and down.

Where are we? How d.d we get here? How long has it been?

I struggle to sit up, but a wave of nausea knocks me flat.

"Fletcher," I croak.

He snaps out of sleep and bolts upright in the chair. Bleary eyes focus on me. "You're finally awake."

Finally?

"H-how long?" My throat is so dry, speaking feels like gargling gravel.

"Three days," he says, the thin line of his lips wavering between a smile and a frown.

"Where are we?"

"Thalijh." He heaves out of the chair and walks to the bed.

I can only manage the barest questioning twitch of my eyebrows.

"They're the best doctors and scientists in the sector," he continues. "And we sorely needed both."

His eyes flick to my left arm. It's cradled in a transparent bag filled with clear fluid. A tight band around my bicep holds the contents inside.

I wiggle my fingers. They're numb. The gash from my dream is barely a jagged seam tracing from my wrist to my elbow. It seemed so real. And the pain...

"What happened?"

"I blew the airlock. Flooded the ship," Fletcher says.

"And Lorn?"

Fletcher's fingers close around a metal railing running the length of the bed in a white-knuckled grip. He shakes his head. "Washed away."

I stifle a sigh of relief. Even though Lorn attacked us, he was still Fletcher's mentor. It was hard enough losing Fallah once. But twice? My lips dip into a frown just thinking of the pain he has to be feeling.

"I'm sorry," I mumble.

He shakes his head.

"And after?"

"I dragged you back to the *Undertow*. Pulled you out of your suit. Stopped the bleeding." He says, then: "It wasn't enough, so I brought you here."

From the twist of his lips, it's clear he left a lot unsaid.

"Thanks."

He smiles.

I take a deep breath. "What now?"

The sudden change in subject seems to ease some of the tension from the air. Fletcher lets go of the metal railing and turns to the window.

"We wait until you get better," he says, staring into the darkness as if there's something to see. "In the meantime, the Thalijh are looking at that bone we took from the wreckage."

"Do you think they'll be able to tell us anything?"

Fletcher shrugs.

I glance down at my arm. "How much longer—?"

"Not long," he says quickly, turning to face me. The smile on his face is strained. Too many questions? Or too few answers? He hurries to the door as if suddenly eager to escape. "I'll let them know you're awake."

It hisses closed behind him.

Once again, I'm alone in a strange place. But it's comfortable. And it feels safe.

Closing my eyes, I relax into the cushioned mattress and puffy pillow. A deep breath eases the tension from my limbs, yet sleep is beyond my grasp. My mind races. Countless questions roar like rushing water, battering me like the deluge that filled the sunken Human colony ship. There are too many to focus on one in particular. Too much uncertainty. Just…too much.

I draw in another deep breath and wish for tranquil silence.

The door hissing open is a harsh denial.

Fletcher enters, followed by a waist-high fleshy mass that's more eyes and tentacles than anything else. A chorus of popping sounds defines its lazy creep across the smooth floor.

"Aiko, this is Prime Orderly Orugh," he says, motioning with his hands to draw my wide-eyed gape away from the being. "He's the Thalijh that's been taking care of you since we arrived."

Orugh is mottled gray, with white speckles, like drops of paint, trailing down each of—His? Hers? I settled on 'its'—wriggling arms. And its saucer-sized eyes are half-covered by drooping lids that make the Thalijh look perpetually tired.

"H—hello," I stammer. The nest of constantly undulating tentacles makes it hard to maintain eye contact.

The response is a rumbling gurgle, accompanied by a synthetic voice. "Greetings. How are you feeling?"

"Good. I guess," I reply. Although…"I can't feel my arm."

I can't even lift it from the bed.

"Normal." The bubbling reply is sickening. "Feeling will return once treatment is complete."

That's a relief, but it doesn't explain the burst of pain earlier. It was only a dream, but—

"And the other thing you're working on?" Fletcher asks.

"Analysis complete," the Thalijh replies. Its lazy gaze shifts to me, then back to Fletcher. "The sample is predominantly hydroxyapatite with trace amounts of magnesium, sodium, and bicarbonate. Extracted DNA fragments are consistent with the Kaisin genome."

Fletcher blinks. "So it's a Kaisin bone?"

"Yes."

Confusion twists Fletcher's haggard face. "You're sure?"

"Confidence is greater than 95 percent," the Thalijh burbles. "Did you expect an alternate outcome?"

"No," Fletcher answers. But he can't keep a frown from his lips.

Neither can I.

The Thalijh is silent for a moment, its tentacles making soft popping sounds as they slowly shift across the smooth floor. Then, it burbles at us again. "Is that all?"

Was that a twinge of impatience in the synthetic voice?

Fletcher nods.

The creature waves an arm at us, then sloshes out of the room. When we're alone, I turn a wide-eyed stare at Fletcher. "A Kaisin bone? Does...does that mean—?"

I can't bring myself to finish the question. Could we be Kaisin? I want an answer. But I don't.

"It doesn't make any sense," Fletcher mumbles.

"Could the Thalijh be wrong?"

Fletcher shakes his head. "Not likely."

"Then…we're Kaisin?" Just saying the words sends a shot of adrenaline through my heart. "How is that possible? We look so different."

"There's an old saying: looks can be deceiving." Fletcher pauses to give me a weary smile that can't hide his confusion. "Guess that applies here."

"So, Humans and Kaisin are the same?" I'm still dumbfounded by the revelation

"But Humans came first," Fletcher adds.

"How do you know?"

"It's the only thing that makes sense," he says, crossing his arms. "They came to this sector on a colony ship named the Kaisin. Then, there's the captain's message."

"You think the humans made it to safety?"

He nods. "And then some."

"Maybe so…" I'm not entirely convinced. There are still too many question marks to count. "Where does that leave us? Where did *we* come from?"

"*That* I can't explain," Fletcher says thoughtfully. "It's the only piece that doesn't seem to fit into the bigger picture."

"Do you think we missed something on the ship? Do you think there might be something else in Lorn's suit computer?"

His lips press into a thin line, and the muscles in his jaw bulge. "I'm not sure."

"What about Gohk?"

"What about her?"

"You said she wasn't telling us everything."

"She probably isn't," he replies, "but that doesn't mean she can fill in *these* blanks."

"We should ask anyway," I urge.

"When we get back," Fletcher says with a nod. "Until then, I'd rather not dwell on it."

"Do you think enough time has passed?"

"That's a good question. I'll send a message in the morning. Till then, get some rest." He considers the chair for a moment. "I'm gonna head back to the *Undertow* and get some real sleep. See you soon, alright?"

Before I can respond, he disappears into the hall.

The deluge of questions return, bolstered by a revelation that I still can't quite wrap my head around. Are we Human? Are we Kaisin? Or are we both? The Thalijh seems to suggest the latter. But how is that possible? It seems our pursuit of Lorn has replaced one fundamental question with another.

Sighing, I cradle my numb arm with the other and swing my legs over the edge of the bed. The cool floor is soothing against my bare soles. At least they can feel *something*. I eye my reflection in the dark window beside the bed. My left arm, cocooned in a clear sack filled with viscous fluid, is numb. Lifeless. Lorn did that, infected by whatever thing the humans brought on board. I step closer and stare at the dark doppelganger. Watching. Waiting.

My reflection moves.

Maybe it's a trick of my eyes from staring too long. Or my mind expecting something to happen. Either way, I stumble back from the window and fall. But even with my reflection gone, the darkness beyond the window continues to shift. *Something* twists and flows beyond the glass. Almost like—

Wait. Are we under water?

Crawling to the window, I cup my good hand against the glass and peer into the dark. Flickering shadows play across my vision. And above, speckled starlight glints on the water's shifting surface, obscured in part by drifting shapes. Suddenly, all the nagging questions from a moment ago fall away, and the tranquility I wished for earlier wraps around me like a warm blanket.

I stare into the silent abyss until the sky fades to soft blue and the darkness is driven away by shimmering shafts of sunlight. Shadowy outlines resolve into creatures of all shapes and sizes. The sea floor is a colorful array of rocky outcroppings covered with entities that sway in the gentle current like delicate, see-through cloth. And between them are all sorts of other things I can't begin to describe.

Fletcher's voice pierces my dream-like trance. "Enjoying the view?"

I tear my eyes away from the window, and reality comes flooding back. My legs are stiff. My right arm is as numb as my left. And fingers of cold have penetrated to my bones. Yet, I feel more rested than Fletcher looks. He stands near the door, just as bleary-eyed as when he left. Maybe more?

"Yeah. Didn't sleep well?"

He grimaces. "Not after what the Thalijh told us. Doesn't look like you slept either."

I shake my head. "Wasn't tired."

"I guess not." His lips stretch into a thin smile, and a tense silence settles over the room.

"Hear anything from Rhuk? Or Gohk?"

"No." Fletcher crosses his arms and wanders into the room. Distracted.

"What's wrong?"

"Nothing," he says quickly, obviously a lie.

I frown. He's definitely holding something back. "You sure nothing's wrong?"

"Why would it be?" he snaps. But then his hard glare softens. "I'm sorry. I sent a message to both of them last night. Expected to hear something by now, but..."

He trails off with the shake of his head.

"Maybe they're just busy?" I don't know what else to say.

He blinks and looks at me. "Maybe."

"So, what happens when we go back?" I ask, before tense silence can return.

The question seems to snap him out of the haze.

"Nothing in particular, I suppose. We'll just be back." He pauses. "Although, I'd really like to hear Gohk's take on everything we learned."

I can already feel the ancient Kaisin's steely eyes judging me. And her harsh words lashing like a whip. "Will she be mad?"

"Mad?"

"About what we did," I reply. "Stealing her pad. Going after Lorn."

"She's always mad about *something*," Fletcher deadpans. "Besides, what we learned is worth whatever grief she gives us. And it's better than staying in the dark."

He doesn't sound convinced. But he's right. Even though the truth is uncomfortable, it comes with a measure of vindication.

We uncovered the truth! Well...some of it, anyway. With any luck, Gohk will be able to fill in the rest. Some of it, at least.

Before I can reply, the door hisses open, and Orugh slips into the room.

"Good morning," a synthetic voice says in time with a sickening burble. Drooping, saucer-sized eyes widen when they spy me sitting next to the window. "You should not be out of bed!"

The Thalijh trundles across the floor in a flurry of wet pops. Before I can protest, a pair of tentacles scoop me off of the floor and dump me on the bed.

"Hey!" I cry out.

The Thalijh ignores me and turns to Fletcher. "I'm going to remove the bag now. You can leave once limb function has returned to normal."

Fletcher nods. "Okay. Thank you."

The Thalijh swivels back to me. Tentacles reach for my left arm. One wraps around my bicep. The other twirls around the bag and gives a gentle tug. I feel nothing as the band slips past my elbow, then wrist. And the expected caress of cool air on the sheen of liquid left behind is eerily absent.

My arm looks good as new aside from a thin, red seam running from wrist to elbow. Though, I still can't wiggle my fingers. "How long before—?"

"An hour," Orugh interrupts. "Until then, stay put."

The synthetic voice sounds almost terse.

I give a silent nod.

"I shall return," Orugh says, waving tentacles as it slips toward the door, half-full bag held aloft, jiggling. Then, the Thalijh disappears into the hall.

"An hour," I grumble.

Fletcher shrugs. "Could be worse."

I want to ask what he means, but suspect I won't like the answer. I change the subject. "So, where will we go when we leave?"

"I'm not sure yet," Fletcher says, rubbing the gray stubble on his chin.

"Back to the station?"

He frowns. "I'm not sure that's a good idea."

"Why not?"

"Gohk said she'd let us know when it was safe to return," he replies.

"But what about everything we've learned?" I press. "Shouldn't we hurry back to see what Gohk knows?!"

Fletcher's brow furrows as he considers the possibility. And he remains silent as a gentle tingle pricks my fingertips. Then my forearm. Then creep past my elbow. The sensation grows to a burn, as if my entire arm has been left in the Alphanax sun for too long. But my fingers move and my arm lifts from the bed, though it feels heavy.

"Good as new!" I exclaim, sluggishly waving it at Fletcher in an attempt to shatter his pensive mood.

His smile is a strained stretch of the lips. "I'll get the Thalijh."

He disappears into the hall and returns moments later with the tentacled mess of a being in tow.

"Feeling has returned?" The Thalijh asks.

"Yeah."

Tentacles snake out and wrap around my arm.

"Can you feel that? And that? And that? And—" Each prompt is accompanied by a sharp prick. I wince at each, until the Thalijh shudders. "Good. Function has returned. You are free to go."

It withdraws and squishes into the hall.

"Let's get out of here," Fletcher mumbles as soon as the Thalijh is gone.

I climb out of bed and follow him into the hall. His lips are turned down in the slightest frown, and his eyebrows are drawn ever-so-slightly together.

"Is everything alright?" I ask.

"Just what you said," Fletcher mumbles. His brow furrows and he frowns. "Maybe Gohk does have the answers we're looking for." He pauses and bites his bottom lip. "Even if she didn't go after Lorn, I'm guessing she did some digging."

"Since you said she wasn't telling us everything?" I chime in.

He blows a breath out of his nose. "Yeah."

"So, we're headed back?"

He nods.

"Even though they haven't called us back?"

"I'm sure everything is fine by now," he replies. "And I wouldn't put it past Gohk to purposefully take her time contacting us as payback for the 'trouble' we caused."

"She'd do that?"

"She's done it before," he scoffs.

"Wow..."

Then, he eyes me, and an amused smile creeps across his face. "Besides, we're going to need to head back to get you a new set of clothes. I don't have anything else near the size of what I gave you before."

I look down at the loose-fitting jumpsuit hanging off of me and clinging to me at the same time. The stark white fabric is thin and soft, yet seems durable enough to last that long, at least.

"Yeah…" I reply with a grimace. It will be nice to finally have something that actually fits.

"Let's go, then."

Without waiting for a response, he slips into the hall and hurries down the oval corridor, boots squeaking on the polished tile underfoot. I jog after him, clenching my fist against the prickling, burning pain still sweeping across my skin. We've been gone for the better part of a week, so there's no telling what we'll find when we get back. Fletcher seems to think everything will be fine, and I want to agree, but we expected our dive to be uneventful, too…

As white walls slip past, sudden doubt shadows my thoughts. We are heading back for answers. I just hope we don't get more than we bargained for.

12

It's hard to sleep while my imagination runs wild. I toss one way. Turn the other. Try to block out the glut of possibilities clouding my mind. They are as plentiful as the stars outside and just as colorful, in all the wrong ways.

Despite the cool air, the blanket pulled up to my chin cloys like a prison. I kick it off and sprawl on the tiny mattress tucked in the corner of my cramped room. But even that isn't enough to quell the restless energy tensing my limbs like coiled springs.

I huff a breath out of my nostrils and sit up. If I can't sleep, what's the point of staying cooped up? Won't it be easier to ignore the storm of thoughts keeping me awake if I'm somewhere else? Like on the bridge? Or staring out of the common room window?

The bare soles of my feet press into the metal deck, just as numb as what's left of the wound on my forearm. The thin line is already barely darker than my skin. More defined in memory. And a concrete tipping point for my mind to slip into a bottomless pit of questions without answers. Ignoring the fall, I shuffle across the dimly lit room.

Darkness oozes from the seam around the door.

I blink. Am I dreaming? Seeing things?

The trickle grows to a stream. Viscous fluid pools at the base of the door and creeps toward my bare toes.

I recoil from the darkness, backpedaling until I bump into the bed. Climbing atop it, I stare in horror as the darkness covers the entire floor. Then, it begins to rise! It makes a hideous slurping sound as it sloshes upward, eager to devour my tiny island of safety.

This can't be! We left Lorn buried under miles of ocean along with whatever had infected him. So, how is it here? And how is there so much of it?

The darkness bubbles over the edge of the bed. I skirt back into the corner, but there's no escape. When the undulating ichor touches my bare toes, it's like fire and ice vying for control of my nerves. The agony sweeps up my calves and past my thighs. It twists my insides into knots and sets my heart racing. Adrenaline sharpens the world to laser focus, and time seems to slow.

I kick at the viscous fluid. Claw at the walls. Scream for Fletcher's help. But nothing can stop the inevitable. Fire sweeps up my neck. Ice tickles the edges of my face. I take one final, deep breath before darkness swallows me.

Pounding heartbeats tick away the seconds.

An urgency to breathe grips my chest like an invisible fist and squeezes. Harder. Tighter. I resist my body's cry for breath, clamping a hand over my mouth and hoping for a last-minute rescue from Fletcher: anything to avoid sucking in a lungful of ichor. But I can't hold on any longer.

Spears of solid ice race down my throat. Fire explodes in my chest. A deeper darkness closes in, overshadowing the one drowning me. Then, everything fades to nothing, an abyss so complete I can't see or hear or feel. It's as if I'm floating in a bottomless ocean without a suit. But where am I really? Sunken in a roomful of the black liquid on the *Undertow?* Or trapped in a dream? A nightmare?

I stare, wide eyed, into the darkness.

Something flickers in the emptiness. Draws closer. Resolves into a familiar shape: *mine.* Too-smooth features and sightless, black eyes glare at me. A lipless mouth gapes in a silent scream. Arms tipped with wriggling tentacles instead of hands reach for me.

There's no air to gasp. There's no ground to stumble back on. I flail, but the dark oblivion's hold on me is complete.

Tentacles snake around my forearms. Trail up to my elbows. Creeping, dull cold pierces the nothingness. Then, a baritone hum fills my brain. It deepens and intensifies until an idea rises out of the depths.

Possession.

I withdraw from the suggestion, but an intense mental pressure squeezes in around me, invisible, yet impossibly large. And irresistible.

The buzzing shifts.

Acquiescence.

The presence sweeps over me like a creeping fog. Insistent. Overwhelming. Inescapable. Just the very thought of resistance sends the nothingness around me tumbling out of focus. Yet the counterfeit clamped onto me remains as sharp as a blade. Its grip tightens. Dark eyes bore into mine. The buzzing reaches a thundering crescendo.

Futility.

The pressure increases. My mind wavers. Begins to slip away. Where am I? How did I get here?

Who am I? Where did I come from?

The figure facing me gives my arms a gentle squeeze. *Answers.* It knows? It can tell me?

Join.

I nod. I have to know.

Tentacles slip past my elbows. Grip my biceps. Pull me closer. *Finality.*

The figure embraces me in a tight hug. The darkness around us compresses. Deepens. And the intense pressure from a moment before releases, shifting to an overwhelming warmth. I relax into it. Let it wash over me. This feels right.

Abstract images drift across my empty thoughts. A cramped room. Crashing waves. Rough stone. A crimson sky. Then, countless faces, all vaguely familiar. One sticks out among the rest. Wide. Flat. Gray, with a streak of blue. And milky, sightless eyes. Kind. Kinder than any other. I hold on to the image. Focus on it. Try to remember who had ever looked at me like that. But I can't.

The face begins to drift away. I strain to hold it in my mind's eye. The warmth surrounding me shifts, and pressure returns. Crushing my will to hold on. I let go, but not because I want to.

The image morphs from a face to the galloping flank of a strange figure. It's sprinting into a barren wilderness, the distant horizon meeting a red sky streaked with ashen clouds. Just before the figure is out of sight, there's a deafening clap. It falls. And doesn't move.

No. This isn't right.

I want to race after the figure, but something holds me back. I can taste bile. Hear cackling laughter. And a muffled, savage voice that sends a spear of fear lancing through my heart. I have to get to her.

Her.

Fallah!

There's no sound as the name leaves my lips, but it echoes throughout my mind and fills the emptiness with a flood of memories, mostly good. And one infinitely bad…

This isn't right!

The pressure redoubles. The dark figure's iron grip tightens. But I'm not under its spell anymore. My mind is clear. Free.

I smile. Fallah is watching over me even now. Her memory has saved me and made sure I'll retain the freedom we both sought. Freedom she paid so dearly to pursue. So, fixing her face in my mind, I push back. Hard.

The invisible, shadowy presence seems to swell. The darkness deepens. The pressure squeezes like an invisible fist. Tentacles tighten. The silent scream balloons to a savage roar. But it's all pretense, as shallow as a child throwing a tantrum. It isn't in control. And it won't be, no matter how much it tries. Can't. Not here.

Fixing a single thought in my mind's eye, I drive it back at the shadowy presence.

Resistance.

The figure in front of me gives a silent snarl.

Relent.

I scowl. This is *my* mind. I close my fingers around the figure's forearms and glare into its black eyes.

Trespassing.

It blinks false eyes.

Expulsion.

The idea strikes the figure like a bolt of lightning. The tentacles wrap around my biceps wriggle free, and it recoils, disappearing into the infinite darkness. Lingering just out of sight.

But the tables have turned. I'm in control now.

Focusing, I soften the darkness around me from oblivion to a moonless night over an endless expanse of soft dirt. I conjure up a familiar sunlit circle. A place I always felt safe and in control.

I take a deep breath of imaginary air. "Come on out," I call.

At first, the silence is defined by the rushing pulse in my ears. Then, the shuffling scrape of uneven steps on dirt that doesn't really exist. Yet I'm still surprised when a familiar face trundles into the light.

Fallah's skin is supposed to be gray, with a bright blue stripe running the length of her spine. But it's as if her entire body has been dipped in ash. Or scorched by fire. Even her eyes are no more than obsidian orbs staring with lifeless emptiness.

This isn't Fallah. Not really. I frown.

"What are you?"

Not-Fallah tilts her head.

I sigh. "Can you even understand me?"

Not-Fallah blinks, then twists wide lips into an awkward word. "Y—yes."

Progress, if only a little.

"My name is Aiko," I offer hesitantly. "What's yours?"

Dark eyes swivel in their sockets, avoiding my gaze. "No name."

"I have to call you something," I mumble. But what? Fallah definitely won't do. Maybe Lorn? No. That doesn't feel right

139

either. I stifle a groan. Fallah had always been better at this kind of thing. Wait! That's it!

"What about Iali?" It's the Quiloh word for darkness.

Not-Fallah stares at me for a moment, then nods. "As you wish."

"Well Iali"—it feels right to call the shadowy presence what it is—"what are you, exactly?"

"I am." Iali replies, twitching ash-tinted eyebrows.

"What does that mean?"

Her—or his, I'm not really sure to be honest—head tilts again. "Words insufficient."

A leathery hand reaches out, palm up.

I hesitate. Is it a trick? Will it try to overwhelm my mind again?

"Will show," Iali insists, fingers beckoning.

Despite Iali's lifeless stare, I sense no malice. Taking a deep breath, I reach out and take its hand. The sunlit circle disappears. And the moonless sky. And the dirt underfoot. Darkness returns. It isn't empty oblivion like before. I'm not alone. Suddenly, I understand what Iali means when it says 'I am'. Because it isn't male. Or female. It isn't one entity. Or many. It simply *is*.

The feeling of togetherness that washes over me is more acute than anything else I've ever felt in my life. It's like sitting in the center of the sunlit circle with Fallah, amplified countless times. It worms into my mind Quells fear. Smothers doubt. Quenches loneliness. In that moment, I no longer need to learn the truth about Humans. Or Kaisin. Or find where I belong. All the answers I needed are in Iali.

But the moment passes like a gentle breeze, and revelation is replaced with something that is equal parts image and idea: weightless solitude. It's endless, as if time doesn't exist. Then, heat sears my skin. Light blinds me. Gravity stretches me as thin as a spider's web. My insides twist at the unpleasantness of Iali's new reality. And the realization that it is going to die.

A lump fills my throat.

Iali begins to fade. Its consciousness compresses to a pinpoint. But just before it is lost to the void, something happens. The image is confusing. Unfocused. There's movement. Color. More darkness. And another presence, but not like Iali. No impression of togetherness washes over me. Only simple life. For a long time, only the pulsing of that single entity fills my mind.

When Iali awakens, it's strong again. It reaches out to the entity and draws it into the togetherness it exudes. Then, like moss growing on a stone, Iali spreads. Time—Iali understands the concept now—flies by. It shapes the entities, until...

Weightless solitude.

Then, the cycle begins anew.

My head spins as light and dark begin to flash by. And it begins to ache as the light strobes faster and faster.

Stop, I plead, but Iali has one more thing to share: the final cycle.

This time, there's light and gravity, but no heat. Entities swarm around Iali. Curious. Insistent. Violent. They invade Iali's reality. Shatter the peace it has enjoyed for so long. So, Iali lashes out.

These memories are crisp. Focused. More than just simple images. The experiences are forced into my mind. My hands tear human flesh. My ears hear their shrill screams. My feet pound metal decking as I hunt them.

There's more, but the images are unfocused. Fragmented. Out of the flashes of light and color, I recognize Lorn's terrified face. And mine.

Iali's leathery hand withdraws.

I stumble backwards, gasping for breath that isn't real. So, this is the darkness that infected Lorn. And now me.

"W—why?" I stammer.

"Preservation."

A parade of images march across my mind. Dozens—Hundreds?—of species poked and prodded from the inside by Iali. Twisted. Controlled. "And all the entities before?"

Iali's large ears flap. "Necessary."

Maybe the *first* was necessary for Iali to survive. But the rest? I stifle a frown. "And the humans?"

"Intrusive," Iali growls.

That isn't the impression I got from the records left behind on the ship. "I meant…what happened to them?"

"Many escaped," Iali replies.

"After that?"

"Unsure," Iali says with a shrug.

I stifle a sigh. It's a longshot Iali will know, but I have to ask. "What happened after they left?"

"Alone," Iali grumbles.

That's it? I frown. "What about Lorn?"

"For a short time," it admits with a shallow nod. "But trapped for very long."

"How long, exactly?"

It sits back on its haunches, and stubby fingers spread as wide as they can reach.

A thought pops into my head and an involuntary word springs from my lips. "Millenium." My jaw drops open. "A thousand years?!"

Standard years. So, is this where the ubiquitous standard Fletcher mentioned comes from?

"That long," Iali agrees.

It sounds impossible. But if everything Iali showed me is true, it spent many thousands of years working its way across space. Jumping from one species to the next. Molding. Shaping. Controlling. It did the same to Lorn. It tried to do the same to me.

I suck a deep breath around the sudden knot in my throat. "What now?"

Iali pauses and looks past me, a twinkle in those previously lifeless orbs.

"Iali?"

Its eyes focus on me, lips split in Fallah's version of a smile. "Freedom."

The word pulls on my heart strings. I wanted freedom so badly, and the real Fallah paid the ultimate price grasping for it. But even so, the thought of letting Iali go free leaves a sour taste in my mouth. Won't it just find another entity to control? Twist? Remake? And another after that? And countless others after that?

No. I can't let Iali go. Not knowing it will steal the freedom of others. Not until I can find a way to keep that from happening.

"You'd be alone again," I say hesitantly.

Iali's ears droop at the proposition.

"You don't have to be," I offer.

Iali blinks.

"You could stay," I tentatively suggest.

"Together?" Iali perks up. Warmth began to tickle the edges of my mind. I can feel its creeping fingers probing for a way inside.

"Not like that," I say, stifling a frown.

Iali's head cocks to the side. "Still alone."

"You're not alone now,' I say. "And you won't be alone if you stay. Things will just be a little different."

"Different…" There's a hint of disappointment in the echoed word. But, eventually, Iali gives a slow nod. "Stay. Together."

I let out a shallow sigh and smile. "It'll be great! You'll see!"

I close my eyes, and when they open, I'm back in my bed on the *Undertow*. Alone. Yet, Iali's presence is still at the edge of my mind, like a heavy memory. When I reach out, it responds with the lightest touch, like fingertips on a pane of glass.

Turning on my side, I close my eyes again, but the gears in my head are already turning. How am I going to tell Fletcher about Iali? And what are we going to do about it? What *can* we do about it? We're going to see Gohk anyway. Maybe she'll know…

13

"Home, sweet home," Fletcher sighs when the station appears against the backdrop of glittering stars. From a distance, the dull cylinder reminds me of the *Undertow*. As we draw closer, its midsection resolves into a belt of hexagonal glass panels. Beneath, spotlights illuminate an array of buildings. And eventually, we're close enough that squinting reveals a flow of tiny dots along the avenues between.

Any other time, I might have relished the view, but there's too much going on inside my head. Even now, I can feel Iali's warm insistence pressing against my thoughts. Without Fallah as my shield—

"Everything alright?" Fletcher's staring at me, eyebrows raised in question.

"Y-yeah," I stammer. "Just thinking."

"What about?"

I can't tell him about Iali. Not yet.

"What's going on with Gohk? And Rhuk?" I lie.

Fletcher still hasn't received a response to the message he sent on Thalijh.

"I'm sure everything's fine," he says, smile wavering as he turns back to the controls. "We'll find out soon enough."

I try to find a comfortable position, but sweat sticks the jump suit to the seat cushion. And my skin crawls just thinking about how to tell Fletcher or Rhuk or Gohk about Iali. What will they say? What will they do?

A wordless question rises to the surface of my thoughts.

Rhuk and Gohk are others. Like me, I reply.

Warm wiggling tickles the edge of my mind, paired with another question.

I don't think so. I stifle a frown. *They probably wouldn't understand. Not after…*

Instead of trying to explain, I offer Iali a memory. Fear. Adrenaline. Lorn. And darkness.

Confusion bubbles to the surface.

The memory didn't work as intended, so I recall another. But this one isn't mine. It's Iali's impression of the Humans.

Its warmth cools at the reminder of what happened a millennium ago. Sudden anger, tempered by fear, scorches the surface of my mind.

It isn't like that. I chew on the inside of my lip until I taste blood. How am I supposed to explain the concept of individuality—and freedom—to a being like Iali? I take a deep breath. I have to try.

To us, togetherness is intrusive, I begin, showing Iali its own memory again to drive the point home. *We are all alone.*

Fallah's face, floating in my memory at all times like a shield against Iali's overwhelming warmth, makes the explanation bittersweet. I really am alone.

Iali's warmth quivers with apprehension. It withdraws slightly.

This is different, I insist. *Friends.*

146

Confusion washes over me again. Iali doesn't understand.

Friends, I repeat, flooding it with warmth.

That's enough to quell whatever lingering fear it feels. And hopefully quiet its curiosity for the time being. My head is already spinning thinking about having to deal with Iali when someone else is speaking to—

"Ready to go?"

I blink the world back into focus to find Fletcher staring at me, eyebrows slightly raised, concern creasing his forehead. The viewscreen behind him is filled with a motley collection of ships. We've landed. And the usual hum of engines has been replaced by unsettling silence.

"You sure everything's alright?"

I nod. "Just a little anxious."

It's the honest truth. And why not? We have no idea what we we're walking into. Are the Kaisin still after us? Have they done anything to Gohk? Rhuk? There's no telling.

Fletcher must have been thinking similar thoughts, because a frown curls his lips. And his brows are drawn down over his steel-gray eyes as rigid steps carry him into the hall. I jump out of my chair and scurry after him, just as eager to visit Gohk and Rhuk. Hopefully, all is well.

The door slides open, and light beams in from outside. Cool air wafts across my face, though it carries a pungent tinge that makes me wrinkle my nose.

"Fuel," Fletcher mumbles, but he doesn't miss a beat, stepping through the threshold and walking down the ramp before it even hits the hangar floor.

I skip to his shoulder, feet rattling in the oversized boots he gave me. They were the only piece of clothing that had survived the dive, but only because I decided to leave them behind.

My gaze darts between the shadows cast by overhanging ships. My ears prick at the echoing ring of bootheels on metal. My heart skips a beat at every set of jittery blue eyes. But no Kaisin gives us any more than a cursory glance. And none stop us.

We pass through the double doors at the far side of the dock and into the grid of buildings beyond. The streets are full, just like last time, but the sense of wonder I initially felt at the overwhelming press is gone. I wipe sweaty palms on my pants and sidle closer to Fletcher's shoulder, scanning the flow of strange beings for the dark-robed Kaisin that tried to drag me away. They're here. Somewhere.

A surge of curiosity pierces the blood thundering in my ears.

I'm afraid of the Kaisin, I say, letting my gaze linger on the next tall, pale figure we pass. Too long. He meets my gaze and holds it, eyebrows furrowing, lips dipping into a frown.

A wordless question floats to the surface.

I tear my eyes away and inch closer to Fletcher. *They don't like humans.*

Another.

I don't know. I frown. We proved the connection between Humans and Kaisin, but uncovered just as many questions. More, actually. Hopefully, Gohk has answers.

We pass the narrow side street leading to Rhuk's workshop and continue along the main thoroughfare until the crowds begin to thin and the buildings shrink. At the next intersection, Fletcher turns left. Then, he slips down a narrow offshoot between two squat, dilapidated buildings. The textured path underfoot has been worn smooth in the center. The walls to either side are scrawled with lettering in so many languages, overlapping so many times that it's hard to tell where one phrase ends and another begins. Then, there's the smell. My lungs want to expel the stink as soon as I take a breath.

"Where are we?" I wheeze.

"Gohk's place," Fletcher mumbles.

"And that smell?"

"I'm not sure. Neither is Gohk." Somehow, he manages a smile. "But she doesn't mind. It keeps the overly curious away."

The alleyway ends at a wide doorway. It seems out of place considering the surroundings. Too new. Too clean.

It whooshes aside when Fletcher draws near. Tepid air washes over us, comparatively fresh. Sucking in a deep breath, I hurry inside. When the door closes, I blow it out in a relieved sigh.

Fletcher's mumble interrupts my relief. "That's strange."

"What is?" I ask, after another deep breath.

"No one's here," he says, walking to the center of the space.

A wide-open floor is dotted with high, chair-less tables. Low booths hug the edges of the room, lit by dim low-hanging lamps. The rest of the space is illuminated by flickering yellow lights, casting a dingy pall over the entire place.

I grimace. "This looks—"

"Yeah," Fletcher groans. "I never liked it either, but Gohk isn't a people person and wants a place that will scare off all but the most determined."

"I'm guessing it works."

149

Fletcher nods. "Almost too well, but there's usually always *someone* here."

He spins in a slow circle. "Gohk?"

No answer.

"Do you think the Kaisin took her?"

"Not sure." Fletcher walks to the counter stretching across the far side of the room. He indicates bottles stacked on shelves along the back wall, all intact. "There's no sign of a struggle. And Gohk wouldn't go without a fight."

But she isn't here.

A chill runs down my spine, and I can suddenly feel invisible—imaginary?—eyes watching me.

"Maybe we should go check on Rhuk. See if he's okay. See if he knows anything."

"Yeah…" Fletcher backs far enough away from the counter for me to spot the concern wrinkling his brow. "Let's head on over."

His tone is even, but his steps are hurried. I have to jog to keep up as he hurries outside. And my longest strides barely keep pace with his determined march. Still, no dark-robed Kaisin intercept us on the way to Rhuk's workshop. Why not? Have they already forgotten about us? Or are they watching us? Waiting?

My stomach is twisted into knots by the time familiar neon letters hanging over a worn door pop into view. Maybe Rhuk will be there? Maybe he'll have answers?

Fletcher jogs the last few steps and slips inside before the door has fully opened. I'm on his heels, eager to see what lies beyond.

Rhuk looks up from his workbench, frowning, bushy eyebrows drawn down in annoyance. When he sees us, the corners of his lips twitch with the hint of a smile.

"Fletcher. Aiko. You're back."

He pauses, then says: "So soon…"

The little alien seems subdued. Troubled. But why? I open my mouth to ask if everything is okay, but sudden alarm jolts my brain like an electric shock.

Iali?

Its warmth quivers at the edge of my mind.

What's wrong?

It withdraws. Shrinks. Disappears.

I blink and shift my gaze to Rhuk. The thin line of his lips accentuates a pensive stare.

Fletcher ignores it. Or doesn't notice.

"We had to come back," he says, breathless.

Rhuk's lips fall. "Why?"

"It's a long story," Fletcher replies, hesitantly. "One we were hoping to tell Gohk as well. Have you seen her?"

"Gohk?" Rhuk shakes his head. "No. We haven't spoken since you left."

Fletcher's brow furrows. "Not even after my message?"

Rhuk looks away. "No."

"Do you know where she might be?" Fletcher asks, wandering deeper into the workshop. "We stopped by her place, but it was empty."

"I don't know where else she could be." Rhuk's eyebrows twitch. "But I'm sure she'll show up eventually."

Fletcher lets out a deep sigh.

"What about the robed Kaisin?" I call. The question echoes in the vaulted space, drawing Rhuk's wide-eyed stare.

"They're still around," he replies quickly.

"You think they took Gohk like they tried to take me?" I ask, a shiver running down my spine. Even days later, I can still feel their ghostly fingers clamped around my biceps.

Rhuk grimaces and shakes his head. But the lack of an answer is telling. Have the Kaisin got to her? To him? Suddenly, Iali's alarm makes sense. We're in danger. We have to get out of here. Now.

The small creature slides off of the stool and trundles toward Fletcher.

"You weren't supposed to come back until *we* called *you*," he says, in a chiding tone.

"This was too important," Fletcher replies.

"You shouldn't have come back," Rhuk hisses.

Fletcher hesitates, a confused frown twisting his lips and brow. He still hasn't noticed.

The small being takes another step forward and pats Fletcher's leg, then slips past him.

Rhuk's warm smile, however strained, is a sight for sore eyes. His outstretched hands are enough to bring me to my knees and sink into his warm embrace. This is the most at home I've felt since sitting in the sun with Fallah.

"You need to leave," he whispers in my ear.

I draw in a shallow breath and open my mouth, but he squeezes me tighter.

"No questions. Run. While you still can."

When Rhuk pulls away, his smile falls and his huge eyes lock with mine. His lips form a single, silent, pleading word: 'Run'.

Fletcher notices the perturbed expression on my face and his eyebrows shoot up in question behind Rhuk's back.

"I'm really glad to be back," I say, throwing my arms around the small being's neck again. I look up at Fletcher as the little creature hugs me a second time and mouth the words, 'We need to leave'.

He frowns, but gives me a shallow nod. "As happy as we are to be back, it's probably best if we stay on the *Undertow*. Just in case we need to make a swift escape."

Rhuk slips out of my grasp. "I think that's a good idea."

Before any of us can move, the door to Rhuk's workshop hisses open, and a pair of dark-robed Kaisin step inside. Then, two more. Four. Eight. Ten. Twelve total stand between us and escape.

Fletcher's shocked stare snaps to Rhuk.

"They've been waiting for you," he says with a defeated sigh. "Your message gave you away."

Fletcher's mouth works. "You—?"

"Tried to warn you without tipping them off," Rhuk snaps.

And so had Iali. I search the edge of my mind for its presence, but find only emptiness. How did it know?

Fletcher inches closer to me, hand out to shield me from the Kaisin creeping closer. There are so many…

"You have to run," Fletcher mumbles under his breath.

I tear my gaze away from the Kaisin. "But—"

"I'll be fine," he snaps. His eyebrows are drawn together, lips twisted into a scowl. He isn't afraid. He's…determined. "Now, run!"

"No!" Not this! Not again! I can't leave Fletcher, or Rhuk, behind!

He doesn't give me a choice.

Firm hands grip my shoulders and shove me past the line of Kaisin. Then, Fletcher barrels into the two that turn to grab me.

"Go!"

His muffled cry pierces the fog of disbelief and spurs me to action.

I stumble through the open door and into the narrow, empty street beyond. The main thoroughfare is within view. If I can make it into the crowd...

Two dark-robed Kaisin—no, four—burst into the open behind me. From inside Rhak's workshop, I can hear Fletcher's strained cries. He's fighting. For me. To give me a chance to escape. One I can't squander

Dancing away from a pair of wild grabs, I sprint toward the flowing crowd. To freedom. My oversized boots hammer the worn metal deck. Recycled air burns in my lungs. But I'm outpacing the Kaisin. I'm going to make it!

I leap into the crowd and let the relentless flow carry me along. Dozens of strange beings jostle me. Hands push me this way and that. Words I can't understand fill my ears as one entity or another warbles at me. Most are taller than I, so it's impossible to see what lies ahead. Or behind. But I haven't run into any dark-robed Kaisin. Not yet. With any luck, I won't. Though, I can't stay on this road forever. Eventually, the Kaisin will think to get ahead of me. Then, escape will be impossible.

Working my way to the edge of the crowd, I slip free at the next side street. It's nearly as narrow as the alley leading to Gohk's bar. But it's clean. And empty. And it doesn't smell.

With a shallow sigh of relief, I jog along the corridor between two unfamiliar buildings. I've escaped the Kaisin, but where am I going? What am I going to do? They have Fletcher. And Rhuk. And Gohk is just…gone.

My steps falter. I'm alone. Again.

A tentative warmth touches the edge of my mind.

Maybe not completely alone.

Where did you go?

Iali shies away from the question.

The beat of footsteps on metal keep me from asking again. A glance over my shoulder reveals a flash of pale skin. The flutter of dark robes. Familiar, yet barely unintelligible, barked speech. The Kaisin have found me.

I stumble into a sprint, hand trailing along the smooth wall, breath catching in my throat. Yet, despite my headlong rush, the Kaisin are gaining this time.

Ahead, the narrow alleyway runs into another avenue. I can see crowds. They're not as thick as on the main thoroughfare, but dense enough to give my pursuers the slip. Again. But how long can I keep this up? How long before they manage to cut me off? Capture me? Best not think about that until it happens.

I barrel onto the street, careen into an alien, and stumble against another, but manage to stay on my feet. The breath burns in my lungs. My feet hurt from pounding against metal. My heart batters against my ribcage. But I can't stop. I shoulder through the press, mumbling apologies to each being I shove aside.

Dark robes flutter ahead. The Kaisin! I spin on my heel and head in the opposite direction, but they're there, too. They're all around me. Closing in. I push against the crowd. Struggle. It's like resisting the current that knocked me loose in the Human colony ship. Irresistible. Inevitable. The Kaisin will have me. There's no escape.

Strong hands snake around me. One slaps over my mouth to muffle my scream. The other clamps like a vice across my chest. Then, I'm yanked out of the crowd and dragged to an alcove on the side of the street, into the shadows...

14

Six dark-robed Kaisin drift out of the crowd and gather into a tight-knit group. Draw closer. Slip past.

What?

I look down at the hand clamped over my mouth and the arm across my chest. Both are pale. Wiry. They belong to a Kaisin. I twist and look up to a familiar face. The ancient Kaisin's permanent grimace widens into a grin that puts yellow, jagged teeth on full display.

"Gohk?!" I mumble against her spindly fingers.

"Shush," she hisses, blue eyes darting along the street. The Kaisin are gone. Gohk lets out a shallow sigh and glares down at me. "Fletcher made a real mess of things with that damned message."

I twist in her grip and turn to face her. "What's going on?"

"These robed Kaisin have been patrolling the station since you left." She crosses her arms. "Which was fine, until Fletcher—"

Her lips twist into a scowl.

"They were on my doorstep minutes later. I barely managed to get away."

For the first time, I notice Gohk's clothes. They're dirty. Stained. Tattered in places. It's only been a few days since Fletcher sent his message. What has she gone through since? I shiver just thinking about the possibilities. "They're still—"

"After you. And Fletcher." Then, she blinks. "Where *is* Fletcher?"

"T—the Kaisin got him," I stutter.

"How?!"

"They were waiting for us at Rhuk's workshop," I reply with a frown.

"So, they got him, too. Poor bastard…" Gohk rubs her chin, and her eyes lose focus. A moment later, they dart to me. "Let's go."

She grabs my arm and steps toward the street.

I resist her pull. "Where?"

"Away from here." She gestures broadly. "Someplace safe."

"What about Fletcher? And Rhuk?" I ask, frowning.

Gohk lets go of my arm and takes a step back. Her stare is cold. "What about them?"

"We can't just let the Kaisin take them," I insist. "We've got to—"

"What?" Her hands find her hips. "Rescue them? Just the two of us?"

She laughs.

"It's better than abandoning them," I shoot back.

She scowls at me. "You want to get captured, too?"

"Of course not."

"Then quit arguing," Gohk snaps, "and trust me."

The thought of trusting anyone right now, let alone a Kaisin—*especially* a Kaisin—leaves a sour taste on the back of my tongue. But I don't have anyone else to turn to. If I don't trust

Gohk, I'll be on my own, trapped on a station filled with Kaisin out to get me. But…

I frown. Gohk is wrong. "I can't leave Fletcher behind."

Not after he dragged me from the sunken ship and carted me all the way to Thalijh.

"Or Rhuk."

"We can't save them," she growls, turning away for a moment, then back. "It'd be you and me against a dozen Kaisin? Possibly more?"

She gives an emphatic shake of the head. "No. We can't."

"*You* don't have to." I back away from her. "*I* will."

"Don't be foolish," Gohk snaps, spidery fingers clenching at her sides.

"I'll go alone if I have to," I threaten, edging closer to the street.

Gohk bares her teeth, then holds out both hands. "Wait!"

Her lips dip into a deep, lingering scowl. "You're stubborn. Just like Fletcher."

I offer her a thin smile. "I'll take that as a compliment."

Tense silence settles between us. Gohk stares at me with cold, hard, jittery blue eyes. And spider-like fingers tap on the seam of her pants leg. But I don't budge. I won't, until I have my way. We're going to rescue Fletcher. And Rhuk.

Finally, Gohk lets out a deep sigh. "Fine, we'll go"—she holds up a crooked finger—"but we're doing this my way."

I open my mouth to agree, but Iali quivers. Caution rattles against the edge of my mind like a stone skipping across still water.

I clap my mouth shut. *Iali? What's wrong?*

Again, it shies from my question, withdrawing from the edge of my mind.

"Aiko!"

A firm shake snaps me back to reality. I'm staring into Gohk's vivid blue eyes. She's waiting for my answer, but the twist of her brow and lips suggest impatience.

"Sorry," I murmur. Iali was right before, so maybe I should listen to it again? But Gohk saved me from the other Kaisin. I can trust her. Maybe it was mistaken? Confused because Gohk is Kaisin as well?

Iali? I take a deep breath, but can't stall anymore. If it doesn't answer, I'll have to make the decision for myself.

For the second time, Iali isn't there.

I cast disappointment into the emptiness and nod to Gohk. "Fine."

"Then follow me. And stay close."

Gohk flips the collar of her tattered overcoat up past her ears and pulls me into the crowd, pacing close to the overhanging buildings lining the street's edge. Some are lit by lamps or neon storefronts, but there are plenty of shadowed alcoves like the one Gohk used as a hiding place. Standing in the shadows, the alcove hadn't seemed so dark, but walking past them is like staring into a void. A Kaisin could have been within arm's reach, and I wouldn't have seen it before it was too late. All of a sudden, our path forward feels as exposed as the barren plains surrounding Alphanax. And just as deadly.

But Gohk's swift, confident steps keep us moving. And her alert, darting gaze keeps us safe.

I stay at her shoulder. Watching for Kaisin. Wondering at Iali's warning. Is Gohk working with the Kaisin as well? Is she leading me into a trap? I stare at Gohk's back. The dark-robed Kaisin don't seem to care too much about subtlety, so I'm relatively safe. For now. But I'll keep an eye out. At the first sign of trouble, I'll run again.

Gohk stops. "We're here."

I don't recognize the intersection. The narrow, nearly empty street we're on crosses another in a "T." All of the buildings are squat. Dark. And most of the light comes from the glow of stars overhead. What little is produced by street lights flickers like candles.

"Where are we?" I whisper back.

A gnarled hand yanks me to the corner.

"Rhuk's workshop," she grumbles, pointing. "We approached from the opposite side of the street. And we're just in time."

The front door creaks open, and a handful of Kaisin file into the street. Two shove Rhuk's diminutive form between them. The last two drag Fletcher, unconscious.

For a moment, the group is remarkably still and eerily silent. Then, in perfect unison, they turn toward where we're hiding.

Gohk hisses in her native tongue and ducks behind the corner, pulling me with her all the way to a patch of darkness between buildings. Her shallow breath in my ear is drowned out by a chorus of footsteps. And the scrape of Fletcher's dragging feet.

The Kaisin move as one. Their steps rise and fall together. Their arms swing in time. None speak. All stare straight ahead, as stiff as statues. It's strange. Unsettling. Sinister. And sends a shot of adrenaline through my already pounding heart.

The group turns right and continues along the street in a slow, methodical march, paying no heed to the scattered beings they pass. Or the strange looks their odd procession garners.

Gohk nudges me with an elbow when they're almost out of sight.

"Let's go," she whispers.

Her steady gait mirrors the Kaisin, keeping us at a safe distance. I pace at her shoulder, arms and legs twitching with coiled energy wound so tight I could have leapt to the top of the nearest building. I take a deep breath. Two. Three. But that just makes me lightheaded. I need to focus.

I scour the dark edges of my mind for Iali. It's there. Withdrawn. Isolated. Not quite hidden in the dark, but...obscured?

What are you afraid of?

I expect silence, but Iali's warmth wafts against the edge of my mind like thick fog. It cools. Shifts toward darkness, like when we first 'met'.

What are you trying to tell me?

The darkness expands. Curls around my mind. Blots out everything else. It squeezes like a vice. Muddles my thoughts. Quickens my heart. Steals my breath. Then, it's gone. There is only Iali. Feeble. Spent from the effort of trying to show me...What, exactly?

I don't understand.

It shivers in frustration but doesn't offer anything more.

I frown and suck an extra-deep breath through my nose. If only there was time to stop, close my eyes, and speak with Iali directly, but the Kaisin's relentless march doesn't let up.

We follow through narrower streets. Past squatter buildings. Thread through less varied crowds. Eventually, we only pass Kaisin. Without skipping a beat, Gohk slips the coat from her shoulders and drapes it around me, pulling the collar up over my head to hide the dark hair falling around my face.

"Stay close," she mutters, before hurrying after the shrinking group dragging Fletcher further into the unknown.

This part of the station is different. Not nearly as much light scrubs away the deep shadows cast by the decaying buildings overhanging the street. Even the metal panels underfoot are worn and warped. I have to place each step carefully to keep from tripping on the crumpled edges.

I shuffle closer to Gohk's shoulder. "Why is this part of the station so...?" I struggle to find the right word.

"Decrepit?" Gohk finishes for me.

"Yeah..." I grimace.

"By and large, Kaisin are xenophobic," she begins.

"Xenophobic?"

"It means they don't like non-Kaisin."

It explains why the Headmistress was so cold toward most of the children at Alphanax. "But why do they hate Hu-?"

"No!" She cuts me off before I can get the rest of the word out. Then, she yanks me to the side of the street. Her voice falls to a savage whisper. "Be careful where you say that word! That's what got us in this mess in the first place!"

I nod and swallow the lump in my throat.

She nudges me back onto the street and falls in beside me.

"Kaisin don't like living with others if they can help it," she murmurs, craning her neck to keep an eye on the group of dark-robed Kaisin further along the street. "This station used to be solely Kaisin, but it grew in popularity as a fuel depot and trading post due to its advantageous location at the sector's edge. Other species moved in, and the Kaisin moved out. Now, only the Kaisin that can't afford to get off station stay here."

I take a deep breath to steel my nerves. "And you?"

Gohk's blue eyes flick to me, eyebrows drawn, lips twisted in consternation. "My years of hating others are far behind me."

She's hiding something. Or holding something back. But I don't press. Whatever it is hurts, like the pain Fletcher carries for Lorn. And the sting of Fallah's death still hanging over me like a laden storm cloud.

The dead conversation gives way to tense silence as we continue to trail the Kaisin. We've been walking so long that the station's outer bulkhead curves up and over us, joining the belt of hexagonal panes of glass above and behind. Yet, the Kaisin continue.

"Where are they going?" I ask.

Gohk frowns. "Not sure, but we'll find out soon. They're almost out of station."

The shadows deepen as the outer bulkhead draws nearer. Crowds thin, and buildings shift from seldom-entered to abandoned, until it's only us and the tight-knit group we're tailing. Gohk slows even further, allowing our quarry to dwindle in the distance.

"Better than being noticed," she mumbles.

Before I can ask what will happen if we lose them, the group slips out of sight.

Gohk belts out a guttural curse and breaks into a jog. I canter at her shoulder.

The street ends at a small cul-de-sac hugged by dark, monolithic structures that can't be called buildings any longer. Directly across the open space, an alley—barely more than shoulder-width—continues into the unknown. Gohk crosses to it and cocks her ear to the empty air. Even without mirroring the motion, I can pick out the echoing tap of a dozen feet on worn metal. And the scrape of Fletcher's limp legs.

"Quietly," Gohk urges, squeezing into the narrow space.

I creep behind, trailing my hands along the scoured polymer siding. Our light footsteps echo like claps of thunder in the enclosed space. Shallow breaths rush like the summer wind on Alphanax. Even my clenched teeth creak like the ancient, settling stone of the orphanage.

A sudden, outstretched hand halts my forward movement. I strain to glance past Gohk's slender form, but the alley is too narrow.

"What's going on?" I whisper.

Her open palm vibrates in a wordless "shush".

Harsh words shatter the muffled silence. Even without being able to see, I know they are meant for us. I can feel the malice in them, as if they're the cold steel of a blade pressed against my throat.

Gohk growls something in response, then twists to look at me. "Go back!"

I turn back and freeze. Shadows flicker in the near dark. Resolve into tall figures with dark robes, pale faces, jittering blue eyes, and spider-like fingers.

Kaisin.

There's nowhere to go. No escape.

They crash into me, shove me toward Gohk, and force the two of us into the open.

I stumble to a halt on a crumpled swath of worn metal decking. Though only a few dozen paces across, it stretches indeterminately to the left and right, dividing crumbling structures from the station's outer bulkhead. The Kaisin crowd around a hatch at its base, but they're staring at us. *Me.* A dozen sets of probing, blue eyes. I meet each in turn, defiant despite the jittering of my heart matching their stares. Rhuk, on the other hand, refuses to meet my gaze. Instead, he studies his shuffling feet. I frown. He has nothing to feel guilty for. The Kaisin didn't give him a choice.

Gohk steps past me and barks something at the group.

A harsh grumble issues from somewhere in the pack, but the Kaisin that spoke doesn't step forward. Gohk calls out again, and I search tight-lipped mouths for the next response. Each comes from a different mouth, given without hesitation as if the Kaisin are of a singular mind. Or maybe it just seems that way because I can't understand what's being said.

Another, clipped growl issues from behind. Spidery fingers grip my shoulder and push me toward the group.

"W-wait! No! Let me go!" I sputter in protest.

Gohk shakes a pale hand off of her arm and spins, fist raised, but the Kaisin plants a solid blow on her temple. She wavers, slurs in her native tongue, then slumps into his arms.

I buck under the Kaisin's grasp. Almost twist free. But a second hand closes on my opposite shoulder. All ten fingers squeeze, digging into the soft meat above my collar bone, until I'm paralyzed by stabbing pain.

"No more struggling," one of the Kaisin calls out. I can't focus through the blur of tears to see which. "You will come with us. Quietly."

A twinge of pressure, and more pain, accompany the order.

I manage a nod, and the Kaisin's grip loosens. But only just a hair. Pain still arcs from my shoulders up my neck and down my arms. It throbs in time with each forced step toward the now open hatch that leads...where?

The dozen Kaisin disappear through the dark opening, Rhuk among them, Fletcher dragged behind. I'm pushed through next. The heavy, shuffling steps of the Kaisin carrying Gohk at my heels.

We descend spiral stairs that plunge through a seemingly infinite abyss to a long, *long* corridor. It's like being in the Human colony ship all over again. Dark. Dank. Endless. I lose track of the number of steps we take. And the number of intersections barely register through the aching miasma. But then, the forced march breaks.

Irresistible hands shove me through a wide doorway. The vaulted space beyond, bordered by a window fogged from age, holds too many dark-robed Kaisin to count. Pale faces lit by starlight turn to us, and a chorus of voices mumble a single word in eerie unison: "Humans."

15

The Kaisin part, their blank stares tracking Fletcher, then I, as we pass through the crowd. All are silent and motionless besides the slow turn of their heads. Yet, as forceful as the Kaisin were, none look upon me with disdain. Or any other discernible emotion. Their faces are simply blank.

I feel the opposite. So does Iali. It has returned to the periphery of my mind, and its scant touch communicates fear. And alarm.

Despite the adrenaline coursing through me—instinct screaming for me to flee—I walk along the path created by the recoiling Kaisin without a hand to drive me forward or barked commands to keep me moving. Curiosity draws me deeper into the space, closer to the fogged window, toward an oval pedestal.

A Kaisin, head and shoulders taller than any of the others, wrapped in a ragged obsidian cloak, glares down at me. Then, his icy stare drifts past. All the while, the mumbled chorus of "Humans" echoes in the vaulted space. Reverberates. Pulses in time with my pounding heart.

Deafening, suffocating silence settles like thick fog when the tall Kaisin raises his hands. The sleeves of his dark robes fall back to reveal thin, wiry arms traced with dark, squiggly lines. Writing?

I search for Gohk among the Kaisin. Her tattered gray shirt stands out among the sleek, dark robes. And for the first time, I notice her wrinkled skin is more yellow than white. Because of her age, perhaps? She's finally coming around, her pale, bald head bobbing as if too heavy for her neck. I catch her attention and tilt my head at the tall Kaisin, eyebrows raised in question. She blinks, studies him for a moment, then gives a weak head-shake.

He barks and motions to the oval's edge. For the first time since stepping inside this room, strong hands grip my shoulders and arrange me into a line with the others. Fletcher is beside me, still dazed, head lolling. Rhuk is beside him, looking small and weak. Gohk wavers on the far end, shoulders back, head held high.

The tall Kaisin's gaze sweeps over us again, lingering for a moment on Gohk. His brow falls ever so slightly in…disappointment? But the appraising stare only lasts a moment before he saunters to the edge of the platform and glowers at each of us in turn. His severe gaze rests on me.

"Are there any others?" he asks, in a surprising, soothing baritone.

"Others?" Gohk calls out. Her tone is harsh. Defiant.

The Kaisin cocks his head at her. "You, most of all, should know exactly what I mean."

Gohk doesn't answer, but the muscles in her jaw bulge.

"So?" the tall Kaisin urges, his unwavering gaze returning to me.

I blink, but can't squeeze an answer past the planet-sized lump in my throat.

His eyes narrow and slide back to Gohk.

She looks away, swallows, and gives a feeble shake of the head. "No."

A satisfied smile curls the corners of his thin lips. "Good."

The tall Kaisin backs to the middle of the platform, but doesn't speak. His gaze, once piercing and severe, is now as empty as all the other Kaisin gathered around us. What is he doing?

A tendril of warmth tickles the back of my mind. Iali wants in.

I stifle a frown. *Why?*

Faint reassurance washes over me. Then, insistence.

I sense no malice in Iali's intent. Or deception. So, against my better judgment, I give in.

Warmth floods through the tiny opening, drowning my thoughts. But then sharp, piercing fingers plunge into the depths. Searing pain bursts like starlight across my vision. Breath catches in my throat. My legs tremble, barely able to keep me upright as Iali sifts through every nook and cranny of my mind.

Clenching trembling hands, I force Iali back and slam the opening shut. Rage bubbles to the surface, which I use to reinforce a wordless question.

Iali quivers but responds with tranquil optimism.

I don't understand. I shoot back.

It nudges the edge of my mind, directing my focus outward.

Blinking, I suck in a deep breath and focus on the world around me. I'm still in line with Fletcher, and Rhuk, and Gohk. We're still surrounded by Kaisin. And ethereal starlight still beams through the foggy glass curving along the outer edge of the vaulted room.

The tall Kaisin is motionless in the center of the platform. And his gaze is still vacant. But the air is filled with a murmuring whisper of the Kaisin around us. No, not the Kaisin. And not a whisper. It's something else.

Is this what you did?

A warm affirmative washes over me.

What am I hearing?

An image of darkness drifts against the edge of my mind.

I don't understand.

The tall Kaisin raises his hands into the air and the sleeves of his robes slide back again to reveal pale, wiry arms. The squiggly lines begin to drip. Darkness seeps from his body. Flows down his arms. Pools beneath his feet. Then, the Kaisin crowded in around us begin to quiver and shake. Blue eyes roll back to white. Mouths open in wordless screams. And liquid darkness wriggles into the open, slithering along the floor in countless gooey tendrils toward the oval platform.

The murmuring grows louder.

The pool at the tall Kaisin's feet shudders and withdraws beneath the hem of his robe. All the tendrils of dark material follow with a sickening slurping sound. His arms, still extended, are swallowed in a sheathe of black goop. Then, the darkness flows out of his collar and covers his pale, bald head.

As a featureless face turns down to look at the four of us, the chorus of voices snap to silence. Even without eyes to glare or a mouth to scowl, malice washes over me. Fear freezes me in place. This is…

Panic batters the edge of my mind. And even though Iali is separated from me, I can make out a single word: *Run!*

171

I stumble backwards. Trip. Fall. The ground is soft with the bodies of sprawled Kaisin. None of them are moving. Are they dead?

Tiny hands grab me. Shake me. Pull me. Coax me out of the pile of bodies. And a voice hisses at me.

"Aiko! Get up! We have to go!"

Rhuk's face pops into focus. His large eyes are wide. His brow twitches. And his jagged teeth are bared in a fearful grimace.

Over his shoulder, still perched on the oval pedestal, is the Kaisin. Completely engulfed. Just like Lorn. But...no...this is different. The darkness doesn't drip. Or shiver. Or shift. It clings to him like a second skin, as if it *is* his skin.

The full weight of Rhuk's tiny body crashes against me, snapping me back to reality.

"Move!"

I scramble over the Kaisin bodies littering the vaulted space. Rhuk jogs beside me. Gohk is a dozen paces off to my right, a scrawny arm under Fletcher's, dragging him along, peppering him with a string of harsh words that need no translation.

The tall Kaisin is watching us, his featureless face cocked to the side, obsidian arms akimbo. It isn't moving, but we'll never escape on foot! Lorn—as old and haggard and spent as he was—proved more than a match for two powered dive suits. The only reason we got away is because Fletcher blew open the colony ship's airlock. The ocean did the rest. But here? We can't open up the station to space. Well...we could, but...

Frowning, I focus inward. *This is what you were trying to warn me about.*

Iali presses against the edge of my mind, its warmth undulating in a frantic affirmative.

I'm sorry. I didn't understand.

But it's too late for regret.

Even supporting Fletcher, Gohk slips through the doorway first. I skirt through on her heels, Rhuk on mine. A flickering button on the wall promises safety. When pressed, thick doors creak on ancient hinges that haven't been used in who knows how long. But they're closing.

Slowly.

A black hand shoots through the narrowing opening, and claws like the dark void of space curl around one half of the metal slab. Then, a different kind of groaning starts. Tortured metal squeals as the door peels back like it's made of cloth. The Kaisin's now featureless face pokes through. Then, it speaks.

"Surrender."

The word rattles in my ears like gravel scraping across glass as it reaches through the gap with its other arm.

"There is no escape."

A small hand yanks me away from the opening and harsh words sting my ears, but all I can hear is its threatening growl echoing in my mind. All I can see is its featureless face staring into me. It is telling the truth. There is no escape. No matter how far we run. How far we fly. How well we hide. *It* would find us. My brow furrows. But how?

Iali's warmth crashes against the edge of my mind. Insistent. Overwhelming.

I stumble but manage to keep my feet. Now isn't the time. I can't focus on running and talking to it.

Later, I snap, fixing Fal ah's face in my mind's eye. I need her shielding presence now more than ever!

The endless corridor flashes by in a blur. The Kaisin is behind us. And though wayward glances over my shoulder reveal emptiness in our wake, I can *feel* its darkness creeping toward me. Like storm clouds on the horizon. Though even at a distance, they overshadow Iali's dogged insistence.

This is bad. Really bad.

Gohk is leading, but she looks haggard. Fletcher is limping along beside her, finally under his own power, but still dazed. Rhuk jogs beside me, his small hand knotted in the fabric of the Thalijh jumpsuit. Pensive. Despite the silence, I'm sure each of their minds are racing as quickly as mine. As quickly as our feet carry us. If we don't reach the hatch before the Kaisin manages to catch up…Well, none of us are in any shape to mount a resistance. Not that there's anything we can do to oppose it.

I suck in a deep breath, swallow against the desert of dryness in my throat, and finally give in to Iali's constant, insistent pressure.

What's your idea?

An image, a memory, floats to the surface: Lorn covered in darkness. He's close to me. Within arm's reach. Outstretched hands are poised to strike.

My arm itches at the thought of what I know happens next.

But the image deviates from real memory. Instead of Lorn's fingers ripping through the flesh of my forearm, I duck under the wild swing and slam both palms into the darkness. A moment passes. Two. Then, Lorn stiffens and topples, the darkness sloughing off of him into an inert puddle.

174

How?

Iali doesn't give an answer.

I offer doubt.

It demands trust.

The itch in my arm grows to a subtle burn. There's no way I'll let the Kaisin get that close. Fletcher and I barely survived the last encounter, and I came away with an unexpected passenger. What'll happen next time? I grimace as my imagination begins a parallel race in time with our wayward sprint.

I slap each image aside and focus on the corridor ahead. It trails into the distance. Narrows to a pinpoint. Then, our salvation springs into view: the staircase. At the top is a hatch. Beyond is freedom. And maybe, safety. We just have to make it.

A whisper, just beneath the echo of our rushed steps, tickles my ear and prompts me to look back. I hope for an empty corridor. But it isn't. The Kaisin is there. In the distance. Sprinting toward us. Gaining.

"Hurry!" I cry, lengthening my stride. Ignoring the burn in my legs. The fire in my lungs. The hammering heart against my ribcage.

Gohk shoves Fletcher at the rickety spiral and motions me past. Rhuk, as well. She brings up the rear. Turn after turn is dizzying. The flickering lights make my temples throb. The burning in my legs and lungs becomes a prickly ache. My heart feels ready to explode. But we're almost there! The shadows above are burned away by starlight beaming through the still-open hatch.

The staircase bucks under my feet. I stumble, clamping a hand on each railing, craning my neck down into the shadows below. A dark shape scrambles up the outside of the staircase.

"Keep moving!" Gohk shouts at my back. "We're almost there!"

Adrenaline-fueled panic keeps my rubbery legs from melting to useless mush. My chest is tight, like a vice is clamped around it, so I can only manage shallow, ragged breaths. My head spins. Stars burst across my vision. And my heart races faster than before. But we reach the top! I stumble through the opening after Fletcher and Rhuk and collapse to my knees. Gohk leaps through after me, spins toward the keypad beside the ajar hatch, and reaches out, but a dark blur slaps her away. She careens from the opening and sprawls across the worn, metal decking.

Iali's presence vibrates against the edge of my mind, and a single wordless shout bubbles to the surface. *NOW!*

Even though instinct screams for me to flee, I tense every muscle in my body, gather my wobbly legs beneath me, and lunge toward the shape looming in the dark opening, arms outstretched.

The world disappears when my hands touch the undulating darkness, and I'm suddenly standing in the middle of a sunlit circle. Iali is just past its edge, huge ears flapping in an invisible breeze. But this time, there's no distant horizon. It's obscured by a billowing, undefined shape. Storm clouds? No. Whatever it is creeps like thick fog. But even from here, I can feel its weight, like every drop of an ocean's water rushing toward me at an impossible speed. There's no way my shining circle of safety will withstand it. I'll be swept away!

I look at Iali. "What am I supposed to do?"

"Push back," it says. "Break its strength."

My knees are close to buckling. "How?"

"You did it once before. To me," Iali answers. "You can do it again!"

The creeping darkness sweeps across the barren wasteland surrounding my circle. It devours the land. Blots out the sky. Buffets me with waves of invisible pressure. Even at this distance, the onslaught is near irresistible—a whole different level from Iali's force of will. How am I supposed to resist *this*?

"You can," Iali insists, staring at me with Fallah's face. With *her* expectant expression. Whether or not it is right, I don't have a choice.

The dark, indelible wall slams against my tiny sanctuary with all the rushing might of the water that flooded the Human colony ship. Only this incessant barrage rattles my mind instead of my body. Intense weight presses against the image of Fallah's face wrapped around me like a shield. It holds, but a host of dark tentacles snake out of the storm to probe at the crimson circle's edge. Embrace it. Squeeze.

A searing pain splits my skull. I stumble, waver, but keep my feet; keep it at bay. For now...

Squinting past the teary-eyed ache, I spot Iali just past the edge of the circle. It's drowning in the dark cyclone. No. It's being devoured. Raging winds scuff its leathery skin. Force it into a hunch, despite four immensely powerful legs. The split-second glance is enough for me to understand Iali won't survive even if I do manage to push the darkness back. The darkness will swallow it and carry it into oblivion.

Wait. No. Not yet. I can't let Iali go just yet.

Springing to the light's terminus, I thrust my hands into the swirling void of darkness beyond. It burns like the embers of a smoldering fire and itches worse than the gash Lorn opened from wrist to elbow. My groping fingers find something. I grab and pull with all my might.

Iali's hulking shape resolves out of the swirling storm and smacks into the barrier with a heavy thud. Tightening my grip, I yank it into the light. Into the quiet safety at the center of the storm. Into my mind.

Iali's wide mouth drops open in a grin. Not sinister. Not triumphant. Happy.

"Thank you," it mumbles, then turns to face the dark swirling around us. "Now. Together!"

The circle's edge is muddled. Fading. And I can feel Fallah's invisible shield beginning to crack.

I turn toward the darkness, with Iali beside me. We pool our collective strength. Push back. Force it away from the edge of my mind. Our mind. It struggles. Flails. Rages at our strength. But there's nothing it can do. The voluminous storm clouds gradually retreat. The horizon reappears. And the darkness shrinks to just a speck above the infinite barren wasteland. Then, with one final surge of strength, we push.

The world snaps back into sudden focus. My head aches as if it's been split in two. And my insides churn like I've been kicked in the gut. My boots slip on the worn metal deck plates, and my hands sink deeper into the gooey darkness. The force of the shove unbalances the possessed Kaisin. He teeters in the opening and tips backwards. As he falls, the darkness wrapped around his body begins to lose cohesiveness, sloughing off like a river of dead skin. Then, the Kaisin—and the darkness enveloping it—drops out of sight.

In the blink of an eye, Gohk is at the keypad beside the hatch, leaning against the gently curved bulkhead, swaying on unsteady feet. With her free hand, she slaps at the glowing keys until the heavy oval grinds shut with a hollow thud.

My wobbly knees give way, and I sink to the floor.

Is that it? Are we safe?

No. Iali's crystal-clear reply echoes in my mind. *Far from it.*

My mouth drops open. *What?*

We only delayed it, Iali replies. *It will come back. Stronger. Angrier. Deadlier.*

16

Gohk's gnarled fingers wrap around my bicep and yank me to my feet. "You alright?"

I manage a weak nod despite the splitting pain in my head. "Y—yeah."

"That was some quick thinking," Gohk continues, offering me a warm smile. "Saved the day."

Pursing my lips, I glance at Fletcher. His drawn eyebrows and shallow frown communicate the same message as Iali's warning: we aren't safe. Not yet. But even without Iali's warning, I'd have been inclined to agree. It took the full, crushing weight of an ocean to escape Lorn on the sunken colony ship. There's little chance a short fall and a shut hatch will render the same result.

"We should go," Fletcher says slowly. Deliberately.

Gohk glares at him. "What's the rush?"

"We aren't safe," I chime in, giving voice to the apprehension we both feel.

She narrows her eyes at me, then slides the skeptical stare back in Fletcher's direction. An unasked question tightens her brow, but his determined expression, and my complementary silence, are enough to leave it so.

"Fine," she says with a sigh.

Fletcher hurries for the line of dilapidated buildings. I jog to catch up and fall in at his shoulder.

"We should leave the station," I whisper, just loud enough for him to hear.

"Way ahead of you," he mumbles back.

Silent agreement carries us through the narrow, mostly deserted streets in this part of the station. Starlight paints the way to wider avenues, bigger crowds, and better-maintained storefronts until our surroundings are familiar again.

The next turn deposits us on the street we left not too long ago. Rhuk's workshop is within view, and the front door is still ajar. But we race past.

The main avenue is packed, as usual, but the straight shot to the hangar no longer feels like a leisurely stroll. And the beings of all shapes and sizes pressing in around our tight-knit group don't inspire wonder. Only apprehension. They jostle us. Threaten to separate us. A rough hand finds one of mine. A tiny one grabs the other. Both pull.

I let the others guide me and watch for dark robes. Pale faces. Jittery blue eyes. Or any sign of the thing we locked in the bowels of the station. But what few Kaisin we do pass are oblivious. To us. To the crowds' press. Even so, I don't relax my guard. We won't be safe until we're off the station.

"Where are we going?" Rhuk hisses.

"To the *Undertow*," Fletcher snaps, barely loud enough to be heard over the unfocused rabble of the crowd.

"Why?" Rhuk demands.

Fletcher casts a grim frown over his shoulder. "We have to leave."

Gohk scowls. "I don't see why—"

"We can explain later," I interject, adding my urgency to his, "but for now you'll have to trust us."

She doesn't seem convinced. Neither does Rhuk.

I shuffle closer. "Please!"

Gohk blinks, as if feeling the chill of the icy fingers gripping my spine.

"If you say so," she mutters.

Fletcher gives me a shallow, appreciative nod and makes a beeline for the cargo bay doors looming in the distance. The massive slabs of metal creak open when we approach, revealing the mismatched collection of ships beyond. The *Undertow's* familiar oblong cylinder is, by far, the largest. And a sight for sore eyes!

Scattered crew toil among stacks of cargo containers and loiter at the base of extended ramps. I only recognize a few beings at a glance. Just as many are strange. Just as many are Kaisin. But none pay us any heed as we pass. And no dark-robed Kaisin appear to bar our path at the last moment, if there are any left after what happened. Nor did the thing we left behind. I suck in a deep breath. Will we actually make it?

The *Undertow's* ramp is springy underfoot, and the vibrations of the others' steps tickle through the thick soles of my oversized boots. Hurrying to the top, I slip inside and listen for the telltale thunk of the ramp slotting into place. There! We're finally safe!

I let out a sigh of relief.

"Get strapped in." Fletcher's command is harsh in the cramped hall.

Without a word, Gohk and Rhuk turn toward the ship's common area. I move to follow, but Fletcher taps me on the shoulder.

"Hey," he says softly, tilting his head at the bridge. "This way."

Surprised, I shuffle after him and drop into one of the chairs along the back wall.

Fletcher settles into the central chair and begins to tap the controls laid out in front of him. The *Undertow* shudders, and the high-pitched whine of engines fills the air. After a moment, he glances over his shoulder.

"Thanks."

I shake my head. "It's fine. We convinced them."

"No." He swallows. "I meant...for coming to get me."

"How did you—?"

"Not Gohk's style," he says quickly, turning back.

"Yeah... Guess not..." I mumble, grimacing at the thought of Lorn left behind for so many years.

The grumbling roar of the *Undertow* lifting off of the dock drowns out the awkward silence that follows, which remains until bright spotlights give way to countless stars. Then, the roar of the ship's engines settle to a hypnotic rumble.

"Well," Fletcher says quietly, leaning back, "ready?"

"For?"

He twists to look at me. "Gohk and Rhuk are waiting for us."

That's right. We originally returned to the station to share the news about Lorn, the Human colony ship, and everything the Thalijh told us. And ask if Gohk has any information to add. But we'd gotten sidetracked.

I swallow. "After everything that's happened, it all sounds so crazy."

Even crazier if they knew about Iali.

"They'll believe us," Fletcher replies. "They'll have to."

He suddenly looks uncomfortable.

I understand. Just thinking about our close call raises the hairs on the back of my neck.

"Okay." I give a weak nod. "Let's go."

The narrow hall to the common area feels never-ending. My heart is pounding when we pass my room. And my palms are slick with sweat when we step into the common area at the far end. Gohk and Rhuk are sitting at the table, across from one another. The shutter covering the window is drawn back, and the glow of starlight washes away the dull gray of the metal walls and floor and ceiling.

They look up when we walk into view.

"You two alright?" Fletcher deadpans, as if he hadn't tried to fight off a dozen Kaisin only hours before. As if we all hadn't collected our fair share of scrapes and bruises fleeing from a monster.

"Fine," Gohk says.

Rhuk merely nods.

"Where are we headed?" she asks.

"Away from the station, for now." He pauses and rubs the back of his neck.

Gohk studies Fletcher, then her severe stare passes to me. I can only meet her gaze for a second before looking away. Her eyes narrow. "You two know what's going on."

"Not really," Fletcher says.

"You have an idea," she snaps back.

"Maybe," is his meek reply.

She frowns. Her gaze flicks to me for a split second, then returns to Fletcher. "What, exactly, did you two find?"

Fletcher's eyes wander the room like a child caught in the act of doing something naughty.

"I'm not stupid," Gohk says with a self-satisfied smile. "I know she stole my pad."

Her head tilts toward me.

"And I'm guessing you went after Lorn. So? What did you find?"

Fletcher's mouth works as he sputters a wordless answer.

"We found a ship," I blurt out. "And Lorn."

Gohk's cold stare burrows into Fletcher. "Is this true?"

He gives a halting nod.

"Lorn was alive?" Gohk's clenched teeth grind out the words.

"How?" Rhuk breathes, eyes so wide that I'm sure they'll pop out of his head.

"That black stuff," Fletcher mutters, "back on the station."

His lips press into a thin line.

"It was on the sunken ship too. It…dripped out of him. Covered him. And then…"

"He attacked us," I continue when he doesn't, ignoring the burning itch racing up and down my forearm.

"Where is he?" Gohk demands. Her white-knuckled hands are pressed flat against the table. She half-rises to her feet. Jittery blue eyes flick between us, her lips quivering between a frown and a scowl.

"Somewhere at the bottom of an ocean." Pain tinges Fletcher's answer. Twists his features. Forces his eyes to the floor.

"Ah." Gohk sinks back into the chair, suddenly looking older and wearier than I've ever seen her before.

"And this black substance? Liquid?" she asks after a long time.

185

Fletcher scoffs. "I have no idea what it is."

I do. More than I ever want to know...

"The humans picked it up in space, and it overran their ship. Forced them to abandon it. Their captain crashed it." He shakes his head. "And until about an hour ago, we thought we'd seen the last of it."

She draws in a slow, exasperated breath. "Wait... Humans?"

Fletcher nods. "It was a Human ship. A Human colony ship. Everything Lorn hoped for. More than we bargained for."

Gohk's silent stare drives his gaze to me. The truth we uncovered—that the Thalijh confirmed—is hard enough for us to hear. How will Gohk react? What will she say?

Looking back at Gohk, Fletcher takes a deep breath. "The ship's name was the Kaisin."

She gawks. "You're joking..."

Fletcher shakes his head.

Bitter laughter echoes in the *Undertow's* common area.

"So, Humans came to this part of space on a ship named *Kaisin.*"

It wasn't a question. Does she know something else about Humans that she isn't sharing?

"There's more," Fletcher says.

The mirth falls from Gohk's face. "Oh?"

"During our escape, Lorn injured Aiko," Fletcher continues.

Rhuk's eyes snap to me

"I'm fine," I assure him. Though, just thinking about what happened makes the hairline scar on my forearm start to itch again.

"I took her to Thalijh," Fletcher adds. "They fixed her up. And while we were there, I asked for clarity."

Gohk's arms are crossed, and her stare is so piercing, Fletcher stumbles over his next words.

"Well?" Rhuk is perched on the edge of a chair far too large for his tiny frame. Small, clawed hands rest on his knees, and he's leaning quite far forward, in danger of toppling to the deck.

"The Thalijh told us we were—" Fletcher's lips purse.

"Kaisin," I finish for him.

"Genetically identical to Kaisin, anyway," he clarifies. "But they couldn't explain *what* we are."

Rhuk's mouth drops open to reveal rows of jagged teeth. But Gohk takes a deep breath, lets out a deeper sigh, and presses her lips together so hard they nearly disappear.

"You knew?" I breathe.

"All Kaisin *know* where you"—she motions at Fletcher and I—"come from. We just don't talk about it. Can't."

Her answer hits me like the thundering wall of water in the Human colony ship. So Gohk hadn't been telling us everything, just as Fletcher suspected. She knew, from the very beginning, what we are and where we come from. And she hadn't told us. But why not? Why was it so important to keep the truth from us? From Fletcher? For so long? My mouth works to ask these questions. And others. But my mind is racing too fast.

"The Thalijh were right," Gohk continues. "You two *are* Kaisin."

She leans back in the chair and crosses her arms. Her gaze drifts to the window, and she stares out at the stars. Past them.

"Every now and then, one of you are born. No one knows why. But—" she pauses. Something akin to pain twists her lips into a scowl. "Your kind is usually taken away within minutes of birth."

"Taken where?" Fletcher finally manages to croak.

Gohk shrugs. "No one knows, only that the babies are never seen again. Usually…"

"Usually?" Rhuk echoes.

She shifts on the chair. Is she uncomfortable? Nervous? Both? After a long, long silence, she looks at Fletcher.

"Your parents weren't willing to give you up, regardless of how different you were. So, they asked Lorn, your uncle, to take you away. To hide you. To keep you safe."

Fletcher's brow furrows. "My…uncle?"

"I urged him to refuse," Gohk continues, ignoring his dumbfounded question. "I tried to tell him what it would mean for us, but Lorn didn't listen. He never has."

She sighs and looks back out the window.

"We took you and fled the homeworld. Even then, we weren't safe. They came for you. For us. We barely escaped a dozen times. It became clear that two Xaisin traveling with a strange baby is too conspicuous. So, we left you in capable hands. For a little while…"

Fletcher's gaze wanders the floor, then jumps to Gohk's face.

"Fifteen years," he mumbles.

"It was necessary," Gohk insists. "For whatever reason, they wanted you and would stop at nothing to make you disappear like all the others. Lorn made sure that didn't happen." Her voice quivers "We gave up *everything* to make sure you'd survive. Just like your parents wanted."

I blink. "You and Lorn—?"

"Were partners," she finishes for me. Her gaze flicks back to Fletcher. "Though once *you* entered the picture, that ended as well."

"What do you mean?" he asks.

"In lieu of you, they took Lorn's sister and her partner. So, on that day he lost as much as he gained. But he needed to make sense of the cost. Somehow..."

A deep, resentful smile twists Gohk's lips.

"Lorn became obsessed with learning exactly what you were. Why you were. It *consumed* him," she spits. "He was never the same. And every little discovery led him further and further away from sanity. From me."

Suddenly, Gohk's lingering, resentful anger makes sense.

"Why didn't you tell us as soon as you found out some Kaisin tried to drag me away?"

"It wouldn't have changed anything," she snaps defensively.

"Wouldn't it?" I push back.

She shrugs.

"And now?"

"There's more to it than before." She surges to her feet, more harsh words hanging on her already parted lips. But they stay there. Despite the anger seething beneath the surface, she turns to face the window. When she finally speaks, her tone is more subdued.

"You. Fletcher. Lorn. The Kaisin. And now this...darkness. Everything is connected. But I don't know how. No Kaisin does."

I know. Well, partially Iali's explanation only covered how the darkness turned Humans into Kaisin. But it didn't explain Fletcher and I. Who could? Maybe...?

"What about the Thalijn?" I offer.

Everyone looks at me.

"That's not a bad idea," Fletcher says with a nod.

"But the Thalijh are scientists," Gohk says. "They work best with tangible evidence. All we have is hearsay."

"They already have *some* data. Maybe knowing about this stuff can help them fill in the blanks," Fletcher replies. "Besides, what other choice do we have?"

"Leave the sector for good," Gohk suggests. "Get as far away from Kaisin space as we can manage. Make a new start. Never look back."

"And if the Kaisin come looking for us?" He places both palms flat on the table.

Gohk doesn't have an answer for that.

"Listen..." Fletcher sucks a deep breath through his nostrils. "I don't know if the Thalijh will be able to tell us anything useful, but I don't want to run from the truth. Lorn died *twice* in search of answers. And we're so close."

His shoulders sag, and he suddenly looks tired. Defeated.

"Please. Let's go to Thalijh. See what they can tell us. Then, we'll leave the sector—leave all of this—behind."

She glares at him, but shows no signs of changing her mind.

I open my mouth, but words catch in my throat. I can see both sides of the argument. Uncovering the truth is important enough that I stole Gohk's pad and prompted Fletcher to go after Lorn. And we found a treasure-trove of information neither of us expected. But what's more, I picked up Iali, and it taught me about the darkness that engulfed Lorn and twisted every single Human into what they are now: Kaisin. So, as much as I want to support Fletcher, I just...I...

"We should go to Thalijh," Rhuk says, so softly I barely catch the words over the rumble of the *Undertow's* engines.

Gohk scowls. "What?"

"They deserve the truth," he says, large, round eyes meeting hers. "And Lorn deserves to see his task completed."

His eyebrows twitch.

"We're this close. Why not go all the way?"

"Come on, Rhuk." Gohk sneers. "You know better than they ever could how something like this ends."

He frowns.

I consider Gohk's self-righteous glare at Rhuk and the small being's perturbed nod.

"Did you know, too?" I ask.

Rhuk's eyebrows twitch again. "I knew Gohk and Lorn were running from something. But not what. Or why. And I never asked about the specifics."

"What about Lorn's obsession with Humans?" Fletcher chimes in. "And me?"

Rhuk shrugs. "We all have our interests."

Then, his wide mouth dips into a frown.

"And you...You were a child in need of a home. They gave you that." He shakes his head. "They never told me what you were to them."

So, even Rhuk had been kept in the dark.

"These things were best kept hidden. Left unsaid," Gohk growls. "As long as no one knew where we were or what Fletcher was, everything was fine!"

She looks at me.

"If you'd kept your damn mouth shut, we'd still be hidden."

"T—that's not fair!" I sputter.

"It's the truth," she snaps.

But it isn't. It can't be! Fletcher didn't tell me the name was dangerous, which meant *he* didn't know. Wouldn't Lorn have said if it was? Wouldn't he have told Fletcher to keep it secret? Wouldn't Fletcher have told me to keep it secret?

I frown. "When we first met, you said Humans were a bad omen and that's the reason why those Kaisin came after us. Was that a lie?"

Gohk's mouth works.

"So the existence of Humans wasn't common knowledge, then?" I snap, sudden burning rage coursing through my veins. "If we're born Kaisin, why did Lorn tell Fletcher he was a Human? Why lie?"

"Because it wasn't a lie!" Gohk's hands ball into fists at her sides. "Even though Lorn didn't have concrete proof, he suspected what the Thalijh told you all along: that the Kaisin *were* Human. Or used to be."

Her jittery blue eyes bore into me.

"As crazy as the theory sounded, it was the only thing that explained the strange children born on the homeworld. But—" The tension twisting her features begins to fade. The resentful scowl gives way to a grim smile, and Gohk shakes her head. "The word 'Human' was never uttered by anyone. Of any race. Anywhere. On the homeworld or off. I'd never heard the word until Lorn ran across it on one of his expeditions."

She lets out a shallow sigh.

"It made sense—to Lorn, anyway—that this is why babies like you were taken at birth. But we couldn't be sure. We couldn't say why. And there was never any solid proof." Gohk pauses and fixes Fletcher with a thoughtful stare. "It was Lorn's idea to say you were Human. He thought any other explanation would be too unbelievable for you to accept. He thought it would be safer for you to believe something, rather than to take the chance you'd eventually go looking for answers on your own. But what I told you before? It's the truth. From a certain point of view..."

Fletcher blinks, but offers no response to her explanation.

A tense silence that even the engine's faint rumble can't dampen settles over the common area.

"So, this group knew about the connection between Humans and Kaisin," Rhuk says softly. "How?"

"The darkness," I say reflexively. Based on everything Iali told me, it makes sense. But even so, perhaps I spoke too soon. Gave myself, and Iali, away. How else would I have made the connection?

I stifle a grimace, expecting suspicious stares and probing questions.

"That's the missing piece of the puzzle!"

My heart jumps into my throat at Fletcher's sudden exclamation. "Huh?"

His elated stare jumps to me.

"Back on Thalijh, something was missing," he says. "The bone we took from the colony ship was Human, but the Thalijh said it was Kaisin. Gohk's story explains where we come from. But not *how*."

He pauses to take a breath.

"The humans abandoned ship to escape the stuff they'd brought on board. But what if some of it escaped with them?"

I stifle a surprised gasp. He's figuring it out. "What are you saying?"

Fletcher's brow furrows. "You saw what happened on the station. That black stuff drained out of dozens of Kaisin. Covered that one. Just like it had Lorn. Maybe it's the missing link we've been looking for?"

The conclusion mirrors the memories Iali shared.

"How do we prove it?"

His eyes jump to Gohk.

She frowns. "What?"

Fletcher grins. "We go to Thalijh and give them a fresh sample."

17

I press my back against the closed door and let out a relieved sigh.

Fletcher's suggestion didn't go as well as he hoped. Gohk started to yell. He yelled back. And Rhuk...Well, he shooed me down the hall before attempting to diffuse the situation. At least, I assume that's why he stayed with them.

A weary shuffle carries me from the door to the bed, where I collapse.

This is the first moment of quiet I've had since Thalijh, but it's far from peaceful. Everything Gohk just told us is rattling around my brain like loose rocks. She knew what Fletcher and I were the whole time, and kept it from us. From him. For thirty years. Longer.

But even so, they'd all be surprised if they knew the entire truth.

You didn't tell them about me.

Iali's crisp, clear words startle me. It has been so quiet.

"No," I reply in a whisper.

Why not?

"I—" My first instinct is to say I didn't know. But that isn't true. "I wasn't ready."

Now that Iali is inside my mind, its thoughts are as open as a cloudless sky. Right now, it's confused. And a little bit doubtful.

Why not? Iali asks again.

Instead of giving an answer, I settle into the bed's warm embrace and close my eyes. Sleep would have been a blessing, but that isn't all I'm hoping for.

I sink into dark oblivion, but a moment later, my eyes snap open. The familiar circle paints the rough ground at my feet, and imaginary sunlight warms my face and skin. Iali is beside me, staring with unnatural, obsidian eyes, but smiling at me with Fallah's wide mouth. It isn't her. I *know* it isn't her. But—

"You should have told them," Iali chides.

"And then they would have told the Thalijh," I counter, looking away from its mostly familiar face. "And they would have poked and prodded you right out of existence."

Concern twists Iali's brow for a moment, then it frowns. "Isn't it more important for them to trust you?"

"They already do."

"Will they still when they find out about me?" Iali asks.

"O—of course," I sputter.

But it makes a good point. *Will* the others still trust me? Will waiting to tell them about Iali change things?

Iali lets out a sudden sigh. "It's just as well."

"What do you mean?"

"The other like you was right about the Kaisin," Iali replies with a grim smile. "*It* is inside of her."

I frown. "Are you sure?"

"I can feel it," Iali insists.

"Ok. So, what do we do?"

"It must be removed," Iali answers.

"That shouldn't be a problem for the Thalijh," I say confidently.

"It must be dealt with *before* we get there."

My brow furrows. "Why?"

"Because if I can feel the small amount inside your Kaisin friend, *it* can likely feel it too." Iali's lips press into a thin line. "Which means it can track us."

A shot of adrenaline launches my heart into my throat. "All the way to Thalijh?"

Iali nods. "And beyond. Anywhere we go, it can follow."

"That's impossible!" It has to be. Because if Iali is actually telling the truth—

"There isn't time for doubt," Iali snaps. "If we don't do something, it will find you. And your friends."

Sudden, sweltering wind swirls inside the circle. This is Iali's will, no longer held at arm's length by the strength of Fallah's memory. Now, it's inside. Unfettered. Powerful. But so am I. This place is mine. My sanctuary. My safety. Gritting my teeth, I push back with all the years of damp chill I endured at Alphanax.

The flicker of a frown tugs at Iali's lips, and the heat subsides.

I blow an annoyed breath out of my nose. "Just tell me what we're supposed to do."

"If you don't want it to find us, you're going to have to remove it from the Kaisin."

"How?" I demand. "And what do we do about it once it's out?"

"You misunderstand," it says. "Pulling it into the open won't do any good."

I frown. "Isn't that the point? Draw it out and destroy it?"

Iali shakes its head. "If even the tiniest bit survives, it will still be able to track you. That won't do."

"Then what?"

A somber expression spreads across Iali's face. "You'll have to absorb it."

"What?!"

"It's the only way," Iali insists.

An involuntary frown yanks the corners of my lips toward the floor "*Absorb* it?"

Iali's lips purse. "Have I steered you wrong yet?"

Iali hasn't. Not really. But I give a defiant shake of the head. "There's got to be another way."

"There isn't." Iali's obsidian eyes meet mine, and Fallah's familiar face pleads for me to relent. "You have no choice."

I frown. Don't I? Surely, letting more of the darkness inside of me isn't the answer. The mere thought of doing so willingly…

"You have to trust me," Iali says, edging closer.

I want to, but can't. "No."

Iali freezes midstep, an arm's length away.

"I can't," I say after a deep breath.

A surge of crimson light and burning heat accompanies Iali's sudden anger. It surrounds me. Squeezes the non-existent air from my lungs.

"Why?" it demands.

I can't breathe. I can't think. And when I try to back out of the circle an invisible fist grabs me. Holds me. No. This isn't right. Letting Iali in wasn't supposed to be like this! Its will encircles me like the summer wind on Alphanax. Darkens the waste around me like the void of space. But this is my body. *My* mind.

Closing my eyes, ignoring the red-hot pain of Iali's overbearing anger, I withdraw and will myself awake.

A sheen of sweat coats my skin and drenches my clothes despite a draft of cool air. And in the deafening silence, I can hear and feel Iali's smoldering resistance burrowing into my mind.

"Be quiet!" I hiss.

Do as I say before it's too late! Iali replies, with the slightest hint of veiled malice.

I won't. Not without knowing beyond a shadow of a doubt there isn't another way.

The pressure of Iali's insistence permeates every corner of my mind. Fills the silence. Drowns out any attempt to turn my thoughts elsewhere. I can't stay cramped up in my room. I have to get out. Go...somewhere.

Slipping off of the bed, I hurry to the door and into the hall. Yelling had given way to the subtle vibrations of the *Undertow's* engines, but there's no telling how long I've been asleep. Minutes? Hours? It doesn't matter. All that does is drowning out Iali's clamoring.

I expect the common area to be empty. It isn't.

Gohk's glassy stare wanders away from the window when I enter. Jittery blue eyes focus on my face, but her expression doesn't change. She's distracted. Perturbed.

I force a smile. "Hi."

"Hey." Hers is more of a grimace.

"Are you okay?" she asks after a brief pause.

My eyes widen, and I start to stutter an answer. Is my internal battle with Iali that obvious?

"I kept a lot from you two," she continues, turning back to the window. "But the truth…"

Gohk shakes her head.

"There was no reason to burden you with what you really were."

I stifle a relieved sigh, but at the same time I feel guilty. I'm keeping just as much from her, and the others, out of my own brand of necessity.

"I'd rather know than be kept in the dark," I say deliberately, then add: "But I can't blame you. You had your reasons."

Gohk's lips purse, and she gives a shallow nod. "Thanks."

A warm smile curls my lips. In this moment, Gohk is almost likable. But her gentle disposition is marred by Iali's prickly voice.

She's dangerous!

Iali's anger still tangles my mind in a burning fog. Its insistence still muddles my thoughts. It's sure of the darkness within Gohk. I don't want to believe.

"What if Fletcher is right?"

Gohk frowns. "He isn't."

"But what if he is?" I insist, Iali's echoing warning drowning out everything else. "What if that darkness is in every Kaisin? Including you?"

"Well, that's why we're going to Thalijh."

Her eyes narrow when I don't answer, and she studies my face. "What's wrong?"

"N—nothing," I stutter, stifling a grimace at Iali's electric persistence.

"Come on," she prods. "Out with it!"

Even though I don't want to believe that darkness lurks within Gohk—or that it'll be able to track us across the stars—the seed of doubt Iali planted is undeniable. It's taken root and is growing in the fertile soil of my mind. As much as I want to discard the notion, there's too much uncertainty for me to do so alone. And Iali has been right so many times before.

I take a deep breath and fix Fallah's face in my mind's eye, creating a bubble of tranquility to keep Iali at bay, if only for a moment. "What if it comes after us? Tracks us to Thalijh?"

"There's no way that thing can follow us," Gohk says with an amused chuckle.

She's wrong!

I ignore Iali's protest. "How can you be so sure?"

"I've seen a lot in my time, but there's no such thing as magic," Gohk scoffs. "It can't come after us without a ship. Or a trail to follow. Even then, we're a speck in the void…"

Her head shakes as she trails off. But her point is made.

Gohk's self-assured answer feels more concrete than Iali's burning rage. I can wrap my head around it. Accept it. Trust it. Especially if it means I won't have to absorb any more of the darkness against my will.

"So, I wouldn't worry," Gohk adds with a genuine grin.

"Okay," I say with a smile and turn to leave.

"One other thing." Gohk's tone is suddenly harder.

I glanced back to meet her unblinking stare.

"That stunt you pulled. With the pad. Don't do that again." Then, the whisper of an amused smile touches her lips. "But hold on to that drive. It'll take you places."

Without another word, Gohk swivels back to the endless expanse of stars. She looks small silhouetted against it: less a terrifying Kaisin and more relatable. Just as fallible and uncertain as I or Fletcher or Rhuk, or any other being I've met. It makes me think, for the first time, that maybe not all Kaisin are as irredeemably evil as I've come to believe. Maybe I can trust this one at least.

The bubble of tranquility slips as I walk back to my room, and the swirling storm of Iali's anger returns.

You're a fool! it exclaims. *It's going to find us and devour us. All of us.*

"I'm not so sure," I whisper. "Besides, we're almost to Thalijh. Once we get there, they'll be able to take care of whatever darkness is lingering inside of Gohk."

A wordless, frustrated growl fills my mind.

"We'll be fine," I insist. "Just trust me, alright?"

Fine. Iali spits as I step back into my room. *But don't be surprised when I get to say 'I told you so'.*

"You won't," I reply, flopping back onto the bed and letting my head sink into the cool, puffy pillow.

We'll see.

Iali's words echoed in my mind, filling the emptiness of my thoughts as I drift into the first deep, restful sleep I've gotten since...

18

Had I not known we were going to Thalijh, I might have thought we'd returned to the unnamed planet where Lorn had gone missing and where the Human Colony ship was submerged. At the very least, the azure globe could have been its twin.

But even so, Thalijh looks more inviting. The water is a shade lighter. The clouds are whiter and fluffier. Even the sliver of atmosphere tracing the sphere's curve is stained a breathtaking, pearlescent white by the distant sun.

"Wow," I breathe.

"That's right. You missed this last time," Fletcher mumbles, as he monitors the collection of hovering projections in a semicircle around him. Then, he grins over his shoulder. "Just wait until we hit the water!"

I grip the belts strapping me into the chair as the *Undertow* begins to shiver and shake. The viewscreen is obscured by fire. And silence is replaced by the grumbling roar of atmosphere whipping past. I close my eyes and relax, trying my best to ignore the sudden drops that send my stomach into my throat and set my knuckles white. But it's hard with nothing else to occupy my mind.

Iali isn't speaking to me. Not since I brushed it off and made my own decision about the potential darkness within Gohk. I can still feel it at the back of my mind. But it has withdrawn all the way to the outer edge, sulking in the shadows.

Still not talking to me?

No answer. As expected.

Despite Iali's stubborn silence, I'm at peace with my decision. For multiple reasons. Not least of which is the fact that I want a say in how to deal with the darkness. This is my body, and Iali is just a passenger. But beyond that, Gohk's confident answer to the possibility made sense, and bolstered my resolve enough to shatter the doubt created by Iali's overbearing insistence.

I push meandering thoughts aside and look up. We're sailing a few hundred feet above crystal-clear water. Then, we dip toward it. One. Two. Three solid jolts shiver up through the soles of my feet as the *Undertow* skips along the water before sinking. Sky blue darkens to navy twilight, pierced by points of brilliant light. Perhaps one of the Thalijh's underwater buildings? Like the one I stayed at during our last visit?

The hulking shadow that looms out of the depths isn't a building. Or is it? The overall asymmetrical shape hints at stone, but the surface is pockmarked by countless tiny divots. Some glint as the *Undertow's* spotlights slide by. Are those…windows? It's hard to tell, though, because of massive, shifting shapes, like the clouds drifting across Thalijh's clear skies. But instead of fluffy white, these are a myriad of colors. Glinting silver. Soft violet. Dripping crimson. Glowing yellow. They intertwine, dancing in and out of the brilliant pools of light, tinting the navy deep.

The water shifts to black and the clouds of teeming life thin, replaced by larger, more timid shadows flickering at the edges of the *Undertow's* spotlights. They give the ship a wide berth until we get closer to the unidentified structure, where they disappear altogether.

It isn't stone.

"Coral," Fletcher says as if reading my thoughts. "The Thalijh live in massive coral deposits. Some are modified for air breathers."

"Is it the same one as before?"

Fletcher shakes his head after a brief pause. "No. Since we're here for something different, the Thalijh directed us to a different habitat. It's a bit deeper," he finished, motioning to the darkness beyond the viewscreen.

A sour taste fills my mouth. So much happened here last time. Now we're back.

For the first time in days, Iali's presence stirs at the back of my mind, reminding me of the warning it gave in our headlong rush away from the station. The sudden, accompanying tendril of doubt tickling my thoughts sends a shiver down my spine. But a flash of light on metal amidst the approaching coral prevents it from lingering.

A polished circle, many times larger than the *Undertow*, made up of multiple slats with curved edges meeting in the center, dilates like the pupil of an eye in near darkness. Beyond, a tunnel curves into the massive structure. Spotlights spring to life as the ship slips inside, marking the way forward. Occasionally, smaller circles dot either side of the rough tunnel walls. All are closed. But ahead, one of the guiding spotlights flashes green and a nearby door opens.

"That's us," Fletcher mutters.

The *Undertow* shudders as he works the controls. It shifts. Leans. Slips through the crystal-clear water toward the newest opening, then through to a small alcove. A flat circle rests in the center of the space, bordered by a gently glowing strip.

Fletcher taps keys and swipes at buttons of light hovering in the air around him. The ship responds, drifting forward and down, shuddering when it comes to rest. Momentary silence is punctuated by the dying whine of the *Undertow's* engines, then joined by a roaring rush. I search the empty water for the source of the sound and blink when the surface dips past the viewscreen, leaving only dripping streaks behind.

Fletcher stands.

"Let's go," he groans, while stretching.

I follow him into the hall where Gohk and Rhuk are already waiting.

The little alien offers me a reserved smile. Gohk's blue eyes slide past me to Fletcher, and the whisper of a frown teases the corners of her lips.

"Ready?" Fletcher asks.

Gohk nods. "After you."

So, they aren't really talking either—

Cool, humid air as thick as damp cloth washes over me when the door opens. The base of the ramp is submerged in a few inches of gently lapping water. And a smell I hadn't noticed during my first visit—salt and some nose-wrinkling odor—permeates the air. Coats my tongue. Thickens, like bile, in my throat. It isn't necessarily unpleasant, but I wonder how I got used to it before.

Fletcher stalks down the ramp to the shallow water at its base and splashes his way to an oval door set in the uneven wall near the side of the ship, Gohk at his shoulder. Like the large door on the outside of the structure, the curved slats dilate as they approach.

Before I can step in the water, I feel a tug on my pants leg and look down to see Rhuk's wide eyes staring up at me.

"Mind if I hitch a ride to the other side?" he asks. "I'd rather not get completely soaked."

I nod, and he scrambles up to my shoulders. I never in a million years thought I'd wind up giving him a piggyback ride. I keep that revelation to myself and pause long enough for him to leap down as soon as we pass the door, before the others have a chance to see.

The wide hallway on the other side is wholly artificial. Smooth, polished floors reflect soft white light shining from strips lining the flat ceiling overhead. Gently curved walls connect the two. Seamless. Clean. The softest gray. We follow the short corridor to another door and pass through to a massive atrium.

A dozen other doors, at least, line walls stretching to a vaulted ceiling of rough coral. The pockmarks on the surface are filled with bubbles of smooth glass, containing a substance that glows soft blue. The shifting light shimmers on the polished tile underfoot like sunlight piercing the deep, as it had on the dive that started all of this.

At the far end of the room, nestled in an alcove, is a shallow pool. In it is a many-tentacled Thalijh. Its saucer-sized eyes wander toward us and a bubbling gurgle fills the air, accompanied by a monotone translation. "Greetings subspecies, how may I assist you?"

I lean down to Rhuk and whisper, "Subspecies?"

"I'll explain later," he whispers back.

"We're here to see Prime Orderly Orugh," Fletcher answers.

"He—uh—Orugh tended to us last time we were on Thalijh."

Submerged tentacles wiggle. The water roils. A deep moan echoes in the vaulted space overhead. Then, silence.

A heartbeat—two, ten, so many I lose count—rattles against my ribs before a rumbling groan splits the air.

The Thalijh floating in the pool perks up, its saucer-sized eyes rising above the surface of the crystalline water.

"The Prime Orderly is on his way and will arrive shortly," the alien burbles. "Please. Make yourselves comfortable."

A tentacle lifts out of the water and waves at the room behind us. Then, it retreats beneath the surface.

I frown at the empty room. "Make ourselves comfortable?"

"Sarcasm?" Rhuk chimes in.

"Polite indifference," Gohk says with a chuckle. When I furrow my brow, she leans close and whispers. "The Thalijh think they're better than everyone else."

After that, she falls silent.

We mill around in the empty space for what feels like hours. Eventually a tell-tale squishing pop draws my blank gaze to an unnerving nest of tentacles sliding across the floor. But I recognize Orugh's distinct coloring and drooping eyelids.

"Greetings," the Thalijh calls out in its dual voice.

Fletcher raises a hand. "Prime Orderly Orugh."

"What brings you back so soon?" the Thalijh asks.

Again, there's a hint of what could have been called impatience in the robotic translation of its burbling native tongue.

"It has to do with why we were here before," Fletcher answers. He quickly scans the empty atrium, gaze resting on the Thalijh soaking in the pool of crystal-clear water nearby, and lowers his voice. "Is there somewhere we can talk in private?"

Prime Orderly Orugh gives a bubbling whoosh, then shimmies toward a metal oval on the back wall. "Of course. This way."

The door opens, and the Thalijh squishes through to another wide hallway. Fletcher follows on the Thalijh's heels...er...tentacles. Gohk is right behind. I pace next to Rhuk. The little alien, however silent, radiates calm, which dampens the apprehension twisting my insides.

As if sensing my uneasiness, a tiny hand reaches out and pats me on the leg, still swathed in the jumpsuit I'd been given from my last visit to Thalijh. There hadn't been time to pick up anything else for me to wear.

"Everything is going to be fine."

"Is it?" The words rush out of my mouth before I have a chance to stifle them.

"Of course," Rhuk replies.

"This is all just so strange," I say with an exasperated sigh, and start ticking things off on my fingers. "The sunken ship. Humans. Their connection to Kaisin. And the darkness..."

I falter, remembering Iali's warning and feeling fingers of doubt creep out of the depths of my mind.

"Sure, all of that's strange," Rhuk says, with an acquiescent nod, "but everything happens for a reason."

My brow furrows. "What do you mean?"

"Take a look at the bigger picture," he replies. "All of those things—however strange—existed before you came along. And they'll remain after you're gone. But why now?"

He emphasizes the question by poking a sharp fingertip into my thigh.

"Why only after you showed up? Hmmm?"

I blink at Rhuk, then shift a blank stare to Fletcher and Gohk, marching single file behind the Thalijh, oblivious to our conversation. So much had passed between those two. So much history. So many omissions. Gohk knew Fletcher's true identity all along and could have assuaged his curiosity at any moment. But instead, she kept things hidden. Allowed him to wonder. Pointed him in my direction. Only after...

"This is all my fault," I whisper.

Rhuk scoffs. "Fault is relative. You simply connected dots that were forgotten."

"But still—!"

"Instead of laying blame, think about your place in all of this." Rhuk's interruption is soft but firm. "Think about what you can do."

"What I can do?" I echo.

Before I can piece together a response, the Thalijh reaches another door and motions us inside. I enter after Rhuk, a confused frown still tugging at the corners of my lips.

Think about what you can do.

"Now, what do you want to discuss?" There's a harsh snap to the robotic words as the Thalijh slithers toward a shallow pool at the far side of the room, breaking the mirror-still surface as it slips inside. I've only seen these beings wriggle along on dry ground, so it never clicked that they actually lived in water. Even though their cities are under it.

"It has to do with our previous visit," Fletcher answers hastily.

"The girl?" Orugh's lazy eyes drift to me. "Her wounds healed properly."

Fletcher grimaces and shakes his head. "Not that. I meant the bone you analyzed."

"The Kaisin bone," Prime Orderly Orugh corrects.

"Y—yeah…" Fletcher stutters, caught off guard. "We have some additional information about that." His gaze flicks to Gohk.

"Oh?"

"Like you told us before, we're Kaisin," Fletcher continues.

Orugh bobs up and down in the water. "Of course."

Even the robotic translation sounds bored.

"They were born to Kaisin," Gohk cuts in impatiently. "Both of them."

"Oh…?" The Thalijh gives a shudder that ripples the surface of the water.

Fletcher glares at Gohk, a scowl twisting his lips.

"Just helping you along to the point," she says, giving him a sickly sweet smile.

"There's something else," Fletcher adds. "About the Kaisin."

"This Kaisin in particular?"

"*All* Kaisin," he says, not breaking eye contact with Gohk.

Prime Orderly Orugh is pressed against the side of the pool, saucer sized eyes wide and fixed on Fletcher.

"There's something inside of them. Like…a parasite."

It isn't. And it is…

"Do you have proof of this?"

Fletcher waves a hand at Gohk. "We have her."

"Ah," Prime Orderly Orugh shimmies out of the pool, leaving a trail of fluid thicker than water behind. The Thalijh stops in front of Gohk. "This is of interest. If you provide a sample, we will begin analysis immediately."

"Sure," Gohk says through clenched teeth, fixing Fletcher with a savage stare. "I'd be happy to."

Obviously, she isn't.

The Thalijh makes a warbling sound that the robotic voice doesn't translate, then wriggles out of the room.

As soon as the door closes, Gohk rounds on Fletcher and hisses at him in her native tongue. Whatever she spouts causes his eyes to widen and his face to redden.

"This is what we came here for!" he growls back, spearing a finger at the center of her chest. "Besides, you owe us this much considering everything else you kept hidden."

Gohk bares her jagged yellow teeth, but doesn't answer. After all, Fletcher is right. And a smug smile proves he knows it. Yet, despite her silent concession, he doesn't gloat. I wouldn't have either. The deep scowl on Gohk's face hints at rage boiling beneath the surface. She's used to having the upper hand. Knowing things others don't. Now though? Fletcher has the edge.

Silence lingers until Prime Orderly Orguh returns.

The Thalijh slithers to Gohk and holds up a small, silver cylinder. "I need blood and tissue."

"Fine," Gohk growls.

A tentacle snakes out and pokes the end of the cylinder against Gohk's pale bicep. She winces. Orugh pulls away a moment later and tucks the object somewhere in its nest of tentacles.

212

"You will be our guests while this is analyzed," the Thalijh says, as it trundles toward the door. "Someone will be along to show you to suitable accommodations momentarily."

Orguh disappears before any of us can protest.

I furrow my brow. "Why can't we stay on the *Undertow?*"

Fletcher opens his mouth to reply, but Gohk cuts him off.

"They don't want us going anywhere."

"Why not?"

"Because *I* am now a scientific curiosity. The Thalijh aren't going to let me walk away until they're satisfied." She looks at Fletcher. "Thanks for that."

He shrugs. "It's why we're here. How else were we supposed to do it?"

"Too late to think about that now," Gohk grumbles and paces to the far end of the room, the tips of her boots hanging over the edge of the shallow pool Orguh slipped into—and out of—earlier.

It's hard to feel sorry for Gohk considering everything I've learned over the past week or so. Some of it is disappointing. Some of it is unsettling. But all of it is the truth, filling in blanks I assumed would remain empty. Even before Fallah insisted that we search for others of my kind.

The unnamed darkness is the final piece of a thousand-year-old puzzle that had been lost to time. Sure, Gohk abhors the idea of it lurking within her. But if it does, maybe the Thalijh can discover a way to remove it. Combat it. Neutralize it.

Is that what you want to do to me?

Iali's sudden question catches me off guard.

"N—no," I stutter aloud.

213

Only Rhuk notices the muttered word and looks up at me. His ears twitch. "Everything alright?"

"Just thinking aloud," I say quickly.

But you want them to remove it from her? Iali continues.

You know this is different. It won't be able to track us once they do.

It's too late for that. Iali's words hold a scolding tone. And something else. Disappointment?

I purse my lips. We left it at the station. Days behind us. Without a ship. How can it follow? How can it find us? By feeling the tiny amount of darkness within Gohk? Iali is so sure, but I'm not. And even after the darkness is removed from Gohk, something else occurs to me that I hadn't thought of before. *What about you?*

The question seems to catch Iali off guard, but it has an answer a moment later. *I can hide from it.*

How?

It doesn't know me.

Are you sure?

Reasonably so. Try as it might, Iali can't stifle a flicker of doubt.

But Iali's uncertainty bolsters my confidence in Gohk's assertion that *it* won't be able to find us.

The door hissing open gives me an excuse to brush Iali's smoldering frustration aside. The Thalijh framed in it is smaller than Orguh, its soft blue skin speckled with sanguine dots. Bright, wide eyes flick to each of us in turn.

"Follow me, please," it says, with a deep, resonating burble.

We follow it along more pristine corridors, empty of even other Thalijh.

"Where is everybody?" I whisper to Rhuk.

214

"Your guess is as good as mine," he replies with a shrug.

Fletcher might have been the better person to ask, but he's at the head of our group, trailing the Thalijh. And Gohk is between us. Even though I can't see her face, the savage pound of her boots on the smooth floor make me happy to be behind her. The answer isn't important enough to change that.

At the next junction, the Thalijh slips around a corner and down a short, dead-end offshoot with doors spaced evenly along the circular alcove.

"These are your rooms," the Thalijh says. "Please make yourselves comfortable."

Even the deadpan tone of the robotic translation makes it clear there isn't an alternative.

Fletcher and Gohk take the two rooms farthest apart and share a brief, burning glance before disappearing inside. I haven't known either of them long, but it's obvious each is stubborn in their own way, enough that they'll probably keep this up for longer than necessary. At least Rhuk and I are left out of it.

I glance down at the small being. He looks up and smiles.

"Well..." he turns toward the nearest door. "Better get some rest. And think about what I said, eh?"

Then, he walks out of sight, leaving me alone with the Thalijh.

I share a blank look with the wriggling nest of tentacles staring back at me and realize I know more about what my dark passenger is thinking and feeling.

Offering a halting bob of my head, I shuffle toward, then through, the last door. The room is as small as my quarters on the *Undertow*. But it isn't cozy. The flat, smooth floor is boxed in by white, blemishless walls. And the entirety of the featureless ceiling overhead exudes a soft glow. In the far wall is another oval, slightly smaller than the door, but covered with the same curved slats that meet at a single point in the center. Probably a window. Beneath it is a cushioned pedestal that must be a bed. Besides that, nothing.

"Great," I mumble, crossing to the bed.

It's softer than the one on the *Undertow*. Too soft. But even so, reclining on the pliable surface teases the tension from my arms and legs and mind, until I teeter on the edge of sleep. What will it hurt? There isn't anything else to do until the Thalijh finish their analysis.

Besides, this is the safest place we can be…

19

WAKE UP!

Iali's yell crashes into me like the thundering flood of water I felt once before.

I bolt upright. Cool air wafts against my sweat-slicked skin.

"What is it?" I groan, blinking my vision clear. The room is empty. Dark. Quiet.

It's here. Fear—no, terror—tinges Iali's words.

"That can't be right," I mumble.

We have to go. Iali insists. *NOW!*

The urgency of its thought forces my feet to the floor. Then, a rumbling BOOM rocks the world, followed by a distant, thundering rush that can only be one thing: water!

In a panic, I stumble to the door and into the hall. The strips of light overhead flicker, struggling to stay lit, and the floor underfoot bucks as if alive. The door to my right hisses open and Gohk appears at the threshold.

"What the hell is going on?" she grumbles, bleary-eyed.

Before I can respond, Rhuk appears at his door, then Fletcher at his.

Rhuk's ears twitch. "What's that sound?"

"Water," Fletcher answers, pacing across the alcove and glancing down the hall. It's empty and silent, except for that horrible, distant rumble.

We have to GO! Iali repeats. *It's coming...*

Iali withdraws as the words fade to silence, until it's barely a whisper in the shadows of my mind. Did the darkness actually follow us? Find us?

Suddenly, the Thalijh from before scrambles into view. Soft-blue, sanguine-speckled tentacles hammer the jittery floor in frantic, wet slaps. The Thalijh calms—or feigns calm—when its wide eyes find us.

"You four," it calls out. Even the robotic translation seems too soothing. "Please come with me."

"What's going on?" Gohk spits over Fletcher's identical question.

"There has been a...maintenance accident." The pause is a heartbeat too long. The Thalijh is definitely lying. "Nothing to be concerned about, but out of precaution, it would be best to vacate the area."

"And go where?" Fletcher asks.

"I will return you to your ship," The Thalijh answers. Then, a bit more urgently: "Come. Quickly."

Past the short, dead end offshoot, the halls are beginning to fill. Other Thalijh lead tight-knit groups in the same direction we're going. Each tentacled alien croons to their respective groups in a different language. But it isn't working. The air is thick, like just before a rainstorm, and tinged with the musky stench of fear.

"Stay close," our Thalijh intones, hugging the wall to squeeze past a pair of beings so tall, their heads nearly scratch the ceiling.

A lilac Thalijh is between them, standing up on the tips of its tentacles, its burbled speech translated into a jabbering, lilting staccato.

"We are almost there," our guide says, turning down an empty offshoot and leading us through a door to the vaulted alcove with pretty blue lights. It's barely recognizable.

The glass orbs set in the ceiling are dark, and their blue glow is replaced by a faint orange-yellow light shining from previously invisible strips on the floor, stretching from the center of the room to each door. Water distorts the even light, sloshing to and fro as the ground trembles underfoot. It spills from the shallow pool, drips from the walls, and seeps from closed doors. One or two are ajar as if forced open, and water spills from those as well.

"Your ship is through there." The Thalijh points across the empty space. "You should—"

Its words are cut off in a warbling scream as it is yanked into the shadows. Water splashes, and the Thalijh groans, but only for a moment. Then, silence. Deep. Sinister. Broken only by the calm trickle of water.

"Run!" Fletcher shouts, but I'm already sprinting for the door.

My heart pounds in time with my splashing steps. Frigid water soaks my pants legs, sending goose pimples racing across my skin. More pours into my oversized boots, freezing my toes. Though muffled by the thundering rush of blood, I can hear the others scrambling after me in a chorus of disturbed water. But there's something else. Calm. Deliberate.

A wayward glance over my shoulder hints at something in the shadows. Darker than the shadows. It is here. It has found us. Just like Iali insisted…

Gritting my teeth, I lunge at the door. It doesn't open. Slamming into the hard surface knocks the wind out of me. As I gasp for breath, Fletcher skids to a stop beside me.

"I—it won't open," I stammer.

"Move," he says, nudging me aside and running thick fingers over a clear section of wall next to the door. A panel pops open to reveal a small crank. Water splashes, and ripples drift into view. Then, it lumbers out of the shadows.

A featureless face turns to Gohk, then Rhuk, then snaps to Fletcher and I. Without words, without sound, I can feel malice pouring off of it. It is here for us.

"Fletcher," I whisper, looking up at the opening he's managed so far: only the size of a fist. "Faster!"

With a grunted curse, he bears down on the crank. The gap surges open. Head-width. Torso-width. Shoulder-width.

"Go!" he spits at me, then turns to Rhuk and Gohk. "You two, come on!"

I don't wait to see if they move. Every fiber of my being wills me through the opening. My soaked clothes snag on the vaned sections of metal. And my awkward, heavy, oversized boots crowd the cramped opening. But strong hands shove me the rest of the way through, to dry ground. A moment later, Rhuk crashes to the floor beside me with a pained huff. Gohk's head appears after him.

"Out of the way," she cautions, before diving through.

"Fletcher," she calls from the floor. "Get your ass in here now!"

Wordless assent is followed by his head and shoulders. It's more than a tight squeeze.

"Grab my arms," he calls.

I take one hand. Gohk grabs the other. We pull.

For a heartbeat, I'm afraid he's too big. Maybe a little too round? Then something gives, and he slips free. We both stumble backwards, and he falls.

A black hand shoots through the opening and seizes one of Fletcher's ankles. All of a sudden, we aren't falling anymore. We're holding Fletcher up. Keeping him from being yanked back through the hole. His face twists in pain as its grip tightens and its pull strengthens.

"Rhuk!" I call to the tiny alien standing dumbly nearby. "Do something!"

But what can he do? None of us have weapons. And there isn't anything nearby he can use as a stand in.

To my surprise, the tiny creature leaps from a standstill onto Fletcher's back, then scampers to his ankle. Rhuk's wide mouth opens to reveal two rows of shiny, jagged teeth, which he sinks into the darkness.

It lets out a bellowing roar and releases Fletcher. We stumble backwards and he crashes to the ground between us, Rhuk clamped to his ankle.

"Get up!" Gohk cries, already scrambling on her hands and knees along the short corridor leading to where we landed.

The door at the far end is still open, so I can see the Undertow and its extended ramp.

"Everybody on the ship!" Gohk urges.

I hurry after her, wade into the shallow pool covering the floor, joined by two more pairs of splashing footsteps. But before we can reach the ramp's corrugated metal, there's a resounding crash from the closed door. Bits of metal spew from the corridor, followed by a roar. Then another, louder crash, and the lights past the doorway flicker and go out.

"UP! GO!" Gohk shouts, waving at the ship.

I turn toward it, dragging my oversized, waterlogged boots through the slightly deeper pool of water beneath it. Rhuk is beside me, nearly up to his waist in the frigid water—I don't remember it being this icy on the way in—and Fletcher brings up the rear.

Gohk is at the top of the ramp when it leaps out of the darkness, landing with a massive splash only feet from Fletcher's heels. Her jittery blue eyes widen, then she disappears inside. I hurry after her, dragging Rhuk along by the collar of his waterlogged cloak. Fletcher dances away from a wild swing and sprints toward me. It sprints after him.

"The dive room!" he shouts.

I sprint through the door and pivot left, but when I look over my shoulder, he turns right, toward the bridge. He dives inside, shutting the door in his wake.

It slams into the wall opposite the door, then lunges in the direction Fletcher fled. It doesn't see us frozen in the hall. And it doesn't notice us as it crashes into the bridge door and begins attempting to tear the metal slab loose.

As quietly as my soaked boots allow, I sneak around the corner into the common area, with Rhuk shivering at my side. We're halfway to the dive room when Gohk emerges with a tool I don't recognize hefted in both hands.

"You think this'll work on that thing?" she asks Rhuk.

"Only one way to find out," he answers, jagged teeth chattering.

The press of a button sends a brilliant arc of light between two long metal poles at the tool's end. Gohk, lips pull back in a wicked grin, hefts it and lumbers toward the hall. There's a sizzle, a roar, a thud, then Gohk sails back into view and crashes into the far wall of the common area. The tool is tossed after her in two pieces.

I can only stare wide-eyed. But Rhuk rushes to Gohk's side. Leans over her. Calls to her. That only draws its attention.

Heavy footfalls shake the metal deck, and a moment later it stomps into view, stopping inches from Gohk's limp form. It bends down, until its featureless face is even with Rhuk. He bares jagged teeth at the darkness and hisses, only to be swept aside with a casual flick of a long-fingered hand. Then, it looks at me.

Even without eyes, its gaze pins me in place. My legs won't move. I can barely take a breath for fear it will charge toward me. It doesn't, and its head cocks to one side. But why? Can it feel Iali? Does it know? Or is it simply looking down on me? A mere human? I would shout the questions at it, if not for the subtle whine from the dive room behind me.

I blink, but don't turn. I can't tear my eyes from its blank stare. Just as well, because I have a feeling if I do—

"Aiko! Behind you! Run!" Fletcher's sudden shout sends a shot of adrenaline through my heart. That's what the sound was: he opened the dive hatch!

Still, I can't move.

A muffled curse echoes over the intercom, then I hear a hiss of a door opening down the hall. The bridge door! What is he doing?!

"I'm over here!" he bellows. "Come and get me!"

It doesn't hesitate.

As soon as it lopes out of sight, invisible ice thaws from my limbs. I rush to the window and watch Fletcher sprint down the slowly retracting ramp. He leaps into the pooled water below, then races under the smooth curve of the Undertow's hull. It squeezes through the quickly narrowing opening and drops to the ground, featureless face searching for him away from the ship instead of under it.

Pushing away from the window, I skid to a stop next to the dive room's open hatch just in time for Fletcher's frantic whisper.

"Aiko!?" He squints up through the hatch.

"I'm here," I whisper back.

He reaches out both hands. "Help me up."

"I—I can't do it by myself," I stammer. "You're too heavy."

His eyes widen, and a frown flickers across his face.

"I need you to try," he says, voice tinged with a note of panic. "Before it notices."

"Okay." I drop to the deck and hang my arms over the edge. "Ready?"

I clench my teeth and give a halting nod.

Fletcher bends his knees, leaps for my outstretched hands, and catches them.

He is heavy!

I bite my lip at the sudden stabbing pain in my shoulders and clamp my fingers around his wrists. But the force of his weight drags me over the edge and I fall, crashing down on top of him with a splash and a surprised, pained yelp.

It hears and spins to face the two of us, letting out a roar that shakes tiny bits of coral from the high ceiling. Then, it charges.

Something about its headlong rush toward us is mesmerizing, like a cascade of water about to sweep us away. I don't move out of the way. I can only stare at the inevitable.

At the last moment, a hand grips my shoulder and shoves me aside. I topple into the shallow pool and push up, gasping for air, in time to witness dark arms wrap around Fletcher in a savage tackle. They tumble in a tangle of limbs and a shower of water, coming to rest with it on top, clawed, spider-like fingers poised to strike.

Time slows.

Iali's voice echoes from the depths of my mind.

I told you this would happen.

I stare at the scene unfolding before me. "What can I do?"

There's only one thing you can do. Iali croons, louder than before. *Absorb it.*

"How?"

I can show you. Iali's voice is deafening. *But first, you must make contact.*

Just the thought of touching the darkness a second time makes my skin crawl. But if I don't… My eyes flick across the scene playing out at a snail's pace. Its claws are inches from Fletcher and creeping closer in slow motion. His battered face is twisted in panic. His eyes are wide with fear.

"Okay," I agree.

Gathering my legs under me, I launch myself at the darkness hunched over Fletcher, bearing down on him. It doesn't see me coming. Doesn't dodge as my outstretched fingers sink into its gooey surface. But this time, touching the darkness burns like fire. Sears like ice. Its taloned fingers ball into a fist and smash into

Fletcher's face, knocking him unconscious. Then, it twists toward me. The world distorts as dark hands grip my shoulders. As taloned fingers pierce the skin of my back. Darkness is already pressing in around my mind as its featureless face bends to mine until our foreheads meet.

That light touch sends me spinning into a void of inescapable darkness.

20

I stumble onto solid ground, but there's no horizon in the distance. No sky overhead. Just...infinite darkness.

And Iali's warmth is gone. I'm alone.

"Hello?" The shout doesn't echo or carry in the emptiness. It simply is, then isn't.

I strain to hear an answer, but the dead air around me is so silent and so still, the rush of blood, the thunder of each breath, and the whip crack of a blink, are deafening.

"Is anyone out there?" I call again, on the verge of panic.

No answer.

This isn't like before. Last time, I appeared in my circle of sunlight with Iali by my side as a thick fog swirled around us. But now...? Where am I? How did I get here? And where is Iali?

I spin in place. Every direction is the same. Dark. Empty. Endless.

Staying put won't solve anything, so I begin to walk. The ground is smooth. And flat. And even though my steps make no sound I can *feel* the vibration of each footfall. Though it's impossible to tell if I'm actually going anywhere.

Yet I walk. And I walk. And I walk. Until...

"Aiko." My name echoes in the infinite darkness as if whispered by a thousand tongues at once.

I freeze midstep. "Hello?"

"Your name is Aiko," the echoing chorus says.

My brow furrows. I've heard this before.

"Who are you?" I shout into the emptiness.

"You know." As the whispered reply fades to silence, the darkness around me condenses into a thick, swirling wall of fog.

I recognize the spinning vortex.

"You..." I don't know what else to say. Unlike Iali, *it* doesn't have a name.

"Us." Even without a face, I can hear it grinning.

"What do you want?" I ask, spinning in place, shying away from smoky tendrils lazily reaching for me. It can grab me in an instant if it wants.

The air shivers when it chuckles, and there's a flash in the fog: a reminder of the many memories Iali forced into my mind.

Iali. "Where is Iali?"

This time, outright laughter booms out of the foggy darkness. *"They were absorbed."* There's a mocking mirth in that final word. An acknowledgement, and dismissal, of Iali's proposed plan.

I stifle a grimace. What am I supposed to do now?

A cackle echoes in the dark as if it read my thoughts. Maybe it did. Maybe it's just toying with me. And if it is...

Think about what you can do.

Rhuk's words bob to the surface of my mind, as sudden as storm clouds on a bright, sunny day.

What can I do? Overpowering it isn't an option. And I doubt I'll be able to trick it—not in this place, at least. So, what? Talk to it? Reason with it? Beg for mercy, if it has the capacity for such a thing? No. None of those things will work. But maybe...

I take a deep breath. "Why Humans?"

It doesn't answer immediately. I'm beginning to fear it won't when the fog swirling around me gathers, compresses, and shrinks into something nearing a recognizable shape. It is still no more than a shadow, and little more than shifting vapor. But it has arms. Legs. A featureless face I can address.

"That is an interesting question," it finally says, in a reserved, almost amicable, baritone. *"One we have not considered in a very long time."*

Its words no longer echo, but fall dead as soon as they're spoken. Just like mine.

"And the answer?" I press.

Its ghostly arms cross. *"We almost did not choose Humans. We thought them fragile. Weak. Ill-suited to the harsh realities of the universe. But they proved us wrong."*

"How so?"

"You have seen our past," it replies. *"Everything we have done to survive. Everything we have done to ensure our proliferation. Symbiosis was necessary. However, the process has proven inefficient. No beings have ever been wholly acceptable. Humans altered that reality."*

Its head cocks to the side.

"They are the most adaptable species we have ever encountered. Even without our aid, they survived. And once they garnered our interest, we discovered their genome to be susceptible to extensive manipulation without catastrophic side effects. It took time, but we managed to mold them into superior hosts."

What I understood of its reasoning makes a macabre sort of sense.

"What about me? Fletcher?"

"Ah, yes." The question seems to annoy it. *"You are the unavoidable result of Humans' remarkable, innate ability to endure. Even though we have painstakingly molded and shaped what they were into what they are, some genetic remnants persist."*

"What do you mean?"

"For some reason, certain genetic combinations invalidate our modifications and prevent us from making corrections."

"So you destroy us?" I ask with a frown.

"We study you," it replies. *"To understand why you are."*

"With the same result."

"Out of necessity," it snaps.

"Out of convenience, you mean," I retort.

It lets out an angry, wordless protest.

"If the Kaisin ever discovered the truth, they'd force you out," I spit. "You'd have to find a new host."

"That cannot happen," it bellows. *"Will not."*

It takes a step toward me, menacing, yet silent as smoke.

"Our secret has never been divulged. We tolerate whispers. And rumors. And baseless conjecture. But not discovery."

It takes another step.

"We will not allow that to change."

Another.

"Even if we have to tear a thousand more of your kind asunder."

Another.

"And sacrifice ten times as many Kaisin in the process of learning how to prevent you."

I stumble away from its wild grab, turn, and break into a sprint. But the darkness around me condenses into the same fog.

Presses in around me. It feels oily against my skin. Tastes sour on my tongue. Dampens each breath.

"You cannot escape!" Its voice hisses in my ear. *"Resist all you like, but your fate will match all the others that have come before."*

The fog thickens. Darkens. Hardens. Squeezes. I can't move. Can't breathe. Can't see. Sweat beads on my skin, while goose pimples cover my arms and legs. And pain, like thousands of needles poking into me, scatter my thoughts.

Countless images merge and overlap: azure water, burnished sand, crimson sky, and countless metal corridors. Faces form and melt like flowing water or shifting smoke. Except for one. Through the searing pain, a round face with a wide mouth, milky eyes, and a bright blue streak running between floppy ears, smiles at me.

Fallah.

I hold her face in my mind's eye and use it as a buoy to endure the pain. And think. What do I do? *What do I do?*

"Absorb it..."

The whisper barely registers, but the voice is familiar.

"Iali?" I wheeze.

"Absorb it..." It repeats, weaker this time.

"How?"

Iali doesn't answer, but I know what I have to do. Be Human. Persist. Adapt. And survive!

No matter how big—how powerful—*it* is the same as Iali. Which means it has the same limitations. And weaknesses.

Taking a breath, I hold the image of Fallah's smiling face in my mind's eye and begin building a safe space. I start with a crimson circle. Add warmth. A rough, stone floor. Dry air. And a pink sky. The same place I was when Iali first made contact. Then, I draw in another deep breath, despite the sharp prick of needles, and will myself into that space.

With a hollow pop, darkness is replaced by light, and warmth, and safety.

Fog swirls along the circle's edge, but can no longer reach me. Not here. Never here.

"You will not escape," it says, countless dark tendrils trailing along the invisible barrier between us.

Running from it might not be an option, but I have something else in mind.

The sky around my small circle of safety is shrouded in darkness, and the horizon is still obscured by swirling fog. It's massive. Powerful. But not without limits. I stretch the circle. Press against it. Force it back. Step by step. It strains with all of its might to collapse the invisible barrier and crush my will. It can't. Not anymore.

But pushing it back isn't enough. Too far and I'll shove it free of my mind. It will escape. Devour me, and Fletcher, and the others in the real world. I can't let that happen. So instead, I let up. Relax my guard. Weaken the barrier. Wait for it to notice.

It takes the bait, surging into the crimson circle with a wicked cackle.

I backpedal until my heels brush the circle's edge. The fog billows to fill the space. Rushes toward me, smoky tendrils reaching out to snatch me from the worn stone ground.

At the last moment, I take a single step back.

It smashes into the invisible barrier. Recoils. Turns to retreat. But it's too late. It's trapped.

232

"*You* won't escape," I say with a triumphant smile.

The fog concentrates in front of me.

"*This cage of yours will not hold me,*" it says. "*It cannot.*"

I ignore the empty threat and spin away from the circle of light—once a haven, now a prison—and walk into the endless, barren wasteland.

"*You think you have won,*" it calls after me. "*But this is far from over...*"

I close my eyes, and when they flutter open, the darkness is gone, the husk of what used to be a Kaisin held upright by my iron grip. It isn't moving. Or breathing. I recoil, stumble, and splash into the shallow pool beneath the *Undertow*.

Fletcher pushes the Kaisin aside and sits up. "Are you alright?"

I nod. "Yeah."

"Are you sure?" His face is stone still, as if he wasn't just mauled by darkness.

"I'm fine," I say.

A distant rumble shakes the ground, and bits of coral rain from the ceiling, pinging on the *Undertow's* curved hull in a hollow, metallic chorus.

"We need to get out of here," I say, eyeing the ship looming over us.

Fletcher gives a stiff nod when the ground shakes again.

He stands, reaches down, and pulls me up out of the sloshing water. Then, he wades to the nearest landing strut and flips open a small, hidden door. When he presses the red button inside, the *Undertow's* ramp extends with a hydraulic sigh.

I follow him up, but walk to the common area instead of the bridge. Gohk is still slumped against the far wall, her breaths shallow and ragged. Rhuk is sprawled nearby, unconscious. At a glance, he seems the worse for wear, but otherwise fine.

Still, I grimace. Iali was right.

Iali...

That is something else I'm not sure how to reconcile. It devoured Iali. And now it is locked away deep inside of me, no more than the whisper of a shadow. Is Iali trapped with it? There's no way to be sure. No way to delve into the darkness to discover if my friend—can I call Iali a friend?—is still alive.

I heave to my feet and pace to the bridge.

"Gohk doesn't look so good," I mumble at the back of Fletcher's head. "Neither does Rhuk."

"They will be fine," he says, not taking his eyes off of the controls.

I frown. "I think they need medical attention."

"We have been directed to a station in low orbit," he replies. "The Thalijh there can take a look at them. For now, see if you can get the two of them secured for our ascent."

It's nearly the same dismissal he gave me when we first met.

I trudge back to the common area, slump against the wall between Gohk and Rhuk, and slide to the floor, relieved. But this is only a temporary respite for the questions Fletcher will eventually ask. Once we get to the station and Gohk is cared for, won't he ask for an explanation? Won't he want to know where the darkness went? Why it just disappeared when I touched it? Won't the others? I can't avoid the questions once they are asked. I'll have to tell them *everything*.

What will they say about Iali? About how the darkness managed to track us all the way to Thalijh? And about my role in our escape? Only time will tell.

My gaze drifts to the window, but the closed shutter hides the world beyond. Moments later, however, the engines shift from a sub-octave rumble to a glass-shattering shriek, suggesting we've risen out of Thalijh's crystal clear waters.

The bulkhead vibrates, but no matter how violently the ship shakes, nothing can dislodge the memories of *it* from my mind's eye, as much as I want to forget. Everything that has happened—to me, to Fletcher, to the Humans—is because of its influence. And despite how much I absorbed, there's still so much more of it inhabiting countless Kaisin. Controlling them. Molding their children. Altering their future. Stealing their freedom.

Fallah died grasping at freedom, and every step I've taken since was to achieve what we promised to do together. Through ample luck, I've managed to find a measure of that freedom with Fletcher, and Gohk, and Rhuk. And even learn more than I ever wanted to know about "smooth skins". But *it*…I never imagined such a thing existed. Could exist. Or how much of an impact it could have on me. And how much of an impact it still had on others.

Think about what you *can do.*

"Aiko." Fletcher's even voice snaps me back to reality.

When I look up, he's framed in the doorway.

I force a smile.

"How are they?" he asks.

"Fine, I think," I say.

"We are almost to the station," he continues, not skipping a beat. "The Thalijh are already aware of the situation and will be waiting to take Gohk and Rhuk."

I want to ask if he told them about me as well. About how I absorbed the darkness threatening us. But a blank stare suggests such questions haven't occurred to him. Yet. So, as long as he doesn't ask, I won't offer.

"O—okay," I stammer, instead.

Fletcher gives a shallow nod.

"I am going to head back to the bridge," he says, turning away before I can even think to respond.

Just as well. I want to be alone. I want silence; what little of it I can get before the inevitable, never-ending stream of questions awaiting me on the Thalijh station.

21

The *Undertow* isn't the only ship the Thalijh redirected to the station. A score of others crowd around the massive cylinder, just like the one Rhuk and Gohk call home.

I frown. Do *all* stations look like this? Or is it just a coincidence?

One at a time, the ships file toward a round opening in the glittering hull. Then, it's our turn.

A metal barrier seals the mouth of the opening behind us, and another opens ahead. Beyond and below, a motley collection of crafts crowd a wide pad in a familiar scene. There's barely enough room for the ships already there, let alone the countless others waiting out in the void. For a moment, I'm worried Fletcher won't be able to find a space. But there's one, near the leading edge of the platform—a painted circle the same shade as Alphanax's sun. Hopefully here, it'll also represent safety.

The ship drops to a lighter-than-usual landing: barely a whisper. Yet, it still prompts a weak groan to my left.

"Rhuk?!" I crawl to the small being.

Unfocused eyes flutter open, scan the room, and find my face. "Aiko."

I reach out and gently sit him up. "Are you okay?"

Rhuk nods. "Fine. What happened?"

"You got knocked out," I reply.

He fixes me with a blank stare.

"We managed to escape," I add.

"To where?" He still looks dazed.

"A station over the planet," I say. "Gohk needs help. And so do you, it looks like."

His mumbled reply is drowned out by a familiar popping squelch as two ochre Thalijh squirm into the common area. Fletcher enters a moment later.

"The Kaisin," he says, indicating Gohk. "And the little one."

"We'll take them both,' the lead Thalijh burbles. The other produces a small bundle from somewhere beneath its nest of tentacles that unfolds into a floating stretcher. They position it close to Gohk, then slowly, gently lift her onto it. Once she's secured with straps, one of the Thalijh turns to Rhuk.

"Can you walk? Or would you prefer to be carried?" it asks, a few of its tentacles twitching. In question? Anticipation? Thalijh are impossible to read.

"I'm fine," Rhuk grumbles and heaves to his feet. Sways. Stumbles. Starts to fall.

The closest Thalijh snakes a tentacle around Rhuk's waist and lifts him off the ground. Yet the little alien ignores the fleshy appendage wrapped around him. Instead, he settles into it, eyes drooping closed. Is he really that injured? He doesn't look it. But if he drifted off so easily after being swept up off the ground, maybe he is.

The Thalijh tucks Rhuk close, grabs hold of the back half of the stretcher, and files down the hall. Fletcher, without making eye contact, follows.

I reluctantly fall in line.

This dock is almost identical to the one at the station Gohk and Rhuk call home. The collection of ships clustered together. The cargo clustered around extended ramps. Crew of all shapes and sizes milling under overhanging hulls. And Kaisin. So many Kaisin.

I blink at the too-familiar scene. Here, too? But…this is a Thalijh station. Maybe it's because we're in Kaisin space?

I stick close to Fletcher's heels as we snake our way to massive double doors set in the far wall. Thankfully, none of the other crews pay us any mind. And no Kaisin gaze lingers. A sigh of relief catches in my throat as I realize everyone likely has their own problems to deal with after what happened below. That's why we're all here, after all.

Our guides slow as they near the bulkhead and wait for it to grind open. On the other side is a wide, open street filled with familiar sights, and sounds, and crowds. Squat buildings stretch to taller towers in the distance. And above, hexagonal plates of glass form an arc that allows a breathtaking view of glittering stars. But there's no sign of the soft blue orb of Thalijh. Shame. I'd have loved to see the planet floating overhead.

Our escort continues through the relentless flow, past buildings that all look the same. Here too, the press seems to ignore our procession, yet they part as if keenly aware of the stretcher gripped between meaty tentacles. And as we walk on, the avenue widens and the crowds thin. Buildings grow until glass and steel reach for the hexagon canopy far overhead.

Finally, the two Thalijh angle toward a nondescript tower. A plain door leads to a familiar atrium, with polished floors and coral walls curving up to a vaulted ceiling. The two Thalijh steer the stretcher past a shallow pool to double doors on the back wall. Beyond is a plain, empty hallway stretching into the distance. We walk, twisting and turning through a maze of corridors until I'm dizzy.

Then, the Thalijh suddenly stop at a door. It opens and we enter a modest room. A wide, comfortable-looking bed juts from the right wall, while a few chairs are lined up against the left. Directly across from the door, a window spans from floor to ceiling, giving a breathtaking view of pooled water far below, scattered skyscrapers in the distance, and the station's bulkhead curving up and out of sight.

I sidle up to the window and look up, then down. Where did the water come from? And how is it so far below the window? Didn't we enter on the ground floor? Was this massive pool just hiding behind the row of squat buildings the entire time?

When I'm able to tear my gaze away from the window, Gohk is already on the bed. The two Thalijh are fussing over her, tentacles poking and prodding her here and there as if able to tell exactly what's wrong with her simply by feel. Then, they begin attaching small suction cups to her arms, clipping wires to those. Finally, they hover even closer, blocking Gohk from view, and when they withdraw, an array of wires and clear tubes are trailing out of the sleeves of her shirt.

Next, they turn to Rhuk, perching the small being on a cot that wasn't there a moment before. After more than a few pokes and prods, they burble back and forth in their native tongue. Saucer-sized eyes blink a consensus, then the two turn away from the bed and slither out of the room.

We're alone for only a few minutes when a familiar, droopy-eyed Thalijh trundles in, fidgeting. I don't know much about the tentacled beings, but it's clear that Orugh is nervous. Or stressed. Or both.

"Good to see you all made it off of the station," the Thalijh quickly gurgles at us, its gaze flicking to Gohk and Rhuk in turn. "Their injuries will be tended to, of course. In the meantime, there are other things to discuss."

Orugh moves further into the room. "The samples provided by the Kaisin were analyzed and did exhibit signs of a foreign substance."

"The parasite," Fletcher says.

"Not a parasite," the Thalijh answers.

"What do you mean?"

"The substance is composed of a complex and senseless mix of compounds." The tips of Orugh's tentacles curl. "However, the substance seems inert. Harmless. Definitely not parasitic."

Fletcher frowns. "That cannot be right."

"Right or wrong, that is our conclusion," Orugh replies.

Fletcher's blank stare turns to me.

Is he going to tell the Thalijh what he saw? His mouth works, but he remains silent.

"Will there be anything else?"

"No," he says.

With a dip of its bulbous head, the Thalijh slips toward the door, but pauses at the threshold. "Your friends will be awake shortly. Make sure they don't move."

It glances at me, then wriggles out of the room without a sound.

I stare at the door for a long time, then force myself to look at Fletcher. He's facing the window, arms crossed.

"Why didn't you tell it?" I ask, unable to keep nervous curiosity bottled up inside any longer.

"Tell it what?" Gohk groans.

"You are awake," Fletcher says, walking to the bed, all trace of animosity toward her gone.

"Tell it what?" Gohk repeats. This time, there's more force behind the question.

Fletcher looks at me, but doesn't speak. Is he giving me the chance to fess up? To tell Gohk what he saw? And everything else I've been keeping secret that they don't know about?

I let out a deep sigh. Now is as good a time as any. But...

"We should wait for Rhuk to wake up," I mumble.

Gohk stares at me for a moment, then looks at Fletcher. He nods.

"We will wait, then," she says, evenly.

It isn't long before the small being's eyes flutter open. He sits up, massages his temples, blinks, and sweeps weary eyes across the room. When he spots us, his brow furrows.

"Why so serious?"

Fletcher and Gohk look at me. Rhuk's gaze follows.

I open my mouth. Close it. Shake my head. Now is the time. I have to tell them everything.

"Let me start at the beginning," I say hesitantly.

Their stares don't waver, and their expressions are still as stone.

I look away, guilt-ridden for keeping the truth from them for so long.

"You remember when Lorn scratched me?"

Fletcher nods.

"Well…" I suck in a deep breath. "It got in me."

Their unchanged faces aren't what I expect. And when none of them speak, I continue.

"At first, I didn't know. I thought its attempts to communicate were nightmares. But eventually, we spoke."

"Spoke?" Fletcher asks.

"In dreams," I reply. "Iali—"

"You gave it a name?" Gohk asks.

"*It* is just like us," I snap. "Iali thought. Felt. Reasoned"—I pause—"sacrificed."

Fletcher tilts his head to one side. "And the darkness on the station?"

"It was different." I clench my fists.

Evil isn't quite the right word to describe its motives. Nor malevolent. Maybe…

"Opportunistic," I finally say with an ambivalent shrug. "It hitched a ride on the Humans that escaped the colony ship and molded them. Into Kaisin."

My gaze drifts to Gohk. She hasn't moved. Surprising, since I expected her to react to the news most of all, considering how many blanks it fills in. She meets my stare. Holds it. But says nothing.

"And we"—I motion to Fletcher and myself—"are just errors in the process."

He frowns. "What?"

"They couldn't completely control Human genetics, and we, people like us, Humans…were the result."

"And it told you all this?" Gohk asks.

I nod. "But only because it expected to overpower me. Devour me."

"It did not," Gohk deadpans. "So, what happened?"

My gaze flicks to Fletcher. "I absorbed it."

Gohk stares. Is she judging me? Disgusted by what I did? Disappointed?

"I had to!" I blurt out. "Otherwise, it would have devoured Fletcher, then the rest of you!"

None of them answer. Or make eye contact.

"I did what I thought was right," I say with a heavy sigh.

After a long time, I work up the courage to meet Gohk's surprisingly steady blue gaze. She still seems unmoved by everything she's heard. But maybe it's everything the Thalijh are pumping into her? She isn't behaving like herself at all.

"So, it is just floating around inside you?" she finally asks.

"Not exactly. It's trapped," I explain, pausing to probe the edge of my mind. Where Iali rested before. It isn't there. Maybe I pushed it deeper than I thought?

"It's dormant," I say, the only explanation I can come up with in the moment.

"Like what the Thalijh found in Gohk," Fletcher muses.

Gohk's stare shifts to him. "What?"

"The Thalijh said they found some strange substance in the samples they took from you," Fletcher says. "They do not know what it is."

I tilt my head to one side. "According to Iali, some of it was definitely inside of you. And that little bit was enough for it to find us."

"All the way on Thalijh?" Fletcher's head shakes slowly. "Not possible."

"And beyond, if it hadn't caught up to us." I should have listened to Iali and absorbed the darkness inside of Gohk when I had the chance. Then, none of this would have happened. We'd still be on Thalijh. Gohk and Rhuk would be fine. And Iali would still be with me.

Gohk stares into an empty corner of the room. Even Fletcher, who would have been well within his rights to scold me for keeping secrets, half-turns to look out the window. But their deafening silence is just as unbearable.

"You did your best," Rhuk says softly. "Better than any of us could have done." His wide-eyed glare drifts to Gohk, then Fletcher, prompting hesitant nods from both of them. Then, he continues. "The question is, what to do now?"

"Why not ask Iali?" Gohk offers with the slightest hint of animus.

"Iali's gone," I say softly. "While helping me subdue it."

Gohk doesn't skip a beat. "Perhaps the Thalijh should take it from here. I am sure they can figure out a way to remove it from you. From both of us."

"I'm not sure that's such a good idea," I say.

"But the Thalijh said what they found inside me was dormant," she shoots back.

"Inert," Fletcher corrects.

"Fine." She looks at me. "And yours is dormant."

"It is, but—"

Her head shakes. "I do not see the problem, then. We take them out now while they are not a problem."

"We can't do that!" I cry. "You saw what it did back at the station. And what it did on Thalijh. If they take it out and can't control it—"

"The Thalijh know what they are doing," Gohk says, then glares at Fletcher. "Are you going to back me up on this?"

Fletcher looks away.

She spins to Rhuk. "You?"

"Perhaps it would be best to put more stock in Aiko's experience with this matter," he says slowly. "She knows more about it than any of us."

"So we should let her, a child, dictate what we do next?" Gohk scoffs.

Rhuk scowls. "We should give her a say. Just as much of one as the rest of us."

Ghok's lips twitch, dipping dangerously close to a frown. "Considering what she told us, we should not be so quick to trust her. What if that stuff is influencing her mind? Controlling her?"

The suggestion angers me. And before anybody can say anything else, I spin on my heel and dash out of the room.

Rhuk calls after me. But I don't listen.

My oversized boots beat the polished floor. Identical corridors slip by in an endless blur. In no time, I'm lost. Alone.

Around the next corner, glass stretches from floor to ceiling. Beyond, buildings of all shapes and sizes and colors ring the massive pool of pale blue water, like a watchful eye peering up at me. And overhead, a myriad of hexagon panels give a clear view of the stars twinkling in the void. It should have been a beautiful sight to behold, but all that sticks out is the deep darkness in between: a reminder of what tried to kill Fletcher and I beneath the waves of a forgotten ocean, and again on a different, yet eerily similar, station only hours before. Even now, the darkness stalks us, though from a different place entirely. From inside me.

I hold up my arm and pull the sleeve back to reveal a hairline seam from wrist to elbow. If only I could reopen the wound and drain the darkness from my veins without endangering everyone. If only I could do a lot of things...

Gohk's words hurt more than I expected, but for an entirely different reason than I expected. A day ago, she praised me for my drive. But now? I'm little more than a liability, as if every ounce of worth she saw in me evaporated with the truth. Worst of all, in the same position she expected understanding. Forgiveness.

She changed her tone so quickly and completely.

I let out a deep sigh and step closer to the window. Soft white light glitters on pale ripples. This whole scene—as beautiful as it is on the surface—is just like my relationship with Fletcher, and Rhuk, and Gohk: superficial. And the freedom I reached for after Fallah's death is nothing more than an illusion. In Gohk's eyes, I'm a child. Less than. Does Fletcher think so little of me, too? Does Rhuk?

"There you are."

I nearly jump out of my oversized boots as the small being sidles up beside me.

"Y—you aren't supposed to be out of bed," I stammer.

"I can do whatever I damn well please," he says with a grin. "I'm old enough to have earned that right, at least."

My brow furrows. His age never occurred to me. "And how old is that?"

"Old," he says with a coy grin. "Which is why those two listen to me more often than not."

I glance down at the little alien and stifle a frown. Why did Rhuk come after me? Why not Fletcher? Maybe he asked Rhuk to come? Or maybe—

Rhuk's deep breath and heaving sigh trip up my runaway thoughts.

"You know, part of being a grown up is making decisions when things get hard." He looks up at me. "And you've done a fine job of that, regardless of what Gohk might think."

This time I do frown. "But how do I know if I've made the right choice?"

"Impossible to say." His tiny head shakes. "Sometimes you just have to go with your gut."

He grins again. "Although, yours seems to have a knack for getting into trouble."

I can't resist a smile. "So, what do I do now?"

"I have no idea," Rhuk admits with a shrug. "But running away from the problem definitely *isn't* the answer."

Rhuk is right. Even at Alphanax, I never ran from the problems right in front of me. And the one time I did, Fallah...Stinging memories wipe away the smile. So, I won't run. But—

"You don't have to make a decision now," Rhuk murmurs, as if reading my thoughts. "Just...think about what you can do."

I nod slowly, but when I look down, Rhuk is gone.

Think about what you can do.

His suggestion—the same one he made before—echoes among crowded thoughts competing for space. But no matter how hard I focus, no clear direction floats out of the turmoil.

Taking a deep breath, sinking my hands into my pockets, I lean my forehead against the clear glass and stare out at the glittering spires amidst gentle waves.

"What can I do now?"

22

I don't move for a long time. Past the point where my legs should have grown stiff from standing still and where the glass should have warmed up against the skin of my forehead. But I don't feel anything. I'm numb. Probably from overthinking.

Sighing, I push away from the window with both hands, expecting a cold jolt from the glass. But the light, even pressure against my palms is strange.

Maybe I just need some rest? But I'm not tired. Or a solid meal? I haven't eaten in...I can't remember. But I'm not hungry. Maybe I'm just too deep inside my own head.

I frown and take a step back from the window. The hallway is eerily quiet. And the air is still as death. Since Rhuk left, no one else has been by. Not Fletcher, not that I expected him. Or any Thalijh. Or any of their guests. It's as if the place is well and truly deserted. Although, I didn't see anyone in their underwater habitat until after the emergency. So maybe it's just my overactive imagination reaching for something. Anything.

Plodding through lonesome hallways, I eventually find my way back. Rhuk is in the tiny cot, eyes closed, the nest of tubes and wires reattached to his arms and chest as if he never moved. Gohk is sitting up now, looking more alert than before. Fletcher still stands by the window, arms crossed, mouth turned down in a pensive frown.

None of them look at me when I enter. Or speak. And it doesn't seem like they were speaking to one another before I arrived, either. There isn't any of the tell-tale tension in the air after a fight. So, what? They just aren't talking?

I pace to the window and stop next to Fletcher, close enough to whisper: "Is everything okay?"

His face is blank when he looks at me. And his unfocused stare seems to be looking past me.

"Yeah," he says.

"No one's talking," I observe.

"No."

I glance over my shoulder at Gohk. Her arms are crossed and she's staring straight ahead, the glimmer of a scowl on her face. Aside from measured breathing, she's motionless.

"Did she tell the Thalijh?" I whisper to Fletcher.

His gaze had returned to the window, but at the sound of my voice it drifts back to my face, still blank.

"About what?" he asks.

"The darkness." I inch closer. "Did Gohk tell them?"

Fletcher frowns. "Darkness?"

My brow furrows. "Fletcher?"

He doesn't answer. He just stares.

What's going on?

"Gohk," I call, turning to the ancient Kaisin propped up in bed.

Her jittery stare snaps to me.

"Did you tell the Thalijh about me?"

"What about you?" she growls.

"You know…the darkness…Did you tell them?" I press.

Her gaze slides away from me.

Gohk is acting strange too? Did the Thalijh do something while I was gone? To Fletcher? And Gohk? And…?

I turn to the Rhuk. His eyes are open and he's looking at me, a vapid smile plastered across his face.

"What happened while I was gone?" I ask.

His lips stretch into a grin.

"Rhuk!" I rush to the bed and grab the little alien by the shoulders. "What happened? Why are you all acting so strange?"

His wide, blank eyes bore into mine. And his eyebrows twitch when he speaks. "Just…think about what you can do."

I let him go and stumble back away from the bed. I remember the words. He said the exact same thing earlier. In the exact same way. With the same tone. And the same smile.

This isn't right. None of this is right. It's a nightmare. It has to be. I must have fallen asleep at the window. Any moment I'll wake up, and everything will be back to normal.

I close my eyes. Take a deep breath. Concentrate. But when I open them, nothing has changed.

My boots squeal on polished metal as I hurry into the hall. Corridors twist like a maze. No matter how many turns I take, or branches I choose, no path leads to the double doors we passed through earlier.

The next turn brings me to the same floor-to-ceiling window I stood in front of before. Beyond is the same breathtaking view. Now, however, I question whether it's real. If any of this is real. But if it isn't, where am I really?

252

I walk to the window and press both hands against the glass. It isn't icy, like I expect. And beyond the same light pressure as before, it doesn't feel like anything, really.

More to the point, *nothing* feels like anything.

The air isn't hot or cold. Or humid. It doesn't smell. Fresh. Or stale. Or recycled. Or salty. And the floor under my boots isn't hard. It's just there, a solid, flat surface to ground me.

But I'm still not sure where.

The Fletcher, and Gohk, and Rhuk here aren't real. They can't be, which explains why they're acting so strange. More like shadows of themselves. Or memories. And the building curled around me like an endless maze is also a ruse. Everything seemed so real when we arrived, so why is everything suddenly different? What changed?

Nothing, really. How could it? When all I did was stand at this window? And—

I blink.

Think. About how things could turn out differently.

That's it! The only thing that changed is me! My thoughts! And if that's the case, then...

With a furrowed brow, I focus my attention inward, past the jumbled mix of thoughts still clamoring for attention, to the depths of my mind. Where *it* should be. Imprisoned. Dormant. But it isn't there. It isn't anywhere.

So, if it isn't trapped, where is it? More importantly, where am I, exactly?

I remember walking away from it. Opening my eyes. Talking to Fletcher. Escaping the damaged Thalijh structure. But was none of that real? If not, I'm trapped in my own mind. Though this hastily constructed fantasy has to mean that it's still a prisoner, stalling for time while it figures out a way to escape.

Which means I need to escape first! But how? I can't wake up. And I can't make my way out of this maze of corridors. What other option is there?

I thump my forehead on the glass in frustration.

The glass! Maybe...?

I pound balled fists on the smooth, flat surface. The glass shudders under impacts that my hands barely register. It seems normal. If I can break it, maybe that's the escape I'm searching for.

My eyes drop to the water far below.

Even if I am trapped in my mind, will I survive the fall? Is there another way? I don't really have the time to waste. If I stay put too long, it will escape. Then, it won't really matter what I do. What any of us might try to do. It's just too strong to resist in the real world. We've barely escaped twice now; I don't want to chance a third attempt.

Sucking in a deep breath of potentially imaginary air, I back away from the window. The far wall interrupts my retreat. I'm afraid. But it's a strange sensation to feel fear without actually *feeling* it. My palms don't sweat. My heart doesn't race. And nothing mars the eerie silence wrapped around me. But my mind jitters as if charged with electricity.

I channel that nervous energy into a headlong sprint, pivoting at the last moment to smash shoulder-first into the window. It ripples like disturbed water. Stiffens. Then, shatters.

A halo of glittering glass falls with me, but not into the water far below. Beyond the window is pure, endless darkness. I twist in time for one final glimpse at the rectangle of light shrinking above me before I'm swallowed by the abyss. I'm either falling or hanging in place. It's impossible to tell without a frame of reference, because my headlong tumble isn't accompanied by any sensation of movement. Or any other, for that matter.

"We told you it was not over." The words rumble like distant thunder. But they aren't confident. Or goading.

"You're still trapped," I shout back, with a satisfied smile.

"Not for long," it growls. *"All we needed was some time to chip away at your meager prison."*

"How did you manage that?" I wonder aloud, hoping the question will distract it or prompt an answer.

"Human genetics might be a challenge, but human minds are easy to manipulate." I can hear its sneer.

"And how many other humans broke free of your deception?" I shoot back.

Its only answer is a seething, echoing hiss, followed by silence. I have to keep it talking. Keep it distracted.

"If you couldn't keep me fooled, what makes you think you'll be able to escape?" I taunt.

"You are no more remarkable than the countless other beings that have been in your place," it snaps. *"We* will *escape. Then we will wipe you, and your friends, from existence."*

It falls silent again, but this time I get the impression it's no longer listening—that its full attention has turned back to escape.

So it's a race, then. To see who can worm free first.

Twisting again, I study the abyss around me. Shards of glass still glint in nonexistent light, tumbling along with me in the infinite expanse of nothing. But the fact they're still here means this place isn't completely nothing. It's a space that exists. That can hold other things within it. Which means it has an end. I just have to find it. And find out how to make my way there.

But how? I can't feel anything in this place, which is arguably worse than being disoriented. At least if there's gravity, I can determine up and down. Without even that, how can I strike out in a single direction? How can I make sure I'll continue heading in that direction?

Maybe that's the whole point? Keep me in darkness? Keep me disoriented? Keep me from reaching the edge of the small space it was able to commandeer in my mind? But it's still my mind!

Shattered glass swirls around me. I focus on the solid bits. Will them to gather into a small bunch. Then, I begin to shape them. One at a time, I compress each bit into a tiny, shining ball and anchor it in space. I fix the next a few feet away. And the next a few feet after that. I keep going, looking back every once in a while to make sure the small spheres are in a straight line.

Eventually, the beginning of the trail of glass balls disappeared into the abyss. Yet I continue to move ahead. And as my precious supply dwindles, I worry that I'll run out before I reach the edge of its makeshift prison.

But suddenly, I'm falling.

Wind whips past my face, snatching the breath from my lungs. My heart jumps into my throat, and a wild pulse thunders in my ears. My throat closes on a scream. And my fingers clench over sweaty palms. Far below is a crimson circle, obfuscated by swirling fog frantically hammering against an invisible wall. Despite the whipping wind and deafening rush of blood, I can hear it slamming against the prison's indelible border, like a hammer ringing on steel. The sound vibrates the air. My body. My bones. My entire *mind*.

Clenching my teeth against the inexorable ring, I will my plummet to a lazy drift and float to a soft landing near the crimson prison. As my feet touch the ground, the fog rushes at the prison's edge again. It smacks against the barrier with a resounding thump. For a moment, the prison holds, then an echoing clap deafens me. And a shockwave sucks the air from my lungs.

Letting out a muffled cry, I sway on suddenly unsteady feet and gasp for breath.

The fog slithers into the open and unfurls as if stretching for the first time after a long, satisfying sleep. Then, the smoky amalgam slams into me, scouring the flesh of my arms and legs like sand in an overwhelming wind.

I fall to my knees, tuck my chin to my chest, and curl into a ball. The chafing burn lashes my back through the thin cloth of the baggy jumpsuit the Thalijh gave me.

"We told you," it croons. *"You are not strong enough to hold us."*

Its voice shifts through the fog. Whispers from a hundred places at once.

"We are far stronger than you will ever be!"

But that's not true! I'm not weak. And I'm not powerless in the face of absolute darkness. I endured years at Alphanax. Survived and escaped a sunken derelict at the bottom of an impossibly deep ocean. Resisted Iali's attempts to overpower me. Pushed back its overwhelming darkness. Twice!

I'll do it again. For good this time.

Punching balled fists into the flat, featureless ground, I heave upright, squinting into the biting gale. In response to my defiant gesture, it bears down on me like so many stinging insects. Every inch of my skin is on fire. My lungs burn with each breath. My mind unravels as it shrieks for respite. But I push feeling aside and find the same, numb emptiness it used to imprison me. And stand.

"*How?!*" Its rageful bellow echoes from all sides.

"You're in *my* mind," I shout.

The fog sputters in response to my harsh words. In fear? I don't care. It has overstayed its welcome, and I'm taking my mind back.

With every fiber of my being, I push against it. Before, I was trying to imprison it, but now I'm trying to overwhelm it. Destroy it. Wipe it from the world for good.

Invisible fingers of thought shred the fog. The disjointed bits scatter as if searching for a hiding place amidst the featureless expanse sprawling into eternity. But there's no escape. Not anymore. I snatch each wriggling piece, molding them all into a ball that fits in the palm of my hand. One by one. Until…

One final bit wriggles toward an escape that's impossible. The frail wisp is light gray instead of black. When I scoop up the tendril, a familiar warmth blooms across my bare palm. Is this…? Before I can make sense of the tiny fragment, it begins to dissipate, like smoke on a stiff breeze. I grasp at the fading tendril, frantic to preserve it from being scattered to nothing.

When I open my fingers, it's gone.

Sighing, I turn my attention to the compressed ball of darkness. I can see it swirling around inside. Scratching at the surface, desperate to escape.

"You aren't going anywhere," I say, closing my fingers around the ball. "And you aren't going to hurt me, or my friends, anymore."

Then, with every ounce of strength, I squeeze.

It pushes back. Frantic. Desperate. But with every millimeter, its strength wanes. And the ball shrinks. Smaller than a stone. A seed. A grain of sand. Finally, it disappears altogether.

For the first time in what seems like an eternity, I'm alone in my own mind.

This time, I turn away with a smile on my face. And I know that when I open my eyes, I'll truly be awake this time. Although, I have no idea what waits for me on the other side of consciousness.

Regardless, I take a nervous breath and close my eyes.

23

Searing pain splits my skull. I gasp shallow breaths and squint through tears. Though blurry, I can see Fletcher sprawled unconscious in the shallow pool beneath the *Undertow*. On top of him is the mangled husk of a Kaisin. The one *it* had used.

All hints of its darkness are gone. And no shadow lingers at the edge of my mind.

With a heavy sigh, I sink to my knees beside Fletcher, letting my hands dip into the cold water lapping at my folded, trembling legs. It's finally over.

Fletcher suddenly sputters. Thrashes. Shoves the lifeless Kaisin off of him. Wild eyes search for the threat that loomed over him moments before, coming to rest on me.

"Aiko?"

I offer a weary smile.

"What happened?" His eyes sweep the empty space beneath the *Undertow* again. This time, they stop on the Kaisin. "How…?"

I frown. "It—"

"Aiko!? Fletcher!?" Rhuk's frantic groans from above cut me off.

"We're here," Fletcher calls back, gaze lifting to the open hatch overhead, the question he asked forgotten for the moment.

"Oh, good." Rhuk's overlarge head pops into view, a wide grin showing jagged teeth. It falters. "When it knocked me aside…"

Fletcher nods and opens his mouth to reply, but I beat him to it.

"What about Gohk?"

"Still unconscious, but she seems fine," he says, the grin creeping back across his lips. "I guess she's tougher than she looks."

Fletcher manages a chuckle and heaves himself to unsteady feet.

"Mind lowering the ramp?" he calls up to Gohk.

"There's no way to open it from the outside?" I ask, remembering…But that was just a dream.

"No," he replies. "Then again, I don't make a habit of parking places where I need to worry about leaving the ramp down."

I nod and trail a few steps behind as he heads for the far end of the ship, skipping a step next to the landing strut he—well, his imaginary counterpart—used to lower the ramp. A simple glance reveals no hidden panel, but I run my fingers across the spot just in case. The metal is smooth. Unaltered.

At the top of the ramp, Fletcher steps toward the bridge. Pauses. Turns back.

"Go check on Gohk and Rhuk. I'll get us out of here."

"Are we going up to the station?" I blurt out without thinking. His brow furrows.

"I don't know where we're going," he says hesitantly, though it's clear he wants to say more.

I stare at his back until he disappears into the bridge, then swivel toward the common area. Gohk is still where she landed, but is finally coming around. Rhuk stands next to her, the concerned look on his face intensifying every time she groans.

"You alright?"

"Bruised. But nothing's broken," she mutters. "Dense bones," she adds with a grimace, that seems like it was supposed to be a smile.

I crouch beside her.

"Can you stand? We're about to—" My warning is cut off by the building whine of the *Undertow's* engines. Then a shiver as the ship begins to move.

Rhuk helps me heave Gohk to wobbly legs and dump her into one of the chairs around the table by the window. I sag into one of the others, the wet jumpsuit sticking to the cool plastic, and glance outside. My stomach drops as dark water lightens, and hulking shadows give way to shifting schools of brightly colored fish. A sky the same color as water. White fluffy clouds. Orange flames. Then, a kaleidoscope of stars. And silence except for the light pinging of the hull.

A moment later, Fletcher walks into view with a frown on his face.

"Where are we headed?" I ask.

"Nowhere yet," he replies. "The Thalijh have asked us to remain in orbit for the time being."

He blinks, then looks at me. His eyebrows lift. "What happened down there? With it?"

It's the question I expect. And fear.

"What do you mean?" Rhuk cuts in before I can offer an answer.

"Aiko was going to pull me up. But I was too heavy. She fell. It heard. Charged. Tackled me." His eyebrows furrow as he recounts what had happened beneath the *Undertow*. "The last thing I saw before it knocked me out was her sprinting toward its back."

All three of them look at me.

In that moment, time seems to stop. If I tell them the truth about what happened, how will they react? Will they understand? Will they accept it? Or will they react how they—their imagined doppelgangers, at least—did? On the other hand, do they really need to know? After all, it's been destroyed. For good. So, there isn't any harm in keeping what happened a secret. Or not telling them about Iali. Right?

I take a deep breath around the lump in my throat. "Nothing happened."

Fletcher gives me a confused scowl. "What do you mean 'nothing'?"

"I sprinted at it. Shoved it off of you. And it just…dissolved…as soon as it touched the water," I lied.

After a few pounding heartbeats, Fletcher lets out a relieved sigh. "So, it's over."

"I suppose so," Gohk grumbles in pained agreement.

But Rhuk stares at me, eyebrows twitching over slightly narrowed eyes. He doesn't challenge my explanation, however, instead giving a small shrug.

"You said the Thalijh wanted us to stay in orbit?" I ask, relieved to change the subject.

He nods. "Only long enough to transfer sample data. After that, we're free to go wherever."

"Back to the station?"

"Probably?" he says, glancing at Gohk, then Rhuk. "What do you guys think?"

"I'm sure it's fine," Gohk groans.

"And if it isn't?" Rhuk chimes in, his gaze lingering on me for a heartbeat longer than I like. Does he suspect something?

"At this point, I'd rather die in my own bed," Gohk spits.

Fletcher grimaces and mumbles something about setting a course, before disappearing in the direction of the bridge.

Awkward silence doesn't have a chance to fully settle before Gohk rises and stumbles on wobbly legs down the hall and into one of the unoccupied crew quarters. That leaves me alone with Rhuk. The small being took his fair share of beating, but seems none the worse for wear. His lips are twisted into a pensive frown that doesn't abate when I stand. Before I can shuffle away, however, he looks up at me.

"You're okay?" His tone borders on suspicious.

I nod.

"What do you think happened to it?"

"I'm just glad it's gone," I reply with as straight a face as I can manage.

Rhuk's smile is shallow. "We all are."

Then, he slowly wanders past me down the hall and into another empty room.

I'm finally alone. *Really* alone. It's gone. So is Iali. And for the first time since Fallah's death, I feel bereft and as far removed from the others as the stars glittering outside the window are from each other. But they remind me how far I've come: from a dank prison on Alphanax to a watery world of tentacled aliens who knows how far away. Along the way, I met new people. Made enemies. And friends.

With all that said and done, it doesn't feel like things are all that different. I traded one prison for another. One struggle for another. Even the freedom I thought I attained is no more than an illusion. Sure, I learned more than I wanted to know about what I am and where I come from. But even those discoveries are within the trappings of someone else's world.

Although, that's a pretty cynical way of looking at things, isn't it? Because, on the other hand, I've gained so much more than I ever dreamed of while still at Alphanax. I grasped the freedom Fallah and I always wanted with both hands. Found another that shared in my thirst for the knowledge of what I am. And came to understand that I'm so much more than a lonely 'smooth skin.'

Fallah would be proud if she were here. I sorely wish she was.

What would I say to her? What would we do? Where would we go?

Where would I go?

I don't know how to answer that question. And I can't think of one on the way back to the station. It gnaws at the back of my mind like a rabid animal desperate to escape from a snare. Burrows into my thoughts like a worm. Eats at me like rot. After three days of interstellar travel, I'm ready to burst. I have to get off the *Undertow*, even if only to wander amidst the station's crowds. At least there, I feel less like an imprisoned orphan and more like one of the fish swimming aimlessly in Thalijh's oceans.

At least then I'll be able to come to terms with my newfound freedom, decide what to do next, and figure out where I want to go.

When we land, Gohk storms off the ship without a word. And Rhuk offers an overly warm smile to both Fletcher and I before sauntering down the ramp He pauses at the bottom and glances back up at us.

"Fletcher, mind if I borrow Aiko for a day or two?"

His eyes narrow. "What for?"

"Does it matter?" Rhuk shoots back. "The girl needs a break from the confines of that tin can. And I could use a bit of company."

"Fine," Fletcher says, with a dismissive wave.

The small being gives a curt, satisfied nod as Fletcher disappears inside the *Undertow*, then spares me a fleeting glance.

"Come on."

I quietly, thankfully fall in line behind Rhuk as he waddles away from the ship.

The streets past the dock are crowded as usual, but this time I walk among the press without the usual awe. Instead, I revel in my renewed anonymity. No beings—not even Kaisin—look my way when I pass in Rhuk's wake. None that jostle me bother to pay me any mind. Or apologize in whatever language they speak. It's as if everything that happened over the past week or so has been nothing more than a dream. A bad one, at that.

The barely ajar door to Rhuk's workshop prompts a slew of mixed memories, yet the little alien doesn't pause at the threshold like I do. No Kaisin are waiting for us inside, but…

"Oh, wow," I breathe at the cluttered mess.

"I figured this would happen." Rhuk sounds annoyed. "Gohk's place is probably no better off."

"I–I'm sorry," I stammer.

"Everything's replaceable. Picking through what's left is what irks me," he says with a shrug, then smiles. "Which is why you're here to give me a hand."

"What?"

"Seemed like you needed a distraction from your own mind," Rhuk says with a grin.

I can't help smiling. "Yeah. Thanks…"

He shakes his head and picks his way into the rubble. "Let's start over here."

The next few hours of sorting and reorganizing are grueling. None of what is strewn across the floor seems important. Though, that's probably why none of it was taken. But Rhuk seems pleased by what is left, smiling and crooning to himself in soft words I can't understand as we restock the emptied shelves on one side of the room. My legs are stiff by the time they're full. And my arms feel like rubber from lifting countless tiny parts. So many of them were so heavy!

Sighing, I sink into one of the chairs we pulled out of the mess. Rhuk doesn't seem the least bit tired.

"How many times have you had to do this?"

"More than I'd like to remember," he replies. "Though, thankfully, it's been a while."

"How long is a while?"

His eyebrows twitch. "A few hundred years, at least."

I stifle a frown. Dream-Rhuk only hinted at his age. "How old are you, exactly?"

He gives me a coy smile. "Honestly, I've forgotten."

"Can you guess?"

The smile wavers and falls.

"Longer than I'd like to remember, but well north of a thousand years. On the standard calendar, anyway."

My initial reaction is to be awestruck, but something about the look on his face suggests there isn't anything to be impressed about. That he's seen far more in his lifetime than he bargained for. That all he wants now is to forget the past and lead a quiet life. I definitely derailed that wish.

Rhuk's sudden smile is forced. "Anyway, now that I've thoroughly worn you out…"

He turns and picks his way to the staircase tucked in the corner behind a metal shelf. The walkway at the top runs all the way to his private room at the far side of the workshop. But I never noticed the door on this side, opposite the stairs.

"In there," Rhuk says. "It'll be sparse. And dusty—no one's used it in a while. But it's a room. With a bed. And a shower."

He starts toward his room and glances back over his shoulder. "There's also food when you want it. Now. Or later."

Instead of watching him walk away—I've been doing a lot of that lately—I turn to the closed door and hurry inside. The room is about the same size as my quarters on the *Undertow*, and just as sparse. A narrow bed juts out from the middle of the far wall. To my right, two skinny slats barely wide enough to call doors lead to a bathroom and closet.

Rhuk was right about the dust. A fine layer of it covers everything, though that doesn't bother me. Dirt and grime were a way of life at Alphanax. And if I'm completely honest, being so consistently clean over the last week or so still feels strange. But I won't turn down a hot, soothing shower. Or a soft bed to lay on.

Damp hair on a pillow makes me think about how things used to be and how they will be. Fallah is gone. And now that Iali is too, she is again relegated to just a fading memory. For a little while, at least, I thought I managed to obtain the freedom we both dreamt of. But the pursuit of the truth and *it* were just temporary distractions. In the end, am I just an accessory to someone else's reality?

But what choice do I have? How can I make my own way in the universe? What purpose can I serve if not to fulfill someone else's desires? Maybe that's my fate. The fate of every child from Alphanax.

I scoff and close my eyes. After everything that happened, I'd be a fool to believe such a thing. The only question is: what am I going to do next?

I'll figure that out tomorrow.

24

Aiko.

AIKO.

I bolt upright, the lingering hiss of incoherent whispers filling the silence and drowning my thoughts. My name stands out among muttered words, uttered by countless voices. But whose? I destroyed it, didn't I?

Turning my attention inward, I frantically search for hints of the tell-tale darkness lingering in my mind. But it is nowhere to be found. I destroyed it. So, where are the voices coming from?

I concentrate on the words. On my name. Follow them like the beads of glass I used to free myself from its dark prison. And eventually...

The voices aren't in my head. They aren't even nearby. Some seem closer than others, but all are far, far away.

"Who are you?" I mumble into the empty air. My words echo, then fade to silence.

"We are." The answer hisses from countless voices in unison.

It! The rest of it. All of it. Everywhere.

Iali mentioned being able to feel its presence. Is that what this is? But how? Did I fail to destroy it like I thought? Did I accidentally, unknowingly absorb it instead? Or did I actually manage to retain some of Iali within my mind before it faded away completely? Or both?

"How?" I ask the chorus of voices, desperate for an answer.

"You are with us," the voices reply. *"Of us."*

"What does that mean?"

"We are," it repeats.

My stomach turns. After everything, it's still inside of me. A part of me. A dangerous part. If it can feel me, it can also find me. Which means it will be able to find Fletcher, and Gohk, and Rhuk too.

I swing my feet to the floor and drop my head into sweaty palms. What am I supposed to do? How am I supposed to protect the others from an enemy I don't even know how to fight?

But I do know how to fight it. I already have. Twice before. Iali, first. Then, it. I won both times. And I can win again. As many times as it takes. Though, I'll eventually have to tell everyone my secret. Or they'll find out on their own. Unless...

I can leave. Go out by myself. Discover, and deal with, each voice echoing in my head. Best of all, it will be my choice. My life. My freedom. All I have to do is stand up. Walk out of Rhuk's workshop. Find a way off the station. And just stay the path.

Easy...

My legs tremble when I stand. And my hands shake when I reach for the button next to the door. The whispering hiss when it opens seems deafening, and the scrape of my oversized boots on corrugated metal is like the rolling rumble of a raging thunderstorm. I creep down the spiral staircase, heart pounding a hundred times faster than my sneaking steps, and across the portion of floor we cleared. Less than a dozen steps from the door, Rhuk's voice echoes in the workshop's rafters.

"Where are you going?"

I freeze as if suddenly encased in a block of ice, though my shivering is from the adrenaline surging through me.

"Well?" he prompts.

"Nowhere!" I say, spinning to look up at Rhuk, perched on the catwalk connecting the spiral staircase to his room. From the disappointed frown on his face to the tiny, balled fists resting on his hips, it seems like he expected me to try and leave.

"For a walk," I add.

"In the middle of the station's night cycle?"

"I didn't know," I say truthfully. Since leaving Alphanax, I've had no real sense of day or night.

Rhuk seems to realize and nods slowly. "Regardless..."

"Do I need a reason to go for a walk?" I snap, a little too defensively.

His eyes narrow. "Do you?"

He starts to pace along the corrugated walkway toward the stairs.

"You've seemed off since Thalijh. And I've had the nagging suspicion that there's something you haven't been telling us." He pauses at the top of the stairs. "So?"

My mouth opens. Closes. Opens again.

"There is something, then?" Rhuk's eyebrows wiggle as he walks down the stairs. "Why not tell me what's going on before you do something rash?"

I consider Rhuk's question for a moment, then turn toward the door.

"Aiko!" he snaps, before I can take a single step.

I turn back.

Rhuk's eyebrows are drawn down, but he isn't angry. "Just...talk to me..."

My head shakes. And my mouth works. But the next thing I know, I'm spilling the entire story: our encounter with Lorn, my injury, the Thalijh, Iali, the battle in my mind—the battle I thought I won—and the whispers that pulled me from sleep.

He blinks. "Hmmm."

"T—that's it?" I stammer. "You don't have anything else to say?"

Rhuk's eyebrows twitch. "Is there something you wanted me to say?"

"N-no. But—"

"You expected me to say something." He chuckles. "Well, Fletcher might not have had a lot to say, but Gohk would have given you enough of an earful enough for both of them."

"And you...?" I trail off into confused silence, unable to work out how he can be so calm.

He makes a dismissive wave with both hands. "I've seen things that'd turn your blood to ice. This doesn't even compare."

"But...it—!"

"Is terrible, to be sure," Rhuk says, a grin spreading across his face. "Though, it sounds manageable."

I blink. "Huh?"

"That's where you were going." It isn't a question.

I open my mouth to reply, but he holds up a tiny finger.

"Very brave. But also very foolish to go off on your own without a word to any of us." Rhuk crosses his arms. "What was your plan, exactly?"

"I...didn't really have one," I admit with a grimace.

"That won't do," Rhuk says with a frown and a shake of the head. "If you're going off on your own, you'll need more than what you've got."

"You aren't going to stop me?"

Rhuk scoffs. "Why would I?"

"Well, Fletcher—"

"He may have rescued you from Alphanax, but he doesn't own you," Rhuk finishes for me. "Your life is your own. And if this is what you want to do with it, who am I to stand in your way?"

An involuntary smile sweeps across my face.

"At the very least, let me prepare you for the journey ahead, because it will be hard," he continues, without missing a beat. "The universe is an unforgiving place. More than Alphanax could have prepared you for. More than you can ever imagine."

He wanders from the foot of the stairs and starts poking through the shelves we organized earlier that day.

"Give me a few hours to prepare something for you. Then, you can leave. Deal?"

I nod, equal parts dumbfounded and grateful.

Rhuk scurries to work, gathering components from the shelves and floor, whisking them all to the workbench along the back wall. There, he tinkers and mumbles for so long, that sleepiness starts to gnaw at the edges of my nervous, elated mind. But before its sharp teeth sink too deep, he spins toward me and holds up a glove. No, a sleeve.

The metal limb is similar to, but far thinner than, the powered suits we wore on our dive. There's even a small screen on the forearm. And a visor attached to the limb by the thinnest wire.

"It isn't much," Rhuk says. "But it should help you along."

He offers it to me.

I accept the sleeve and slip it on. It's light. Snug. Comfortable. And it doesn't limit the movement of my fingers, wrist, elbow, or shoulder. And miraculously, it stays put. I half-expected it to slip right off.

"It's nearly as strong as the limb on the full-sized suits," Rhuk says. "And the panel on your wrist is capable of many of the same functions, with a few extras. Although, the translator will probably be the most useful."

He points at a blue cross hatched texture on the panel curved over my shoulder.

"It's powered by an internal capacitor that needs to be charged via sunlight every once in a while."

I flex my fingers and twist my arm. "Thanks.

Rhuk shakes his head. "Don't mention it."

Then, he takes a deep breath.

"You know, I had no idea you'd take my words to heart, but I'm glad you did."

Frowning, I think about which words he meant. They immediately spring to mind. "Think about what you can do."

"You really did," he says. "The words rolled off Fletcher and Gohk like grease on water. But you acted on them. And you're going to continue acting on them."

A sorrowful smile stretches his lips.

"Part of me wishes you'd stay, like Fletcher and Gohk stayed after Lorn's disappearance, but—"

The words catch in his throat.

"I have one more thing for you," he continues after a moment. "To get you started on your way. Wait here."

In a flash, Rhuk bounds to the top of the spiral staircase and bolts across the walkway to his room. Moments later, he reappears, small hands clutching something I can't make out, until he pushes a small pouch into my hands.

I stare down at it, eyebrows raised in question.

"Credits," he says. "For passage offworld. And supplies. They'll last a while if you're careful, but you'll eventually have to find a way to make more."

"Thank you." I'm barely able to whisper the words.

Rhuk shakes his head, then spreads his arms wide. Dropping to my knees, I give the small being the hug he wants. The hug I didn't know I needed. After everything that happened, he's the one who understands me the most. Understands what I have to do. Supports my decision.

"What will you tell the others?" I mumble into his silky fur.

"The truth," he replies, pulling away. "That you left in the middle of the night. That I have no idea where you went."

"And...everything else?"

"Gohk had her secrets for long enough. I think it's only fair I have mine." He grins. "Don't you?"

I laugh at that. For the first time in...I can't remember. But it feels good. Really good.

Standing, I turn back to the door. Hesitate.

Rhuk sidles up beside me. "Let me walk with you. Help you find a ship."

Nodding, I step out onto the street. And for the first time, someone follows me. The feeling is bittersweet. I'm finally walking toward the freedom Fallah and I always talked about, but I'll be grasping it alone to fulfill a destiny I never wanted or expected. It's scary. And exciting. And...

I have no idea what the future holds for me. What dangers I might face. What adventures I might have. But after years of waiting, that future is finally mine!

Epilogue

It's strange to walk down a ramp that isn't the *Undertow's*. And doubly so to hear boots that fit scrape uneven ground, where last I trod barefoot.

"I won't be long," I call over my shoulder, before trudging along worn paving stones toward a squat, stone building in the distance. But that place isn't why I'm here...

At some point, I turn off the path into the endless expanse of wasteland stretching toward a ridge of mountains on the horizon. The ground gently slopes down and away from the path. Loose dirt and rocks skitter under my feet, but the rubber soles of my boots grip the rough ground, keeping me upright.

In the near distance, the slope steepens. I'm getting close.

Slowing, I scan the uneven ground for a tell-tale ruddy splash.

Dirt has dried and shifted, but not the stones. They haven't forgotten the violence that happened here.

Kneeling, I trace the bare fingers of my right hand along a faded stain, nearly invisible under the sun's crimson light. There's another within reach. And a third nearby. I don't remember it being so large.

I soak in the sun's warmth for a long time and focus on the stone's rough texture under sweat-slicked fingertips. It hasn't been that long since I knelt in the damp dirt, my hand resting on the warm, leathery flank of someone I loved. Someone I planned to spend the rest of my life with. I take slow, measured breaths, because if I don't, the tears will come. And never stop.

With a weary, long-overdue sigh, I heave to my feet, but can't tear my gaze away from the stained stones, the only solid evidence that Fallah ever existed.

"Can I help you?"

I stiffen at the Headmistress' familiar voice, though her tone is far friendlier than I remember. Perhaps because she's speaking to a potential client instead of one of her children?

Drawing in a deep breath, I turn to face her.

Her jittery blue eyes meet mine and she smiles, oblivious.

Am I really that different? Sure, I'm wearing clothes that fit, my dark hair is pulled back into a ponytail, and a wide-brimmed hat is pulled down to shield my eyes from the brilliant sun, but I'm still the same girl from just a few weeks ago. Why can't she see that? Has she forgotten me already? After years of calling me strange?

I smirk. "I heard that a few children tried to escape not long ago. Can you tell me what happened to them?"

Her vapid smile melts into a frown.

"One of the children—a Quiloh, I believe—was unfortunately shot during the attempt." She pauses and blinks in confusion. "I think it was right here, actually—"

"And the other?" I press.

"She was a strange child," the Headmistress says, pinching her chin with a thumb and curled finger. "After the attempt, she couldn't stay, so I—"

She stops short.

"You what?"

"The girl was adopted," she finishes quickly, leaving something unsaid.

"Do you know what happened to her?"

"No, I…"

My smirk splits into a grin when the Headmistress trails off. Her blue eyes study my face. Widen.

"It's…*you*," she finally whispers.

I don't give her the satisfaction of confirming. Instead, I motion to the stained rocks at my feet. "What happened to Fallah's body?"

The Headmistress hesitates.

"Well?" I snap.

"Disposed of," she says. Her lips quiver and her eyes fall to the ground.

"How?"

She shakes her head, but doesn't answer.

I want to demand one, but don't. Maybe it's best if I remember Fallah like this, instead of learning whatever horrible way the Kaisin dealt with her body. The thought can't keep a scowl from twisting my lips.

"You know, I'm sorry it happened," the Headmistress mumbles, looking everywhere but my face. "I would have preferred to let you two go, but…"

I glance over my shoulder to where the ground steepens and swoops behind a ridge. What would have happened if we both escaped back then? Would we have survived? Or would the wasteland have claimed us both? Suddenly, I'm not sure whether the Headmistress' preference is better or worse.

"That doesn't matter anymore," I say, shaking my head. "I only came to pay my respects, not overstay my welcome. I'll be on my way."

"Wait!" The Headmistress calls after I've taken only a few steps. "I think I have something you might want."

I stop. Turn. "What?"

"Something that belonged to the Quiloh."

"Fallah," I say.

She nods. "Fallah."

"Where?" I ask, already knowing what the answer will be. The only thing it can be.

"Back at the orphanage," the Headmistress replies. "Follow me."

I trudge in the Kaisin's wake, boots scraping over the loose ground. In the distance, the squat stone building looks smaller than I remember. And it doesn't get much bigger as we approach. The worn stone tiles trace a path from the ship I hired—thankfully still on the landing pad—to the wooden double doors that are far less threatening than I remember. Even when they creak open, my heart doesn't race.

The Headmistress walks halfway down the hall and pauses in front of a door I've never seen opened. Iron keys jingle on the ring at her waist as she grabs one and pushes it into the lock. With a quick twist, the door drifts open.

Inside looks no different from the rest of Alphanax. Worn stone floors stretch to featureless, monolithic walls. In front of the far wall is a hefty wooden desk, dried from the heat and chipped in places from age and overuse. A small lamp sits on the corner of the desk, which the Headmistress lights.

So, she lived no better than the rest of us, just as much of a prisoner to these stone walls as every other child trapped in that coliseum only steps away.

Skirting the desk's edge, the Headmistress pulls open a drawer and rummages inside, eventually pulling out a small item.

"Here," she says, walking around the desk and pushing it into my hands.

It's a small pendant made of wood, with a single symbol carved on the polished surface: Fallah's name. She wore it every single day. It was as much of a part of her as her milky-white eyes or the blue strip running down her spine. I forgot all about it. How could I? I should have remembered it before! Taken it when I left Alphanax the first time.

"Thank you," I mutter, stuffing the pendant into the pocket of my jumpsuit, letting my fingers trail across the smooth surface before pulling them free.

The Headmistress offers an awkward smile. But it's genuine.

And I have something to offer in return.

Stepping forward, I take her hand in mine and concentrate. On the roughness of her skin. Its warmth. And the darkness lurking beneath. There isn't much—not even enough to come close to being one of the countless voices whispering in the back of my mind—but I draw it out of her anyway and crush it out of existence.

The Kaisin doesn't notice—Why would she?—and places her free hand on top of mine. Her smile widens, more warm and genuine than ever before.

"Thank you for coming back," she says. "It's always nice to see what's become of the children that leave Alphanax. Especially ones so…unique."

She pauses, bright-eyed.

"Maybe you can come back again?"

"Maybe," I lie, smiling and gently pulling my hand away. I don't offer the Kaisin any additional thanks. And I don't look back after I turn toward the door. I only came to pay my respects to Fallah's memory, such as it is, not make peace with my time here.

I'm unsure of the Headmistress' gesture. Is she really sorry about what happened? Is she really glad to see me? Does she even care that I'm still alive? Whatever the case, I appreciate the small piece of Fallah she granted me.

Before, I was afraid Fallah's memory would fade with time. That I'd eventually grow to view her as a fixture of the past. But the pendant she always wore…That's something real. Something I can see. And touch. More than a simple memory.

Smiling, I dip the fingers of my right hand into my jumpsuit pocket. The wood is cool despite the hot wind and overbearing sun. And the polished surface is slick, almost like water-worn stone.

Maybe, just maybe, this path won't be as lonely as I thought after all.

Acknowledgements

The world of *Aiko's Dive* began as a piece of flash fiction only about a thousand words long. Yet that brief snippet caught the hearts and minds of enough people to push me to explore more about Aiko, Fletcher, and their universe.

I always intended for Aiko's Dive to be an origin story, but determining its final form took over five years and at least two complete rewrites (with many smaller revisions in between). And just like Aiko, I received more than a little help along the way.

Stuart White was one of the first people outside of my close circle of writing associates to read any of Aiko's Dive. I submitted it to him as part of a fledgling mentorship program called Write Mentor. And while he didn't select Aiko's Dive to mentor, his kind words kept me moving forward. Beyond that, his continued support over the years, along with the support of the Write Mentor program and community, pushed me to continue refining Aiko's Dive into the story it is today.

I first met Jason Byrne in a writing forum in 2015; over the years, he's remained one of my closest writing colleagues and has become a dear friend. His unflinching positivity has buoyed me through many storms, and his creative thinking has helped me through plenty of writing rough spots. I wouldn't be the writer I am today without Jason's companionship.

Bracken Sallin was a fantastic college roommate—he introduced me to Ruroni Kenshin, Steve Vai and Joe Satriani, and The Elder Scrolls III: Morrowind—but over the past few years he's been an even better critique partner. His meticulous attention to detail and to-the-point feedback is always appreciated. Because of his insights, I've become a far better storyteller.

My wife, Astrid, has been my biggest supporter throughout my writing journey. She's listened to countless, rambling monologues about every novel I've worked on. She's been my rock through the highs and the lows of the writing, editing, and querying process. And she never had any doubt that I'd be a success, even when I couldn't see past the next rejection. I couldn't ask for a better partner in writing or in life. Infinity +1.

Finally, I'd like to thank everyone else who has ever supported me or worked with me on one of my novels and every writing community that has welcomed me with open arms. And I'd like to say thank you to the Vulpine press team, as well as my editor, Josh, who believed in my work enough to give it a chance. It means the world to me.

Chase Gamwell grew up in Huntsville, Alabama, just down the road from NASA's Marshall Space Flight Center, where his father worked. Take your kids to work days and summers exploring the U.S. Space and Rocket Center cemented his love of science and science fiction. At university, he studied microbiology, but he quickly decided a life of pipettes and petri dishes wasn't for him. Since then, he's worked in a variety of STEM fields, though crafting science fiction stories remains his true passion. When not writing, he plays way too many video games and collects *Star Wars* Lego sets that he refuses to open.

Currently, he lives in Texas with his wife and dog.

Find him online:

Twitter and Instagram @elaqure

Tiktok @cgamwell

or on his website at chasegamwell.com